"Don't you do this!" she cried out, lifting herself to grasp Rhys's shoulders and shake him. *"Don't you take yourself from me, you selfish, stupid ass!"*

Rhys stared up at her as if she had sprouted a second head, but then he shifted and they rolled farther away from the cliff's edge. However, the motion also caused her to move beneath him and now she was pinned by his weight.

"What is wrong with you, woman?" he barked, his warm breath heating her already flushed face. "You could have killed us both by attacking me in such a foolhardy fashion."

"So you weren't about to do yourself a harm when I pulled up to the cottage?"

"No! I would certainly never think to do something s___ I was merely about to dive off the cliff. I ___"

"O___ ___ore.

As ___ to realize she ___ by her husband' ___ was utterly naked.

Later she could be angry, later she *would* demand answers. Right now she just wanted to hold this man and be held by him.

Romances by **Jenna Petersen**

The Unclaimed Duchess

Jenna Petersen

AVON

An Imprint of HarperCollinsPublishers

AVON BOOKS
An Imprint of HarperCollins*Publishers*
10 East 53rd Street
New York, New York 10022-5299

Copyright © 2010 by Jesse Petersen
ISBN 978-0-06-193499-5
www.avonromance.com

First Avon Books paperback printing: September 2010

Avon Trademark Reg. U.S. Pat. Off. and in Other Countries, Marca Registrada, Hecho en U.S.A.
HarperCollins® is a registered trademark of HarperCollins Publishers.

Printed in the U.S.A.

10 9 8 7 6 5 4 3 2 1

For my Mom, my biggest cheerleader and sometimes first reader. For Miriam, whose encouragement has kept me marginally sane, and honestly that's the best you can get with a writer. And for Michael, my reason and my heart. Thanks to you all for supporting me, no matter how much I stumble.

THE UNCLAIMED
DUCHESS

Prologue

1796

Anne Danvers had been very good, as good as any six-year-old girl could be expected to be after the two-day journey to the estate of their host, followed by a forced march to a picnic site. She had even remained quiet and demure while the grown-ups talked endlessly of farming conditions and servants and politics.

But Anne was bored and it was becoming increasingly difficult to pretend that fact away. She wanted to run to the lake's edge and splash her toes in the water. She wanted to go into the copse of trees in the distance and see if she could catch a frog or chase a bunny. She wanted to stop being a "little lady" and simply be a little girl like her mother and father allowed her to be in the back garden of their London home.

Suddenly there was a whooping war cry and a small group of boys burst from the trees in a mass of flying arms and running legs. They had wooden swords and were swinging them recklessly as they charged the lake.

Anne sat up straighter on the picnic blanket, longing to join the other children. She grasped her mother's gown sleeve and tugged gently. Her mother looked down at her, then followed Anne's forlorn expression to the boys a few hundred feet away. She smiled at her daughter, her eyes filled with love.

"You want to play with the others?" she asked softly.

Anne nodded.

"They're older, you know," her mother said.

"I don't care, they have swords," Anne whispered, still in awe of the careless way the boys slapped the wood against one another. Little girls rarely played so robustly.

"Very well," her mother said with a light laugh. "But do try to keep your dress clean."

As Anne got to her feet, one of the other women in the party smiled at her. It was the Duchess of Waverly, and Anne shifted beneath her scrutiny. The duchess had been staring at her since their arrival earlier in the day, and Anne didn't know what to think of it.

"Are you going to play with the boys?" she asked.

Anne bobbed a proper curtsy. "Yes, Your Grace."

"That tall one there is my son, Rhys," the lady said, motioning.

Anne looked. The boy was taller than the others by a few inches, with dark hair. He was obviously the leader of the group, directing them at their play with unquestionable authority.

"You know, one day you are to marry him," the duchess said.

Anne stared first at the lady and then at her mother. Her mother's eyes had widened, but then her expression softened.

"Go ahead, dearest. Go play."

Anne departed, loath to be kept from the fun for very long, but as she scurried away, she thought she heard her mother murmur, "Your Grace, we had not intended to tell Anne about the betrothal yet."

Anne ran at first, but as she got closer to the boys, she slowed her pace, suddenly shy. Finally she reached them, and they stopped playing to look at her with the unmasked disdain only eleven-year-olds could master.

"Who are you?" one of the boys asked with a scowl.

"I'm Anne Danvers," she said. "I'm here with my mother and father."

At that, the one the duchess had pointed out, Rhys,

straightened up. He looked at her, dark eyes focused and sharp.

"How old are you?" he asked.

Her gaze went naturally to him, it would have even if she hadn't known who he was. "I'm six," she said, suddenly defensive. She folded her arms.

One of the other boys groaned. "She's a *baby*. And a girl baby at that. Go away, baby!"

Anne stomped her foot, outraged. "I am *not* a baby. And I want to play."

"No," another of the boys said. "Go away."

Anne stood her ground. "I *want* to play."

Suddenly one of the smaller boys marched up to her. Without preamble or warning, he shoved her. She wasn't ready for the attack and fell backward onto her bottom in the grass.

As she looked up, there was a flurry of activity. Rhys rushed the boy who had pushed her and thrust him aside, sending him reeling away. Then he forced his way through the group of arguing boys and reached down to help her up. Although his palm was rough, he brought her to her feet gently and didn't let her go until she was steady. When he did, he spun on the other boys with a scowl.

"Hey!" he cried, bringing their chatter to a halt. "You don't do that! You *never* do that to someone smaller! And one day Anne will be my wife. You treat her with respect. She'll be a duchess one day."

Anne stared. So it was true. Was she really going to marry this boy someday? She tilted her head to look at him more closely, trying to picture a day when they would be married like grown-ups. Like her parents.

He turned away from the boys and looked down at her. "Did he hurt you?"

She stared, still mesmerized by the fact that she would one day be this boy's wife. He blinked at her when she was silent too long.

"You hear me?"

She shook away her thoughts. "No, I'm not hurt."

"Good, now go back to the blanket with your mother."

"But I want to play," Anne protested. "There aren't any other girls here."

He frowned at her as his gaze moved up and down her frame. "Look, you're too little to play. You might get hurt."

Anne folded her arms and returned his frown with one as dark and stubborn as his. His eyebrows lifted at the expression, but there was a grudging respect in his eyes. He cast a quick glance at the boys waiting behind him before he leaned in closer.

"There are some servant children who are your

age and they play behind the icehouse every day after luncheon," he whispered.

She narrowed her eyes. "With swords?"

His lips pursed, but then he nodded. "I've seen them with swords. Go play with them. If they tell you no, tell them *I* sent you. Then they'll fall in line."

With that, he turned his back on her, and he and the others rushed off to continue their battle. Anne stayed in her spot for a long moment, simply staring after their group. Her eyes never left the tallest boy. The one who had defended her just before he dismissed her.

She turned and began to trudge back up the hill. If she was really going to marry that boy someday, she wondered what kind of match it would be. But by the time she reached her mother she had decided.

Her parents were a love match and Anne would settle for no less herself.

Chapter 1

1816

Until the day he returned from his honeymoon, Rhys Carlisle, Duke of Waverly, had lived a life relatively free of disappointment. It was a charmed life, some would say, and many others would claim that Waverly's luck was most undeserved.

But Rhys had never cared about the petty jealousies of lesser people. He *knew* who he was. *What* he was. He was a man of power. He was a man who inspired respect and even fear. *He* was the Duke of Waverly.

As he stepped down from his well-appointed carriage, he sighed deeply, the sigh of a much contented man, for at the relatively young age of one and thirty, he had fulfilled one of his main obligations as duke. He had married the young woman his family had chosen for him.

He turned and offered a hand back to his new bride. Anne Carlisle, formerly Anne Danvers, smiled at him slightly as she departed the carriage with a graceful step.

She was everything a man could want in a wife. Well respected by her peers, she had been one of the most popular of her debut group. Rhys had always admired how easily she could defuse a tense situation or coax a smile from an upset friend. The very few people who didn't think highly of her were not worthy of notice.

And then there was her beauty, which was undeniable. She had brown hair with just a hint of gold in certain lights, and it always seemed to be arranged to perfection, even when she had taken it down on their wedding night. Her eyes were equally spectacular, a beautiful green-blue that sparkled with humor or darkened with concern when those emotions were merited.

Other men had wanted her when she came out, Rhys thought a few might have even been in love with her, but none could have her, for she was meant for him. She had been almost their entire lives. His fellow gentlemen could only comment on how lucky Rhys was to have been betrothed to such a prize.

Anne's feet touched the ground. He thought her smile wavered ever so slightly when he released her hand once she no longer required his assistance, but he ignored that.

Yes, things were going very well for Rhys. The wedding had been perfect, the honeymoon trip short, but entirely pleasant. He had few complaints as he and his new bride entered their home side by side and into the life they would now lead as duke and duchess.

His butler gave a smart bow as he quietly closed the door behind them.

"Good afternoon, Your Grace, Your Grace," he said with another quick bow for the pair. "Welcome back, I hope your trip was satisfactory."

Rhys stripped off his gloves and handed them over. Out of the corner of his eye, he saw Anne doing the same, tugging her fingers free of the white satin one by one. His gut clenched unexpectedly at the sight of her slow reveal of pale skin, but he cleared his throat and shoved those inappropriate urges away with force.

"Yes, Gilmour," he said to the servant. "Quite satisfactory."

He thought he saw Anne blush slightly as she pulled her hat pins away and removed the headpiece. She handed them to the butler.

"We are most happy to be home, Gilmour," she said with a warm smile for the servant. "Were there any callers or messages while we were away?"

The butler nodded and removed a small pile of correspondence from the tray on a nearby table. Anne flipped through the missives and notes quickly.

"They mainly appear to be felicitations on our marriage and a few invitations for events in the next few days." Her brow wrinkled. "But there are several messages from the Duke of Billingham." She glanced up and met Rhys's eyes. "Simon knew we were away, I wonder why he would send so many missives."

Rhys frowned. Simon Crathorne, Duke of Billingham, was the best friend he had ever had in this world, and the other man had experienced quite an upheaval recently. Not only had he discovered his beloved father had sired several bastard children, despite his reputation for piety, but Simon had met and married a woman in a whirlwind just before Rhys's own wedding. While Rhys did not entirely approve of Lillian Mayhew—now Lillian Crathorne—he still hoped his overly romantic friend did not regret his choice so soon into the marriage.

He smiled at Anne slightly. *He* certainly did not regret his. Anne would be the perfect bride, the perfect duchess. He had always known she would be.

"Actually, Your Grace," Gilmour said softly, "the Duke of Billingham is here, awaiting your arrival. He has been here for almost an hour, despite my explanation that I wasn't certain of the specific time of your return."

Rhys shot a glance at Anne, and the same worry he felt was as clearly outlined on her face. She had known Simon nearly as long as he had, and it was evident she had her own concerns for their friend.

"I hope he has had tea and any other comforts he required," she said as she smoothed her hands over her hair in preparation for receiving a guest.

"Of course, Your Grace," Gilmour said. "He has asked that I tell you to take your time in coming to greet him, as he knows you have had a long journey."

Anne waved a hand. "Posh, of course we'll go to him straightaway."

Although he was concerned, Rhys couldn't help but smile as he accompanied his wife down the hallway to the parlor where his friend awaited. Anne was already seamlessly taking on the role of lady of his household. Yes, his family had chosen well for him indeed.

He opened the door and stepped inside the parlor, motioning for his wife to go before him. As she moved into the room, the Duke of Billingham rose from his seat. Billingham was a tall man, just a touch taller than Rhys, with black hair and green eyes that had always captured the interest of women, though Simon had seemed immune to that until Lillian Mayhew came into his life. Once more, Rhys wondered if Lillian was the reason for Simon's apparently urgent visit.

"Billingham," Anne said with a broad smile while she crossed the room. "How good it is to see you."

She offered his friend a hand, which Simon lifted to his lips briefly. "Anne, or should I say Duchess Waverly, at last. I apologize for my abominable manners in coming here uninvited."

Anne shook her head. "Of course not, Simon. Don't be silly, you're welcome in our home any time you call."

His friend smiled, and then his gaze lighted on Rhys. For a moment the two men held stares, but Rhys was surprised when Simon's flitted away suddenly. Guilt and pain lined his friend's face, and Rhys's smug euphoria at being home faded a fraction. It seemed whatever had brought his friend here was serious indeed.

If Anne sensed the tension between the men, she made no mention of it. Instead she took a seat and motioned the two to take theirs.

"How is Lillian?" Anne asked as they all settled in.

There wasn't a hint of emotion in her voice, but Rhys saw her lean forward a fraction. It appeared her thoughts echoed his, that perhaps Simon was unhappy in his new marriage.

But at the mention of his bride, Simon's eyes lit up with a love so powerful and a passion so intense that Rhys looked away from it. He had never been comfortable with such strong emotions, it wasn't the way his father had raised him to behave and it seemed improper.

"Lillian is more than well, thank you, and I believe she is much looking forward to calling on you if you would allow it," Simon shot a brief glance at Rhys even as he spoke to Anne. It was no secret Rhys hadn't approved of Lillian.

But she was a duchess now and Rhys wouldn't sabotage her.

"Of course!" Anne said, and there was genuine affection in her tone. "I would dearly love to see Lillian again once we're settled. I shall send word to her this afternoon and we'll make the arrangements. I'm pleased to hear you are doing so well. And by the looks of it are very happy with your choice."

"I am," Simon said softly, and all the love he felt for Lillian was again powerful in his face.

Anne's gaze flitted aside and she swallowed hard. Then she stood. "Well, if you gentlemen will excuse me I have much to do and arrange. If I don't see you again before you depart, Billingham, then I will say good-bye."

It was evident Anne was allowing the two men privacy, and as they got to their feet for her departure, Rhys inclined his head toward her in silent thanks.

She offered her hand to Simon again and he pressed a second kiss to her knuckles briefly. "Thank you, Anne. Good afternoon."

Anne gave Rhys a brief glance before she slipped from the room and shut the two men in alone together.

For the first time in his memory, Rhys actually felt nervous as he looked at his friend. If it wasn't troubles in his marriage that brought Billingham here at such an inconvenient time, then Rhys wondered at the cause. It couldn't be good.

"Cigar?" he asked, motioning to the ornate box on a table across the room.

Simon shook his head slightly. "No." He retook his seat and leaned back as he looked up at Rhys. "So, my friend, how is married life?"

Rhys drew in a sharp breath as he slowly returned to his own chair. "Of course it is exactly as I hoped. Anne is the perfect hostess, the perfect lady, the perfect—"

"That isn't what I meant," Simon said as he leaned forward to drape his elbows over his knees.

Rhys pursed his lips in displeasure and discomfort. Neither he nor Simon had been raised as a libertine. They didn't discuss conquests or crow about the women they bedded. And yet Rhys recognized Simon was asking him if he and Anne were compatible in ways beyond her infinite suitability as Duchess of Waverly.

His body stirring unexpectedly, Rhys made an attempt to block out the images his friend's question inspired. Ones of his wedding night when he had taken his wife's innocence, when he had first heard her sighs of pleasure. Those things had driven him to the very outer reaches of his considerable control, but he had managed to rein himself in. Barely.

That near lack of restraint actually alarmed him a little. He wasn't a man prone to succumb to his animal instincts, he had been taught better than that. Those desires were meant to be purged with a mistress or a lightskirt, not a proper wife, a woman meant to be treated with reverence.

Still, despite her propriety and innocence, Anne brought out powerful desires in him, and it was a constant struggle to remain as unruffled as a man of his station should be. He hoped that over time, his passion for her would wane and they would fall into a comfortable, distant union more like his parents had shared or that a thousand others in their social sphere enjoyed. It was better that way.

When he looked at Simon again, he found his friend was staring at him, head cocked, with a look of concern on his face. "Waverly?"

Rhys shook away the memories of Anne in his bed and shrugged. "Of course I am perfectly content. But somehow I doubt you came here, the very day of my return to London, to discuss such a mundane topic. I can see you're troubled. Tell me what is wrong."

Simon didn't reply for a long moment, but merely stared at Rhys. He had an expression Rhys rarely saw from his friend, a mixture of sadness and regret, but also true affection.

"You have always been able to read me," Simon finally said softly.

Rhys shifted. Emotional exchanges were something he avoided at all costs. Normally his friends respected that, but today Simon was pushing for them both with his questions about Anne and his current comments. It was entirely uncomfortable, especially when coupled with the fact that Rhys had no idea why his friend had intruded upon his home.

"What is going on?" he snapped, his tone as sharp as the one he generally used with those below him in rank.

Simon smiled, but it was sad and distant. "Yes, I apologize. I have avoided this unpleasantness long enough. You will recall that before you married I uncovered some painful truths about my father. Despite his exalted reputation, he sired several bastard sons, as well as engaged in political intrigues and manipulations."

Rhys nodded as pity filled him. He couldn't imagine his friend's pain and didn't want to. "Of course. Have you learned more about his unsavory past?"

Simon swallowed hard before he answered. "I did. I have obtained more information about the identities of his other sons."

Rhys's brow wrinkled. "Why?"

Simon stared at him. "I want to meet them, Waverly."

"*Meet* them?" Rhys drew back a fraction. "Why in the world would you wish to do that? They are certainly not of your quality, your rank. If you allow such people into your life, you are only opening yourself up to the potential for blackmail and pain. I would hate to see you suffer for your father's sins."

Simon shut his eyes. "Well, you may be correct about that, my friend."

Rhys cocked his head. "What do you mean?"

"I shall start at the beginning," Simon said, almost more to himself than to Rhys. He got to his feet and began to pace the room with a restless energy that made Rhys's own heart quicken.

"Just after you wed, Lillian and I went to the offices of one of the solicitors who held some of my father's information. While there we . . ."

Simon hesitated and took a long, deep breath. Rhys watched the struggle line his friend's face, and the pain there touched even *his* distant heart. Simon had been like a brother to him for years, Rhys hated to see him in such a state.

"We uncovered the identity of one of my illegitimate brothers," Simon finally finished, his voice breaking as he turned to face Rhys.

Rhys's eyebrows lifted. "I see. But there is clearly more to all of this than you have yet said."

Simon nodded. "A day after I uncovered the truth, I received an anonymous note. You said that my investigation into this matter could lead to blackmail and it appears you are correct."

Rhys bolted to his feet and moved on Simon in shock. "My God!"

Simon nodded. "It appears that my coming to the solicitor's and obtaining my father's papers set off a chain of events. The note said that a man would contact me in a month's time and he would expect a rather large payment to keep silent about the information I now have."

Rhys swallowed hard past the bile that had filled his throat at the idea of blackmail. "I wonder why he gives you a month before he makes himself known."

Simon shrugged, though the anxiety in the lines on his face belied the nonchalant action. "Perhaps he wants me to stew on the idea that he has such damning information about me and my family. After a month of contemplation, he might think I am more apt to surrender to his demands."

Turning away, Simon continued, "And then there is the fact that the solicitor who was steward to the papers was an American who inherited them from some distant relative. Perhaps the blackmailer might be located away from England. Travel would take some time, especially if the charlatan of a solicitor had to send him word of my recovery of the documents."

"Wait, you think the *solicitor* is involved?"

Simon nodded, his expression grim. "I returned to the man immediately to demand who else had access to the papers he had provided me, but found his offices abandoned. I have used the entire scope of my influence in an investigation, but he has all but disappeared from the face of the earth. I can only assume he played some role in this."

Rhys drew in a deep breath. "I am sorry, my friend. How terrible for you. But . . ."

"But?" Simon asked.

"This does not have to equal ruination. After all, what can the man say but that your father had a bastard son? Most of the men we know have a few children from the wrong side of the blanket. It damages your father's pious reputation, but it will not necessarily reflect upon you if you release the information in the proper fashion yourself."

Simon flinched and turned away. Rhys watched him, uncertain as to why his friend would be unable to meet his eyes. Why Simon would be so pale and sick.

"You are correct. If the situation only involved myself, I would likely reveal the truth. God knows my father doesn't deserve protection. But there are other things to consider. You see, the man who is actually my brother is important. He is . . . he is titled."

Rhys stared for a long moment as the force of what his friend was saying hit him. Bloodlines were the driving force of the Society he and Simon kept. Although a gentleman who was born into a legitimate marriage would not be stripped of his title, if the truth was revealed about his unfortunate birth, the scandal would be more than devastating. All who saw this person from that moment on would know he did not deserve his rank and the privileges he had been granted. He and his family could very well be shunned, their name tied to fraud and ruination for as long as they lived and even beyond.

"A man of rank . . ." Rhys breathed, almost unable to say it. "It is highly regrettable, but—"

He broke off, knowing how differently Simon felt about the importance of birth. Still, his friend *had* to know the consequences.

"The man is a bastard by birth and should not be given the consideration of his title, no matter what the law says," Rhys finally finished slowly. "Those around him have a right to know that he is only masquerading as something he is not. Revealing the truth won't only protect you against this blackmail, but it's only fair. This person must face the consequences—"

"He is a friend," Simon interrupted.

Rhys staggered back. "Someone we know? My God!"

"No, Rhys, not someone we know . . . Rhys . . ." Simon seemed to struggle. His hands shook and his face was a sickly shade of green, as though he was only just controlling the urge to cast up his accounts. "Rhys, *you* are my brother."

It took a moment for the words to fully pierce Rhys's mind because the statement was so entirely unfathomable that it almost seemed like a foreign language to him.

"What?"

"You heard me," Simon whispered. "You're my brother."

All the denials and reasonings in Rhys's mind faded away as his friend's words sank in. He stared at Simon, his eyes widening and his blood pounding in his ears.

"That isn't funny, Billingham," he finally said, his voice low and dangerous. "I don't appreciate you coming here and wasting my time with this nonsense. This little joke of yours has gone too far."

He pushed to his feet and turned on his heel toward the door, but he hadn't gotten two steps when Simon spoke again.

"Damn it, Waverly, you've known me for almost twenty years. Do you think I would do such a thing as lie to you about *this*? Or make light about what is the greatest pain of my life, and what I know full well will be the greatest pain of yours?"

Rhys froze. If Simon didn't truly believe what he was saying was true, he wouldn't come here and repeat it. Slowly he pivoted to face his friend, who was now standing, arms open in a pleading gesture.

"Then you have been misled, my friend," Rhys said softly. "Because there is no way that I could be your brother in anything more than spirit. If someone has told you otherwise, then they have played a cruel hoax on you. Perhaps the blackmailer arranged this, perhaps—"

Simon reached into his coat pocket and withdrew

a packet of papers. Rhys noticed his friend's hand trembled as he offered him the bundle.

"Rhys, I have irrefutable proof that you are my brother. You *are* one of my father's by-blows."

Rhys snapped his gaze to his friend's face, then down to the papers he still held out, waiting patiently for Rhys to take them. But Rhys didn't. He dodged the offering as if it were a hot poker that would burn.

"This is unacceptable, Billingham," he said as he paced away. "To imply such a thing about my mother and your father . . . If you weren't my dearest friend I would call you out this instant."

Simon lowered his hand with a sigh. "I realize it is difficult to accept. When I first discovered the truth I hesitated to tell you because I knew it would destroy your world. But with the blackmailer threatening, this might come out on its own. I thought you deserved to know the truth and help me determine how to handle it. And I thought you would want to know who you are from a friend, not some blackguard demanding payment for silence."

Rhys crossed the room in a few long strides and grasped Simon's collars. Although Simon was the larger of the two men, he didn't resist, even when Rhys shook him.

"Shut up, do you hear me? Keep your lying mouth

shut! I *know* who I am. I am Rhys Carlisle, Duke of Waverly. I am the son of one of the most feared men in the Empire. I *know* who I am."

Slowly Simon lifted his hands and pushed Rhys away. Smoothing his coat, he took a long step back.

"It will take a while to accept. And while you digest it, please know that I am working to uncover who the blackmailer is and how to handle him, so you don't have to worry about that until you are ready."

When Rhys didn't answer, Simon sighed. "I'll leave these things here for you. You can look at them when you feel inclined, see that I am not wrong and then come and speak to me. Day or night."

Rhys stared as Simon gently set the packet of papers on a nearby table.

"I'll take my leave," Simon said softly. "But Rhys?"

Rhys looked at his friend wordlessly.

"I know that this is not what you would ask for, and I would never ask for it, either. But I am happy you are my brother," Simon whispered. "No matter what happens, you always will be."

Rhys stared at him, the one person he had truly called a friend and meant it. And in that one moment, he recognized Simon was telling the truth, even without looking at the so-called evidence he had produced.

He thought about all the times Simon's late father had dodged him, avoided speaking to him, all the times he'd caught the former Duke of Billingham watching him . . .

"Get out," he said softly.

Simon inclined his head gently and left Rhys alone. Alone with the bound papers on the table that looked so innocent. They called to him, and even though Rhys knew they were a siren's song, meant to dash everything he had ever been, every way he had ever defined himself and his place in life, still he couldn't ignore them. He had to look, had to see.

Slowly he crossed the room and untied the string that bound the information together. Inside he found letters between the Duke of Billingham and his mother, a solicitor's ledger, and an unexpected and certainly unneeded payout from Billingham to his mother just a short time after his birth.

The more he read, the sicker he felt. And the more he lost himself with every word. He wasn't Rhys Carlisle. And though the law would continue to see him as Duke of Waverly, in his heart he would never see himself as that again.

Who was he, then? *What* was he? The questions plagued him, echoing in his mind until he wanted to scream. So he did the only thing he could: he called for his horse and he ran.

*   *   *

Anne Carlisle frowned as the maid pushed the door open.

"And this is your chamber, Lady Anne," her long-time maid, Malvina, said. Then she shook her head. "I mean, Your Grace."

Anne ignored the woman's correction as she stepped into a very lovely room, done in her favorite shades of blues and golds. Normally she would have been enchanted by the big bed that was the centerpiece of the room, draped in a gauzy fabric that spoke of princess dreams and wishes.

On any other day, she might have oohed and aahed over the big dressing table with its large mirror and carefully arranged perfumes and brushes.

But not today. Because she had spent only one night in her new home before she and Rhys departed for their wedding trip, and that was her wedding night. But it hadn't been here; no, she had been in Rhys's chamber. She had thought *that* room would be the one she inhabited once she took her permanent place here.

But Malvina had brought her to a room a few doors down from her husband's.

She moved forward to the window and looked outside. Although it wasn't what she expected, the chamber had a delightful view of the garden behind the home and the beautifully tended yard beyond that. But she didn't want a view. She didn't want a chamber of her own.

She wanted Rhys. She wanted to be a real wife, a love match, although she knew what a silly and romantic notion that was in today's modern world. So the beauty before her was tainted, no matter how much it sparkled.

"Are you certain this is correct?" she asked softly, avoiding her servant's gaze as she moved forward. "*This* is to be my chamber?"

Malvina nodded. "Yes, Your Grace. We have been preparing and unpacking your things since the wedding, and His Grace's instructions were quite clear. Do you not like it?"

Anne sighed as she turned to face Malvina. She forced her usual bright smile. "Of course I do. It is lovely, everything a chamber should be. You've done marvelous work, as always, my dear Malvina."

Her maid blushed before she moved to the trunk a servant had delivered and began to unpack Anne's honeymoon things with swift efficiency. As she worked, she talked, a constant stream of cheery observations about the house. Anne nodded, occasionally murmuring an encouraging platitude. Normally she would have listened, for Malvina always had the best tidbits of information, but today she sank down at her dressing table and stared at her reflection with unseeing eyes.

"Are you worried, Your Grace?" Malvina finally asked.

Anne started before she gave her maid a side glance. The servant had worked as Anne's attendant for almost a decade, since both of them were little more than girls. After her mother's death, Anne had come to view her servant as a friend, something Rhys had always disapproved of. He believed ranks were made for a reason.

"Am I so obvious, Mally?" She laughed, reverting to the friendly nickname she had given the girl years ago.

"Only to one who knows you well," Malvina said. "You're worrying over the chambers, I think."

Anne stiffened. Only her servant knew her secret and they rarely spoke of it.

Slowly she nodded. "Yes. I hadn't realized it would be like this. I had hoped . . ."

"That the man would change his pompous colors after your wedding trip and tell you he was in love with you, after all?" Malvina asked.

Anne lowered her chin. In most households that kind of impertinence would result in punishment, but Malvina only spoke Anne's own heart. If anyone should be punished for such foolishness, it was she.

And she was, every day, by disappointed wishes and aching dreams.

"He was very good to me while we were traveling alone together," Anne admitted. "And very gentle and giving to me when we—"

She broke off. After her mother's death, her father had been careful to ensure Anne understood all the things she would need to know to be a good duchess. A string of women had instructed her in those elements over the years.

But the things that happened between a man and woman were not things she'd been all that prepared for. Without a mother to explain, she had been a bit in the dark, though she had very much enjoyed the intimate touch of her husband. Still, she wasn't ready to have a conversation about it.

"Well, I mean he was gentle, and he certainly didn't have to be. I'm his; he could have been coarse or callous if he cared nothing for my feelings," she said with a blush. "I suppose I foolishly hoped that might mean something more was developing between us."

Malvina shrugged one shoulder. "Lady Anne . . . *Your Grace* . . ."

"You needn't keep correcting yourself," Anne said. "In private I see no harm in the old forms of address."

The servant flushed with pleasure before she continued, "Lady Anne, you are dealing with a man of ice, you've known that for years. For whatever reason you believe he has a heart under it all, but you aren't going to reach it in a week of marriage. It might take years to break through that nasty façade and find the man within."

Anne nodded. It was true, Rhys Carlisle had a reputation for being distant, cold, and obsessed with maintaining the sanctity of rank. Everyone knew that, many had suffered from it. And while she had occasionally seen glimpses of more within the man— glimpses that had helped her develop greater feeling for him over the long years of their engagement—she wasn't so naïve as to think that he wouldn't be a difficult nut to crack when it came to making him love her. To making him see her as more than the "perfect" duchess and more like the love of his life.

"You are right, Mally," she mused. "But luckily I have all the rest of our lives to change his mind."

"Hmph," Malvina huffed as she unfolded the last garment from the trunk. She snapped the lid shut. "I suppose."

Anne ignored the incredulous tone of her maid's voice as she smoothed her hair. By now Simon would likely be gone, and perhaps she could have a few moments alone with Rhys.

She slipped from the room and down the stairway.

She had visited this house so often that the turns of each hallway were like second nature to her. She had memorized them, memorized everything about the life she would one day live here, since she was a girl.

She found the parlor where they had met with Simon, but when she opened the door it was empty. She moved to Rhys's office a few doors away, but it, too, showed no signs of its master. She frowned and called for Gilmour.

When the butler arrived, she smiled at him. "Gilmour, will you tell me where I can find His Grace?"

The butler's gaze flickered down a fraction, but not before Anne saw a brief glimpse of pity in his stare. She cocked her head. Why in the world would the servant pity her?

"I'm sorry, Your Grace. Not half an hour ago Lord Waverly called for his horse and rode off. I have no idea where he has gone or when he will return."

Chapter 2

Three days. It had been three days since Anne's husband of a week had gotten on his horse and abandoned her. In that time she had hardly eaten and rarely slept, watching and waiting for his return and pondering all the worst scenarios of what could have happened to him. But after all these years of careful observation, Anne knew Rhys. If she set out on a full-scale search for him it would cause the gossip he abhorred, and that was the last thing her husband would want.

So that was how Anne found herself in a beautifully appointed carriage with the Waverly crest emblazoned upon its door to declare to the world its inhabitants, pulling up on the drive of the London home of Simon Crathorne, Duke of Billingham.

She was unannounced and uninvited, but that was how Anne had planned it. Simon was the last person who had seen her husband, she didn't want to give her friend a chance to concoct some story that wasn't true if he knew why Rhys had left.

Left her.

The servant who greeted her didn't seem put off by her unannounced appearance and led her to a cheery parlor to wait while he fetched his master. Anne paced the room, wringing her hands as she pondered what she would say to Simon when she saw him.

What she wanted to do was fly at him, beat her hands on his chest, and demand he tell her where her husband had gone. But she wouldn't. Her near-hysteria wouldn't give her the answers she desired and would only increase her humiliation.

The door behind her clicked as it opened and Anne spun around and moved forward a step. But to her surprise and disappointment, it wasn't Simon who met her, but Lillian, his new wife.

Normally Anne would have been happy to see the pretty blond woman, for in the weeks before her wedding, the two had begun a friendship Anne was sure would bloom and grow. But in the fraction of the first moment Lillian saw her, Anne noticed her friend's golden hazel eyes flash pity and sorrow.

It took all of Anne's strength not to burst into tears right then and there.

"Good afternoon, Your Grace," Lillian said as she entered the room and shut the door behind her

"I didn't expect you today, but I'm pleased to see you."

Anne drew in a shuddering breath. She had long been raised to be polite, ladylike, and those lessons were difficult to forget. She smiled as brightly as she could manage.

"I-I do apologize for coming unannounced, Lillian," she choked past dry lips. "But I'm afraid I have a matter of great import on my mind."

Lillian hesitated, staring at her before she motioned to two chairs beside the fire. Anne ignored her offer.

"You do seem troubled," Lillian said softly. "Is there something I can do?"

"Not you, unfortunately. I came to see Simon," Anne whispered, her gaze flitting to the door. "In fact, I'm certain it was *he* I asked for when I inquired as to your residence to your servant. Please, is he home?"

Lillian stepped closer, but it was a wary movement. In that moment Anne could only imagine how she looked, eyes wild, face pale. Her anger, her fear, her utter confusion clawed at her at present. She felt those emotions throbbing as powerfully as she felt her own heartbeat.

She dragged in a gasping breath and clenched her fists at her sides. She had to control these feelings. She didn't want to show them to Lillian or to Simon or to anyone else. Hadn't she been humiliated enough?

"Anne," Lillian said softly.

"I . . . want . . . to see . . . Simon," Anne gasped out. Blood heated her face at the raised, broken tone of her voice, but her patience and propriety had finally reached its frayed end. "I *need* to see him, immediately!"

Almost as if on cue the door to the parlor opened and Simon himself entered the room. His face was bright with a welcoming smile as his gaze fell on her, but it was less than a moment before it vanished. He rushed to her in three long strides and caught her hand.

"Great God, Anne, are you well?"

She wrenched her fingers from his, unable to bear his touch in her current state. It felt like sandpaper on her skin when all she wanted was the truth, not some empty show of comfort.

"You should know," she whispered. "*You* saw him last. Where is he? What did you do? What did you say?"

Lillian and Simon exchanged a brief, confused, and concerned look before Simon returned his attention to her.

"I'm sorry, Anne, I don't understand your question. Please, be seated, calm yourself and let us talk about what is troubling you. I want to help, but—"

"Help? How can you help me? You did this. You—
you did this," Anne repeated, but now she did sit
down. Collapsed was more like it. The entire situation
was like a weight, constantly crushing down upon
her. She couldn't breathe, she could hardly think.

Simon sucked in a sudden breath and sank down
into his own chair. Lillian moved behind him and
pressed a hand to his shoulder in a gesture of support and love. Anne flinched away from it, from
the closeness she had never had and was beginning
to believe was no longer possible in her own young
marriage.

"Anne, tell me what has happened and I'll do my
best to assist you any way I can," Simon said, his
tone low and soothing.

She clenched her fists in her lap and stared at him
evenly. Simon did seem genuinely confused, and who
could blame him? She was ranting and raving in the
middle of his parlor. Clearly she hadn't explained
herself well enough. With much effort, she took a
deep breath and started over, determined to make
Simon understand and then obtain the answers she
required.

"Three days past you came to my home. What
did you say to my husband?"

In an unguarded reaction, Simon physically recoiled from her before he regained his composure. He shot a brief glance up at Lillian and then slowly shook his head.

"I'm sorry, Anne. You know I view you as quite my own sister, but I wouldn't feel comfortable in sharing that conversation with you. You should ask Rhys."

All attempts at calm vanished as Anne flew to her feet. *"Ask Rhys?"*

Both Simon and Lillian leaned back at Anne's unexpectedly violent reaction. Simon was on his feet in an instant, reaching for her as if he feared she would topple over in her current state, but Anne jerked away.

"Yes," he said, watching her. "I think it would be best if you take this up with your husband.

Anne barked out a laugh, but it was inspired by anything but humor. "I would do if I knew where he was! Tell me, Simon. Tell me what you said to him that sent him flying from our home with no explanation and no return? That sent him from London, apparently. From all of his estates! Please tell me what you said, what you did, to make him disappear like this!"

Aside from his shock at her behavior, Simon had been cloaking his own emotions quite well during this exchange. But now . . . now the façade fell and his green eyes brightened with heartache.

"Rhys is gone?" he whispered in disbelief. "I knew he was upset, but I never thought . . . Are you saying he's quit London entirely?"

Anne nodded. Somehow hearing another person state that fact out loud helped. It renewed her focus on her duty, and that duty was to find her husband. Tears and screaming and letting herself surrender to her pain would not aid in that responsibility, and might even hinder it.

She struggled for a moment, swallowing her tears, calming her breath. Her heart slowed from its wild beating to something more natural, and that was when she finally spoke.

"Yes, he is gone," she whispered. "The afternoon of our return, I sought him out after you left, only to be told that he had called for his horse and ridden away with no explanation or hint of his plans to return. At first I simply waited, assuming he would come back, but when morning came, he hadn't returned."

She squeezed her eyes shut, ignoring the clawing panic that raged up inside her once more. "I sent word around to his clubs, discreetly inquiring if he was there, but to no avail. I even asked his mother, but she was as in the dark as I am. No one seems to know where Rhys is, and now it is three days past. And nothing. Not a word of or from him, Simon. So

I ask you again, what did you say to my husband? Because before you came to visit us, Rhys seemed perfectly contented."

Simon shook his head. "I'm sorry, Anne. It isn't that I don't believe you deserve to know, but it isn't my secret to reveal to you. Rhys must tell you, not I."

Anne stared at him, suddenly overcome by a rage she hadn't even known she could feel. Simon was staring at her with such calmness, dismissing her demands as if she wasn't owed an explanation.

"You bastard," Anne said. Her voice was quiet, but it shook and wavered. "Did you tell him not to love me? Not to want me? To leave me?"

She moved toward him without realizing she was going to do it, but before she reached him, Lillian intervened, scrambling to embrace her.

Anne tensed, not wanting to be comforted or placated, but as Lillian smoothed a hand along her back gently, Anne went limp. All the pressure and pain of the past few days, the humiliation of abandonment and the fear that she had lost her future, flooded her. She clung to Lillian, sucking in breath after breath. But she didn't cry. She refused to cry.

"I'm sorry," Lillian whispered as she held her. "But trust that Simon would never hurt you. He adores you, he would never bring you pain on purpose."

Anne looked over Lillian's shoulder. Simon stood,

ramrod stiff, looking at her with a devastation in his eyes that reflected her own so perfectly that she felt it even more keenly. It burned in her, searing every part of her like a fire, only there was no way to put it out. No way to end it.

Not unless she found her husband. Because in the end, as much as she cried out to Simon to tell her the truth, as much as she resented him for saying he couldn't . . . it was *Rhys* who had left her. It was *Rhys* who owed her explanations for why. And transferring her feelings onto Simon as a surrogate was not satisfying.

Although she feared confronting Rhys would be no more so.

With a great shuddering breath, Anne removed herself from Lillian's embrace. She touched the other woman's arm briefly, a gesture of thanks.

"I'm sorry," she whispered, her comments directed to both the Billinghams. "I realize it must be quite shocking to have me arrive here in such a state, not to mention to have me tell you that a friend has vanished."

Lillian shook her head, even as she stepped back to stand beside her husband. "You deserve those feelings, Anne. I cannot imagine how I would behave if Simon disappeared."

Lillian shivered, and Anne nodded. "Then you

understand why I'm desperate to know why he did this. Any inkling of what set Rhys off could help me determine where he might have gone."

It was Simon who stepped forward this time, and Anne allowed him to gently place a hand on each shoulder. He looked down at her, his gaze kind.

"I *do* understand. But I have been friends with Rhys for so long, Anne. You must know I cannot betray a confidence between us."

Anne's chin dipped down, and when a pained moan filled the air, she was shocked to discover it was her own.

"I can tell you that I do think what we spoke of likely did bring this situation to pass," Simon continued. "And that . . ."

He hesitated, and the uncertain tone of his voice made Anne jerk her gaze back to his face. Simon's expression was torn, as if he was trying to make a difficult decision.

"What is it?" Anne whispered, trying not to hope too much that he might give her some glimmer of information.

He cleared his throat. "When he was a very young boy, Rhys's mother used to take him and his sisters to a cottage by the sea. While deep in his cups, he once confided to me it was the one place in which he was most happy."

Anne drew back. Rhys must have been deep in his cups indeed to confess something about his happiness. Her husband often dismissed all emotion as weakness in one broad stroke.

"Do you think he might have gone there?" she asked, her voice hoarse and cracking.

Simon nodded. "If you have made inquiry at all his estates and with his clubs, then it is possible. Few know of this cottage. If Rhys was hiding to lick his wounds, I think it's a good guess as to his whereabouts."

Anne let out a gasp of hope and relief. "Then I must go there. Tell me its exact location and I will depart today!"

Simon's eyes widened. "Anne, it is three days' travel, two of them quite hard. You will need an escort and—"

She shook her head. "No, Simon. You cannot deter me, though I appreciate your reasons for doing so. I must go to Rhys. And I shall do it whether you assist me or not. Ultimately I *will* find out where this cottage is and I'll go there. But I'm asking you this one thing, to make my search easier."

Simon shut his eyes briefly and let out a low sigh. "Anne—"

Before he could finish what was clearly going to

be a statement of protest, Lillian quietly touched his arm. "Simon, tell her."

He shot a glance at his wife. "What?"

Lillian nodded. "This is between them now, Simon, and I think you can see in Anne's eyes that she is telling the truth about her determination to uncover the location of this place in one way or another. I know if it were me, it would take hell itself to stop me from finding you. You should tell her where the cottage is."

Anne stared at the other woman in stunned thanks. She had met Lillian Crathorne only a few weeks before, but in that moment a swell of friendship welled up in her so powerful that she realized it would never quite fade. She would feel some part of it toward the woman for the rest of her life.

"At least let me escort you," Simon said softly, clearly on the brink of surrender under the attack of both the women.

Anne pondered that thought for a moment, but then she shook her head. "I admit it is somewhat comforting to think of you coming with me and helping me confront Rhys if he is there. But it is clear that whatever has precipitated this problem has to do with your friendship, and if you came with me, you and Rhys would have to focus on that. And for once, I don't want my interaction with my husband to have anything to do with you or with Society or with my father or his father . . ."

She clenched her fists at her sides as she trailed off. She sucked in a calming breath and continued, "As Lillian said, this confrontation must be about me and my husband. And he *is* my husband, whether he wants to be or not. I must go alone."

Simon stared at her for a long moment, and then he sighed. "Very well. But I'll feel better if you at least allow me to send you in my carriage. My driver is very discreet, and the fewer people who know about this, the better."

Anne opened her mouth to object, but then shut it. Perhaps Simon was correct. She didn't want to face the utter humiliation of having her own servants know she was chasing her husband across the country. As she would likely never see Simon's driver again, she would never have to face the fact that he knew her pain.

"Yes," she said with a brief nod. "I can agree to that."

"And," he added, "I want you to send word to me when you do find Rhys. If you don't send word or you don't return within a week, I'll come there myself to search for you."

Anne's eyes widened, and this time she had every

intention of arguing, but Simon lifted a hand to silence her. "It is not open for debate, Anne. Rhys is my . . ."

When Simon trailed off, Anne tilted her head. She had never seen the other man so pained. It echoed her own emotions, and she flitted her gaze away, uncomfortable.

"He is my friend," Simon finished, his voice cracking. "The best I have ever had. I want to be certain that you are both well."

After a moment's hesitation, Anne nodded. "I'll do that. Now I shall return home and make some arrangements. Will you send your man there in an hour or so?"

Simon nodded. "Yes."

Anne turned to go, but Lillian's voice stopped her. "Anne?"

She looked back and found that Lillian was approaching her. Once again the other woman's arms wrapped around her in a tight embrace.

As she held her, Lillian whispered, "You are strong, Anne. Stronger than you think, in both your character and in your love for him."

Anne flinched, hating that her emotions had been so clear to someone who was almost a stranger. Lillian released her when she stiffened, but smiled as Anne backed away.

"You'll need that strength," Lillian continued. "Hold on to it."

Anne stared. It was obvious from her tone and the pity in her stare that Lillian knew the secret Simon wouldn't tell her. Anne wasn't certain how she felt about that, but she pushed it aside, for another feeling was far more powerful in that moment.

Fear.

It was becoming rapidly clear to her that whatever she would face when she did find Rhys was going to be difficult indeed. And she wasn't sure if her one-sided love for him could overcome it.

Chapter 3

Rhys stood on the high cliff, staring down at the sea below as it crashed with violence and power on the rocky beach. The angry slam of it reflected the wretchedness of his own heart, but it gave him no comfort.

In the week since Simon had come into his parlor and utterly destroyed his life, Rhys had been grappling with what he now knew about the shocking details of his birth. Every moment he was awake, the truth ate at him, forcing him to reflexively read and reread the documents that proved he was not the man he had always believed himself to be.

And the nights were worse. It was a struggle to find sleep, even when exhaustion clawed and burned his eyes. When he did collapse, sometimes with the help of alcohol, restless dreams kept him from any real respite.

And so he paced the cliffs, torturing himself not

just with the facts he knew, but with all the uncertainties that now plagued him.

He had been Rhys Carlisle his entire life and the Duke of Waverly for several years. He had built his whole person on those facts. He had behaved a certain way because that was his world. Damn, he had even formed the "Duke Club" as a boy, allowing only other first sons of dukes to join because at least they understood the majesty of what he would one day become. He had actively excluded "lesser" men from his circle, cutting sometimes viciously in order to maintain the sanctity of rank.

His father . . . except the man who had raised him wasn't his father . . . Thomas Carlisle, Rhys supposed he should now think of him as Thomas Carlisle. Either way, the elder duke had encouraged Rhys's arrogance, even going so far as to punish him if he showed empathy or friendliness to people of lower status. The last Duke of Waverly had reminded Rhys at every moment of every day that he *deserved* more than other people because he had such impeccable bloodlines. Because his ancestors and his title made him special.

So if none of that was true, if everything he had ever thought or felt or been taught about himself and his place in the world was a lie . . . then who was he? What was he? Where did he belong . . . or did he belong anywhere at all anymore?

And those thoughts didn't even begin to touch upon the possibility of blackmail. The idea that someone would try to obtain money for this shameful secret turned Rhys's stomach every time he thought of it. Thank God Simon was handling that problem at present. Whatever else he thought of his friend . . . *brother* . . . right now, he trusted him to handle that matter until Rhys came back to London.

With a frustrated shake of his head, Rhys walked to the edge of the cliff. There was but one safe place to dive, a small cove where the water far below was deep, there were no rocks, and the currents kept the waves from rolling in like fists of nature's fury. He had discovered it with the help of some village youths one summer long ago when he came here with his mother, before the concept of rank would have kept him from playing with those children.

Right now he wanted to feel the air across his cheek as he plummeted into the sea. He wanted the cold snap of the water to wake his body and erase the circling thoughts that tormented his mind. He found the spot, long ago marked with an unusual rock by the people who came here to take advantage of the same excitement.

Standing at the edge, Rhys stared at the water as he tugged his shirt over his head and tossed it aside on the grass. His trousers went next onto the pile.

For a moment Rhys thrilled at the pure exhilaration of standing nude at the edge of a cliff, about to dive fifteen feet into the icy water below. It made him feel alive and that was what he wanted, what he *needed* more than anything.

He moved into position to jump and was about to go over the edge when a piercing scream echoed through the still air around him. He pivoted in surprise to face the voice and perhaps offer some kind of assistance to its owner, but what he saw shocked him enough that he rocked back on his heels.

A carriage was now parked at the top of the gentle slope next to the cottage that had been his home since his arrival here a few days before. That would have been a surprising enough sight, since he had told no one of his coming here and very few people even knew this place existed.

But it was the person who had intruded upon his privacy that shocked him all the more. It was his wife who had thrown herself from the vehicle, not waiting for assistance or even shutting the door behind her before she sprinted down the hill toward him.

"No!" Anne screamed as she tossed a reticule aside and grasped her skirt in one fist to keep from tripping over it.

Rhys caught his breath at the sight of her wildly racing toward him, brown locks tumbling around her cheeks in the breeze, the blond highlights catching the sun and almost sparkling.

"Anne?" he said, staring.

She didn't answer, but instead hurtled herself at him. He wasn't ready for her and staggered back, very nearly going over the cliff. Somehow he managed to lurch to the side before he landed flat on his back, his wife splayed over him.

And for a long moment, there was only silence.

Anne struggled to catch her breath, semi-stunned as she lay across Rhys's prone body. She hadn't exactly planned to greet her husband in such a way when she encountered him. But then neither had she expected to find him at the edge of a terrifying cliff, ready to jump to his death.

The very idea of that disintegrated her remaining shock and forced her to action.

"Don't you do this!" she cried out, lifting herself to grasp Rhys's shoulders and shake him. "Don't you take yourself from me, you selfish, stupid ass!"

Rhys stared up at her as if she had sprouted a second head, but then he shifted and they rolled farther away from the cliff's edge. However the motion also caused her to move beneath him and now she was pinned by his weight.

"What is wrong with you, woman?" he barked,

his warm breath heating her already flushed face. "You could have killed us both by attacking me in such a foolhardy fashion."

Her brow wrinkled as she stared up at him. Her frightened mind was beginning to clear.

"I-isn't that what you wanted?" she asked.

"To die?" He drew back and his eyes narrowed. "Of course not."

"So you weren't about to do yourself a harm when I pulled up to the cottage?" she asked, reliving that horrifying moment in a sudden burst that made her shiver.

His face softened a fraction for just a moment, such a rarity that she drank it in, but then whatever he felt was erased and he glared at her.

"No! I would certainly never think to do something so rash. I was merely about to dive off the cliff. I have done so since I was a child."

"Oh," Anne said, and said nothing more for she could think of nothing.

As her fear faded, she was startled to realize she was lying on the grass, covered by her husband's hard, muscular body . . . and he was utterly naked.

It was something that hadn't happened all that often in their new marriage. And now that her terror was fading, other feelings were making themselves known. Other reactions in her confused and exhausted body.

Like she wanted to open her legs and let Rhys seat himself there. Like she longed for him to lean down and kiss her, let her feel that he was whole and alive after the last week of worry and anguish. Later she could be angry, later she *would* demand answers. Right now she just wanted to hold this man and be held by him.

Their gazes met and she thought she saw a flicker of something heated in his normally stoic stare. As if he, too, had just realized that he was utterly bare over her. That it wouldn't take much to flip up her skirts and touch her in the way a husband was meant to touch his wife.

"Rhys," she whispered, her voice shaking with emotion.

He blinked, as if his name had snapped him from a haze. Without preamble he jerked himself to his feet. She stared because she couldn't help herself, watching as he bent over to snatch up his trousers. His bare skin was a temptation indeed.

"What are you doing here?" he asked as he covered himself.

The harshly spoken question yanked her from any reverie or fantasy that was in her mind. The anger

Anne had promised to save until later returned in the face of his arrogant nonchalance. He acted as if he had simply stepped out for a walk, rather than vanished without explanation for so many terrifying days!

"What am *I* doing here?" she repeated in utter shock. "What are *you* doing here? You are meant to be home, starting a new life with your bride. At least that was the plan, wasn't it? I never received word that you had changed it."

He jolted at the directness of her reply, but then he reached down to offer her a hand. He remained shirtless and she stared at the strong hand, the bare arm, the naked chest that rose up over her. Then she took his offering and allowed him to help her to her feet. Of course he immediately released her as soon as she was steady. Oh, he was always the chivalrous gentleman . . . except when it came to anything real. And except, apparently, when it came to abandoning her.

"Anne," he said, breathing heavily through his nose, almost like an angry bull. "Go home."

She stared at him, unable to keep her mouth from dropping open in utter shock. Go home? *Go home?* She had trekked across Lord only knew how many awful miles, her mind spinning with the horrible possibilities of where her husband might be and what he might be experiencing . . . She had cried for him; she had ached for him. Hell, she had thought he was going to throw himself off a cliff and made every effort to save him.

After all that, after all her years of dutiful companionship and unrequited love as she awaited their wedding, he thought he could dismiss her by saying, *Go home*?

He turned away to go back up to the cottage. His shoulders slumped as he walked up the hill, but he didn't look back. She watched him take every step and contemplated her options.

She could do as he said. After all, she had vowed to obey him in a church not two weeks before. Doing so would avoid at least some of the massive humiliation he had created with this situation. She had many friends who would take her side in London and her father would certainly take her back . . . and perhaps even demand satisfaction from Rhys when and if he ever returned to the city.

That was no doubt the easier route. But Anne hadn't spent two decades in love with this man to simply take the easier route at the first sign of trouble. She had come here because he might need her, and now, seeing him, she was more certain than ever that he did.

After all, he hadn't shaved perhaps for days, his

clothing, when he put it back on, was disheveled and wrinkled. He had been about to jump off a cliff *naked*.

No, the man who had pinned her down, the one walking away from her . . . he wasn't the bold, arrogant, oh-so-proper duke she had married. He wasn't the hard man she had loved despite his numerous faults.

And she wasn't about to walk away and regret it later. For the first time in her life, Anne realized she was going to have to fight.

With her heart throbbing so loud that it drowned out the crashing sea behind her, she jogged to catch up with Rhys. Reaching out, she caught his bare shoulder and pulled, forcing him to face her.

"No," she whispered, her voice shaking. She cleared her throat and shook her head. "No. I won't leave, Rhys."

His eyes widened and she knew why. He wasn't accustomed to anyone disobeying him, much less her. But these were desperate times and she couldn't do the things that were expected of her anymore.

"Anne," he ground out through clenched teeth. "I said you should go and I expect you to do so. Now leave!"

She shook her head a second time. "No. I won't no matter how many times you demand it. I have come all this way for an explanation as to why you abandoned me in London, but also to help you if I could."

She realized her tone was elevating until she was almost screaming and she hated herself for being unable to control her anger and pain, but it was so potent, so powerful that it overwhelmed all reason.

"I don't want your help," he said, his own voice becoming louder. "I want you to leave me alone. I promise you, Anne, it will be all the better for you. I swear you do not want to do this."

Anne recoiled. There was the "lord of the manor" she had come to know. Rhys had always believed he knew best for anyone and everyone around him. At times she had found this quality charming; it had even given her hope, for if he inserted himself in the troubles of others, it meant on some level he actually cared about the welfare of even those beneath him.

But now, having him turn that "duke knows best" attitude toward her, especially in this charged moment, she felt no gratitude for it. In fact, just the opposite.

Her hands went to her hips. "How would you know what I want, Waverly? In all the years we've been together, you have never *once* asked me. Well, now I'm going to tell you whether you ask or not. I want to be here, I want to be with *you*, and for once I am doing the thing *I* desire. Nothing you say shall move me or force my hand."

He opened his mouth as if to continue his protests, but before he could, the driver who had brought her here stepped around his carriage. He stared at the couple with obvious concern, as well as interest.

"Y-Your Grace," he called out, tentative. His gaze flashed from one of them to the other, as if he wasn't certain who he was addressing. "Are you well? Are you in need of some kind of assistance?"

Anne flushed so hot that it felt as though her cheeks were on fire. She had all but forgotten the stranger who had been her escort, and now she and her still-half-naked husband had been exchanging harsh words not ten feet away from him like a common fishwife and her beleaguered groom.

And if she felt horror, it was nothing compared to the expression on Rhys's face. He stared at the man at the top of the hill, his eyes wide and cheeks pale.

"Who the hell is that?" he asked, spinning to face her again.

She shifted uncomfortably. "Simon's driver," she admitted. "Our friend wouldn't allow me to come here without some representative from him."

"Simon," Rhys repeated dully, but in his eyes, dark and dangerous emotions swirled unexpectedly.

Anne had known both men for so long, but she had never seen even a hint of discord between them. Now Rhys, who was normally so cool and even-tempered to a fault, was almost shaking when he heard his friend's name. And she recalled Simon had seemed brokenhearted when he spoke of the man before her. It was curious and she intended to get to the bottom of what had torn the friends apart and sent her husband fleeing to this savage place.

"Simon told you about this cottage?" he asked, interrupting her thoughts.

She nodded. There was no use denying it. "Yes."

"One more betrayal," Rhys muttered.

She stared at him. "You consider it a betrayal that Simon sent his servant to escort me?"

Rhys barked out a humorless laugh. "No, I consider it a betrayal that my supposed friend revealed this place's existence to you at all, let alone encouraged you in a foolhardy endeavor of coming here to 'save' me, or whatever it is you think you're doing."

Her nostrils flared, but Anne refused to give in to her baser desires and shout again. Instead she folded her arms and stared at Rhys evenly.

"Well, the least I can say of Simon is that he helped me. He didn't simply *abandon* me. At this moment, I appreciate that more than *you* could ever comprehend."

Now it was Rhys's cheek that twitched, indicating her barb had hit, and for that she was more pleased than was probably healthy. She had been in such pain, she found she actually enjoyed inflicting some shadow of it on him.

But instead of replying or fighting or anything else, he grasped her hand and yanked her up the hill. She tugged back.

"If you force me into that carriage," she said, enunciating each word carefully, "I swear to you that I will hurtle myself from the moving vehicle and *walk* back."

Rhys snapped his gaze to her wordlessly and then stopped before Simon's driver. The man actually took an almost imperceptible step back, and for that Anne did not blame him. Rhys looked like he could kill at the moment.

"*You*," Rhys said, his tone back to that of the cold, dismissive duke she had always known, as if they hadn't just exchanged their most emotional, passionate words ever.

"Yes, Your Grace?" the driver squeaked out.

"Go back to London, your services are no longer required," he growled. "Tell your master I shall deal with him when I return."

"Y-yes, Your Grace," the other man stammered.

"And if I ever hear you breathed a word of what

you saw, or the fact that you brought my wife here to me, I will make sure that your life is painful, disappointing, and possibly brief. Do I make myself clear?"

For a long moment all the driver could do was stand and stare, swallowing reflexively. Then he nodded. "Clear as crystal, Your Grace."

With that the servant threw himself back into his place and urged the horses to turn the carriage and go. Anne stared as the vehicle rumbled down the rocky path toward the main road, sending up a plume of dust in its wake. A strange sense of both relief and terror filled her as her only means of escape disappeared from view.

She had done it, somehow she had won. Rhys was allowing her to stay.

"And *you*," Rhys said, forcing her attention away from the road and back to him. His dark eyes were alive with emotion, anger, and pain so palpable that she felt the throb of it. "Come with me."

She wasn't given the chance to answer or protest before he dragged her into the cottage and slammed the door behind them.

Chapter 4

The cottage was a small affair, with only two rooms, so when Rhys hurtled Anne through the door, she staggered off balance and landed sprawled across the rumpled bed where he had been sleeping since his arrival. He stared down at her and had a most unexpected reaction.

Through his anger, through his frustration with her utter refusal to leave him alone, he was completely aroused. Never before in his life had he so wanted to lie his body across a woman's and rut with her until he was overtaken by the oblivion of pleasure.

In some ways, he supposed it was a normal reaction. After all, Anne's hair had come down in the scuffle during her arrival, so it bounced about her shoulders in fragrant waves, and her clothing was cockeyed, as if she had already been touched and loved and left in disarray from it.

She was soft and beautiful and her face was filled

with as much emotion as he was trying to suppress in himself. Her intensity wasn't something he had seen before. Oh, certainly Anne was quicker to laugh than he, and he had seen her eyes fill with tears at a memory or a sad occasion, but those flashes of emotion were different from this.

This was wild, out-of-control, completely untamed feeling. And it was because of him, directed at him, which was also an uncommon occurrence. Since he controlled his own passions so thoroughly, he had never thought to inspire such things in other people.

"Are you going to speak to me or just stare me to hell?" Anne whispered as she struggled to sit up.

He arched a brow. His new bride had never been so defiant in all the years they had been betrothed. Her pliability was part of her perfection for the position as his duchess. But he found he rather liked the tart tone of her voice, the snap of rebelliousness in her eyes. Why, he had no idea. No man in his right mind would want to be married to a woman who didn't recognize his authority.

He folded his arms and pulled himself back together as best he could. He would handle his strange reactions to Anne once he got rid of her, and get rid of her he must, before she uncovered the reasons that he had come there. He wasn't ready for anyone to know the truth of his birth . . . not yet.

"There are a few people in the village who I think could have their silence assured with enough blunt," he murmured, more to himself than to her. "If I sent word home, a driver and your own servant could meet you along the road in a day or so."

Anne stared at him, then got to her feet. "So you are still determined you shall send me back? Then why tell Simon's driver to depart?"

He sucked in a breath as she said his best friend's . . . his brother's name. She had no idea how deeply it cut him every time he heard it.

"Because I don't want my Simon involved in this," he growled as he turned so he could wipe his emotions away as best he could. "But you must go back."

He felt her hand on his shoulder, and in that moment he realized he still hadn't put the shirt he clenched in his hand back on. He turned to face her, mesmerized by how soft her hand was on his skin. How her fingers lingered for a moment on the muscle of his shoulder as she looked at him, face upturned in the glittering sunlight that came through the clean window behind him.

"Rhys," she whispered. "I told you already that I won't leave."

He opened his mouth, but her fingers came to his lips, two of them pressing there gently to stop the words on his tongue. But now he wanted to do something different with that tongue, like dart it out and taste her. Draw her between his lips until she shut her eyes and buckled to his will one way or another.

Instead he stood stone-still and tried to think of anything he could that would make the raging ridge of his blooming erection less noticeable.

"I'm not some reticent child who you can simply send away," she said softly. "You and I married not two weeks ago. When we were announced as husband and wife before God and our friends, it changed everything. I won't abandon you, even if you claim you desire it. That was my promise to you and I keep my promises."

She slowly withdrew her fingers and let her hands fall to her sides. Rhys stared at her, her words slithering through his pain-addled brain like insidious snakes. He had been so alone since Simon told him the truth of his birth. There had been no comfort, no friend, no confidant to share these deep and powerful pains with.

He had never called Anne any of those things, but he knew she *could* be a friend and confidant. He'd seen her be both to other people. Her character was such that if he told her the truth, she would offer him support and consolation without hesitation.

She would do it, even to her detriment.

It was a bewitching idea, that he could hand over

all his heartbreak and let her bear it for a short time. That he could depend upon her.

"Rhys?" she whispered.

He shook his head, and the action cleared his mind. What was he thinking? He wasn't about to pour out his heart like some kind of foolish romantic hero. Or give over his secrets to anyone, not even his wife. And not only because it wasn't in his nature to be so maudlin and weak.

No, he had to keep his secrets from her in order to protect her. This *thing* he now knew about his birth was bound to come out, especially with a blackmailer poised to spread the secret like a fire through Society. When that happened, his entire world would fall apart . . . and Anne's, as well.

But if he kept her in the dark, if she had no idea of what he knew, then she could easily claim her innocence in the matter and be believed. When she was seen as a victim, not a conspirator, Society would pity her for her bad luck in a husband.

Of course they would separate. He would grant her a home of her own in London and they would move on as if the marriage had never occurred. Once that was done, Anne had enough friends and a powerful enough family that she might be able to weather the storm and even find acceptance again one day.

It would be a long road, but one that could lead to a better life for her.

But only if he did not allow her to become a partner in his scandal. Rhys would be destroyed one way or another by the time this situation was resolved, but if he could protect Anne even in the smallest way, he would.

She reached up and with one trembling hand cupped his cheek. He stared down at her, wanting her with a power so strong that it was almost frightening, especially when coupled with the fact that he had just decided they couldn't be together.

"Please say something, Rhys," she whispered. *"Please."*

He swallowed hard. What he was about to do would be seen by her as cruelty, but he meant it as kindness. This was the only way, even if it would be difficult.

"I-I don't want you, Anne. I don't want to be married to you."

She blinked, those green-blue eyes widening with shock and dilating with hurt. She stared at him for a long moment, utterly silent as her face crumpled. He hated himself for doing it, for crushing her in such a way, but it was for the best, it was the right thing to do, it was . . .

Before he could finish the thought, Anne yanked her hand back and slapped him.

"How dare you?" she said, her voice nothing more than a low whisper. "How *dare* you speak to me like that?"

He nodded as the sting in his cheek faded. He deserved her anger, and perhaps now she would go. Except, God, how he didn't want that. He had never seen her eyes so alive, so sparkling. He had never seen her skin so flushed. He wanted to breathe that in, fill himself with it and with her.

"Anne—" he said, hoping to regain some purchase on the situation.

Instead of answering, she lifted her hand and swung a second time, but this time he caught her wrist and tugged her against him to keep her from striking him. She tried to free herself with an admirable struggle, but he held fast, keeping her wiggling body firmly against his bare chest.

When she realized it was hopeless, she stopped fighting. In that moment, with her in his arms, with her face upturned, her breath coming short . . . he didn't care about all the reasons he had for her to go. He just wanted one taste.

He didn't realize he was moving in to kiss her until their mouths met. And it wasn't a chaste, shy, welcoming kiss, either. No, it immediately exploded into an openmouthed, panting, warring kiss. His arms came around her body, her hands clenching against his skin as she lifted up on her tiptoes to get closer.

Her body was so damned soft in his arms. Before when he made love to her, when he claimed her as his bride, he had tried to focus on other things when he touched her, to disconnect some part of his mind and prevent his emotions and desires from raging out of control.

But now . . . now he was incapable of such a thing. He was too raw for control, and so he felt every inch of his wife and reveled in every arch of her back and sigh from her lips.

He delved deeper, fisting her hair in his fingers and tilting her head back so he could angle his mouth more firmly over hers. He sucked her tongue, he tasted her breath, he crushed her against him, and he forgot, in that one glorious moment, all the pain and lies that had brought her here to his side.

Yet, even as lost as he was, grinding his mouth over hers, his body against hers, he knew this couldn't last. Some small part of him remained in utter and total control, and that part finally forced Rhys to pull back abruptly.

He didn't try to right Anne as she staggered when he released her. It wasn't because he wanted her to fall, but because he feared if he touched her once more that he wouldn't be able to listen to that small voice in his mind that still clung to the virtues of propriety. He feared if he even so much as touched her arm, he would end up on the bed behind them, her skirts around her waist and his body pushing into hers.

It was an impossibility. They could never make love again. He had to treat her as if she was no longer his wife.

He shook his head at the thought and looked at her. She had managed to right herself, and now she smoothed her skirts with shaking hands before she lifted her gaze to his. He expected horror to light her eyes because of the way he had molested her with so little finesse. He expected fear or even anger.

Instead her green-blue gaze was filled with triumph. She folded her arms and speared him with a stare and a tiny smile that made his gut clench with renewed desire.

"You're right, Rhys," she finally said softly. "I can see that you don't want me."

He expelled a frustrated breath at her quiet sarcasm. How he hated complications, and this one he had put upon himself because he hadn't been able to control his need for her.

"Anne," he said through tightly clenched teeth. "You don't understand."

She shook her head. "Then explain it to me, Rhys. After all our years together, you should know I'm not stupid. I want to understand why you have run from your responsibilities, from London, from me. And since I'm not planning on leaving, you will have a great deal of time to give me all the details you so fear to share."

Rhys stared at her for a long moment before he scrubbed a hand over his stubbly face. "Why, Anne? Why can't you just trust me that it is better for you to return to London and forget all this. Forget our betrothal, forget our marriage."

Her face crumpled again, but this time there was no anger to line it. There was only pain, a pain so intense that Rhys was almost mesmerized by its power.

Until she spoke and turned his world upside down.

"Because I love you, Rhys Carlisle," she said, as matter-of-factly as if she was announcing she was going for a ride. "I have always loved you."

The moment she said the words, Anne wished she could take them back. Oh, she had always imagined she would one day confess her heart to Rhys, but not under these circumstances. And she had certainly never pictured, in those girlish fantasies, that he would stare at her, spearing her with the same look he often gave to people who disgusted him.

"You don't mean that." His voice was even and quiet, controlled as he was always controlled. He didn't even sound like he cared that she had just handed over her heart.

In fact, quite the opposite.

She shut her eyes. She had already spoken once out of emotion, she wanted to be certain she didn't repeat that mistake. She had to consider all her options before she responded.

And she did have options. She could open her eyes and smile in an empty fashion and tell him that no, she didn't mean what she had said. And then she could return to London. It would make Rhys happy, she was certain.

But she had spent her life trying to make Rhys happy. And her father. And Society. And everyone else in the world but herself. Longing had been her companion in her bed at night as she pondered her future. A longing for Rhys's love, a desire for those glimpses of goodness she saw in him to overtake his less savory aspects. She had reached for a match based on affection, for all the hopes and dreams that a thousand fairy tales and novels had instilled in her. If she left now, longing and regret would remain her only friends, her only lover.

"I can't," she whispered as she opened her eyes.

Rhys stared at her. "I beg your pardon?"

She shook her head. "It would be easier for you if I didn't love you."

His cheek twitched, and a flicker of something darkened his gaze. "It is a foolish inclination, Anne. Ours is an arranged marriage, made by our parents when we were still children. I've never pretended any more or less. But if I somehow misled you—"

She interrupted him with a laugh that held no humor. "No. You have *never* made me think you loved me. When we were younger, you could be friendly. When my mother died, you were sympathetic, even kind when you thought your father wasn't looking. And sometimes over the years I caught you watching me . . . but you always looked away, and I knew I was only putting my own hopes into your face."

He winced, as if what she said hurt him, but he didn't respond. She wasn't sure if he was quiet to allow her to speak or if she had simply struck him dumb with her confession.

"The heart feels what it feels, Rhys," she whispered. "And mine has loved you since I was a child, almost as long as I can remember."

Rhys's eyes squeezed shut and his mouth twisted. "Please don't say these things."

"Why?" she asked, her dull tone not reflective of how much it hurt when he was tearing her heart out with his cold dismissal of everything she had ever felt for him. "Because you never allow such emotions to touch you? Because you shun love as much as you do anger and pain? Because something has now happened to make you feel those things and it—"

"No!" He grabbed for her, catching her upper arms in a powerful grip. She stared up into his face, wild with desperation and all the things she had accused him of avoiding. "Because I *can't*, damn you. You don't understand, but I'm trying to protect you."

She shrugged away, pushing from his arms. "You always say that, as if you somehow know best. But you don't. What you don't understand is that I don't want your protection, Rhys. I want something far deeper, far more meaningful than that."

He stared at her, unspeaking for close to a full minute. Then he turned on his heel and left the cottage. Left her. Again.

Chapter 5

Rhys crouched down on the beach, letting the sand push between his naked toes as angry waves crept toward him, moving closer with each crash. He wished he was capable of expressing his own anger with such loud clarity.

Because Rhys *was* angry, and he was angry with Anne. Why did she have to love him? More to the point, why the hell had she felt compelled to confess her feelings? His entire life was already ravaged. He had gone from understanding what he was and what his future would hold to having nothing but uncertainty all around him.

In the midst of that confusion, in the middle of this hell, the last thing he wanted was Anne's love. That kind of emotion was too powerful. Too dangerous. He just wanted to pack it away, along with every other feeling he could no longer control. He didn't need these things.

"Hello."

Rhys stiffened at the sound of Anne's voice, soft behind him. It had been nearly an hour since he stormed from the house and he thought perhaps she finally understood he wanted peace. Apparently not.

Slowly he straightened up and turned to find her standing at the base of the path, her slippers and stockings in hand. She had rebound her hair, but it was looser now, not as impeccably coiffed as it normally was. He supposed that made sense. There was no servant here to fuss over her, so Anne had made do on her own.

The softer style suited her, for she looked more beautiful than he had ever seen her. Oh, she had always been beautiful, but now Rhys saw her . . . *truly* saw her, and realized it was perhaps for the first time. Anne had never been anything to him but an accessory to his future. At times she had been a distraction, but he had managed to squelch those feelings when they made themselves known.

This afternoon there would be none of that. Now he couldn't help but see the softness in her eyes, a kindness and a gentleness that had always made her so well-liked by the *ton* at large.

Yet beyond that, there was also strength, something deeper than most possessed. After all, Anne had come here after him, faced off with him, and never once backed down, even when he hurt her and probably frightened her. She had even been willing to save his very life when she believed he was about to throw himself off the cliffs in desperation.

And then there was the passion. The dark green-blue of her stare had always been pretty enough, but Rhys had never recognized one key aspect that Anne held there. Passion.

She might not show it in ballrooms, she might not know or fully understand it, but when she had come screaming down the hill to save him, when she had reeled back and slapped him after he hurt her, when he had kissed her in the cottage, and above all when she had confessed her love for him . . . Rhys had felt Anne's deep and abiding passion. All these years he had judged her as the kind of woman who didn't allow deep feelings to trouble her. But instead she had merely been masking them.

He understood something about that. And now, as he stood looking at her on the sandy beach, he wondered how he had been so blind as to not see these things in all the years they had spent betrothed.

"R-Rhys?" she whispered.

He blinked, shoving away his thoughts. "Hello," he finally responded. "I thought you might have gone, after all."

She shrugged one shoulder, but he could see she was

biting her tongue to keep herself from arguing about her departure once more. Instead she said, "When I came out of the cottage, I noticed the driver had left my bag when he departed. I hadn't even noticed."

Rhys blinked. Normally he was observant, but he hadn't noticed, either, so distracted had he been by both arguing with and desiring Anne.

"At any rate, I took it in and unpacked it."

He stared. "Yourself?"

Her gaze settled firmly on his. "Yes, Rhys. I'm not so incapable that I couldn't put a few things into a drawer. But when you didn't return by the time I had finished, I thought to look for you."

He nodded, awkward and unable to think of a good answer now that he was standing here with her, this woman who loved him. He hadn't even known that, so he wondered what other things she had kept to herself over the years. Did he know Anne at all?

She paced past him to the edge of the water. Lifting her skirt just a fraction, she allowed a wave to splash over her bare feet. Rhys swallowed at the glimpse of her bare toes, her ankle, a little calf.

"It's beautiful here," Anne finally said after it seemed like the uncomfortable silence would last a lifetime.

He nodded. *That*, at least, was a subject he could address.

"My mother used to bring us here every summer for a week. She said every child, no matter their rank, deserved to run free for a little while."

He shut his eyes. He could so clearly picture his normally staid mother running down the shore, laughing and playing with him and his sisters.

But now his image of her was tainted. Had *she* run wild here? Was this where he had been conceived, or some other place where she went to escape her husband? And had she had a tryst only with Simon's father or were there other men?

Great God, what her indiscretion had wrought. For him, but also for herself and for his sisters, when and if this *thing* came out into the open, they would all be punished for her shocking lack of control.

"What about your father?" Anne asked, coming closer to his thoughts than she likely knew.

"My father . . ." He hesitated. "The Duke of Waverly didn't accompany us."

"Never?" she asked with surprise in her tone.

Rhys shook his head. "He disapproved of the 'savage' surroundings and said that this little place was beneath us, but my mother insisted. He allowed it for a time, but when I was thirteen it ended abruptly."

He remembered the day his mother had told him he could no longer go to this place. She had been crying, he thought. And after that, she laughed even less, but he had never put much thought into her happiness or lack thereof. Now he wondered about it, about her, even as he burned in anger and betrayal toward her.

"Why did it end?" Anne asked, turning toward him with empathy in her eyes. Not pity, for he hated that, but something else.

"We came home that year and I was talking foolishness about making friends with some of the village children, perhaps even inviting them to one of our estates some year." Rhys shrugged. "The duke had never supported the idea of me coming here. He didn't like it that I consorted with children who had no rank and believed that my wild behavior was below my station."

Anne's brow wrinkled. "Didn't it matter to him that you had a little happiness here?"

Rhys's shoulders stiffened. He had confessed that fact to only one person. It seemed Simon had felt compelled to share it with Anne. The idea that she had such a glimpse into the weaknesses he had been taught to hide was troubling.

"Happiness is irrelevant. The duke was correct. At thirteen, I wasn't a boy anymore. It was high time to forget such foolish notions and begin to truly prepare myself for the future my father saw for me."

Anne's gaze dropped and she slowly turned to look

at the ocean again. "How sad your father thought joy was a foolish notion. And sadder still that he convinced you his opinion was gospel."

Rhys didn't respond, but instead stepped a fraction closer and looked out with her over the water. The afternoon was waning now, beginning to cast a faintly orange glow over the waves in the distance. They were quiet for a long moment, but unlike when she first came to the water's edge, there was nothing uncomfortable about it.

When some time had passed, Rhys looked down at her. "I'm not trying to hurt you. It was never my intention."

She didn't look at him. In fact, she hardly reacted to his statement at all, just continued to look out to sea. Finally she nodded.

"I know that. In fact, it's obvious from simply looking at you that *you* are the one who is hurt. Deeply enough that you would run away not just from me but from everything important in your life. And it says something that when you ran, you came to a place where you were happy almost twenty years ago. Where you weren't stifled by the ideals of rank and propriety that were so important to your father that he would crush any other instinct you might have once had."

Rhys frowned. That was actually a remarkably

good assessment of what was happening here, especially coming from a woman who wasn't fully aware of the entire situation. Was he so easy to read?

Slowly she turned toward him and lifted her face to his. Her hand fluttered at her side, almost like she wanted to touch him, but held back. He found himself wishing she would cup his cheek or take his hand, but then he pushed those desires away. This was what heightened and unchecked emotion did, it made one imprudent.

"Rhys," she said quietly. "No matter what you feel about it now, I'm still your wife. Clearly something has happened that has driven you to these uncharacteristic actions. Perhaps I could help you."

All the anger she'd expressed upon her arrival was gone, though he suspected much of it lurked beneath the surface. Still, in the strength of her face and the flash in her eyes, her passion and the love he did not want remained. If she had once hidden her heart to protect herself or to make him more comfortable, those days were over.

He shook his head. "I can't tell you why I'm here, Anne. Or why I left."

She nodded slowly. "Then don't. But allow me to stay. Let me be with you while you do whatever it is you came here to do. Perhaps you'll change your mind about revealing the truth to me, but perhaps you won't. Either way, I want to be here for you."

He scrubbed a hand over his face, suddenly aware of how exhausted he was. Since his arrival, he had hardly slept, and now this war with Anne had sapped almost all his remaining energy. The idea of fighting with her for the next few days about staying or going wasn't a pleasant one.

And truth be told, the thought of having her here with him . . . well, it wasn't as *unpleasant* as he might have thought. As long as he didn't reveal his secret or make love to her and risk creating a child, perhaps there was little harm in her staying.

"Fine," he said softly.

Anne's face lit up with a smile, and Rhys stared at the expression for a moment. When she looked at him like that, he could almost forget his own misery. He could almost see how making her smile could be a man's life pursuit. Some other man. Not him.

He shook his head. "But if I allow you to stay with me, you must obey me from here on out, Anne."

Her bright smile faded to a more controlled one and she nodded enthusiastically. "Of course, Rhys. That was one of my vows, after all, and I take my vows very seriously."

Anne restlessly stirred the fire and looked around the cottage once more. She was alone, Rhys had gone to "take care of an errand." Her initial response was to chase after him, but she resisted. He had only just agreed to let her stay; she had to remain calm if she wanted to slowly gain his trust . . . and perhaps, one day, his heart.

Still, she couldn't help but fear he would run away again, and this time perhaps to a place where no one could find him. But every time she stared out the window, she could see his horse moving about the paddock in the distance. Wherever Rhys had gone, he had walked, so there was little chance he could find means of escape tonight.

She sighed as she picked up a wrinkled shirt and moved it to a hamper in the corner of the room. For a man who was usually so refined, Rhys had been a bit of a mess since his arrival here, and his cottage reflected that. She wasn't certain if that was a symptom of his upset or just about the fact that he didn't often tend to himself, just as she didn't.

She smoothed the bed's cool coverlet. Despite its small size and current state of disarray, the cottage was a comfortable place. Cozy and homey.

"Still, it's odd that you loved it here," she mused aloud as she sat down on the edge of the bed. "It's so different from the life you live in London, from the man you have become there."

She heard a swift, certain step outside and scrambled to her feet with a blush. The door opened and Rhys stepped into the room. He had forgone his jacket, leaving him only in a linen shirt tucked lazily into black trousers. The first two buttons were open, leaving a glimpse of his chest and making her think of that moment earlier in the day when his naked body had pinned her down. He held a big basket under one arm as he swung the door shut behind him.

"Food," he said, and his voice was rough.

She shook her thoughts away and stepped forward to take the basket he offered.

"Goodness," she murmured as she carried it to the plain wooden table through the open door in the other room. "It's quite heavy."

He nodded. "That's why I was gone so long. There is a woman in the village who has been cooking for me. Normally someone from the family brings me a late supper, but I wanted to be certain you had enough to eat after your trying journey. When they heard my wife had joined me . . . well, the family went into a state to prepare something extra special."

Anne lifted her gaze from the fragrant basket that had been slowly seducing her with its succulent choices. She found a small but amused smile unlike anything she had ever seen on Rhys's face.

"You like them, the family you visited," she said as she returned her attention to the basket before her.

She unloaded item after item onto the plates that had been sent along with the food.

"Don't be silly," Rhys protested as he moved forward and took a place at the small table. "They're pleasant, of course, but peasants. I played with their eldest son as a child, but things are different now."

Anne glanced at him as she took her place, but said nothing. This was the second time he had mentioned friendships he'd shared with village children. And though he dismissed them now as foolish, it was clear they had once meant a great deal to him.

Now Rhys's ideas about the sanctity of rank matched his late father's. They were well-known, he had never hidden them. Still, she sensed he retained a bit more feeling for the village family than perhaps he was ready to admit even to himself. Once more her hopes were fed by this brief, unintentional glimpse into Rhys's soul. If he could still care for a family so beneath him, surely she could give him reason to care for her.

They began to eat. Anne couldn't help her silence. The last time she'd eaten was a not particularly pleasing luncheon along the road just before her arrival. Now darkness had overcome the countryside, and the smells of the hearty country fare made her stomach growl.

Still, the quiet wasn't uncomfortable. In fact, as she dabbed her mouth with a rough napkin, she realized it might be the most intimate meal she and Rhys had ever shared.

"You know," she said as she gathered the empty plates. "I don't think we've ever shared a meal without ten other people at the table or a newspaper or book between us."

Rhys glanced at her with a shrug. "It's difficult to obtain a good paper in these parts."

She frowned as she searched for a place to put the tableware. That wasn't exactly what she meant.

Rhys motioned to the door. "I put them in the basket outside. The village family . . . Parks is their name . . . they collect it when they bring the next basket. I've also arranged for them to tidy up the cottage when they come tomorrow. I don't mind its current state, but you deserve more comfort."

She nodded and did as he had suggested. When she returned to the cottage, she found he had turned his chair to face the entryway and was staring at her.

"We'll need to discuss our sleeping arrangements, Anne," he said as she shut the door.

Anne looked around them and then speared him with a look. "Because there are so many choices?"

She thought his lip twitched with suppressed humor, but then it stopped.

"I realize the accommodations aren't up to the standard I would normally provide—"

She held up a hand to stop him. "I love it, Rhys," she interrupted. "I do."

His eyes widened with surprise, but then he continued, "Well, I'm glad for that, but it doesn't resolve the problem. You see . . . well, there is only the one bed."

Anne folded her arms and tried unsuccessfully to keep a tinge of bitterness from her voice. "Yes, I see that. What is the issue exactly? We're married. It isn't the arrangement we have back at your—*our* home in London, but we won't be here forever. We can share a bed for the time being."

Actually she very much looked forward to sharing that bed. It wasn't overly wide and they would have to lie close together.

Rhys pushed to his feet. "I realize we're married, Anne . . ."

Anne blinked. Rhys was actually uncomfortable with this discussion. She had never seen him squirm and fidget so, like a boy who had done something wrong and knew he was about to be caught for it.

"But?"

He cleared his throat. "But you see, what I said earlier about not being married . . . I meant it. Legally, of course, it would be difficult, if not impossible, to end the union, unless you would be willing to lie and make a case for annulment."

Anne stared at him, eyes wide and mouth open. There were only a few reasons the court would allow for such a thing and none of them was a circumstance she was willing to swear to, or even consider. When she was silent, he shook his head.

"I thought not," he continued. "But even if a legal termination is out of the question, our marriage *can* be ended in every other way."

Anne staggered back three steps. She would have gone farther but she hit the door behind her and was forced to a stop. She had thought his earlier words were mere fancy, a way to lash out at her in his frustration. When he said she could stay here, she had believed that to have passed. But now it was clear he had thought this through with a cool and logical head.

"You mean to permanently separate from me?" she whispered. Suddenly the food she had so enjoyed churned unpleasantly in her belly.

He nodded once, and Anne squeezed her eyes shut with a low groan. There were some in their circles who lived separate lives as he suggested, but those who did often suffered the social consequences. The rumor and censure Rhys abhorred would be visited upon them for years to come. And for what? She still had no inkling as to what would drive him to such extremes.

"I don't understand," she whispered.

He dipped his chin. "Anne, I know this is difficult for you, but there are forces at work that may *demand* we end this union. And for your own protection, it would be best."

"Best?" she repeated. Her voice sounded far away to her own ears, as if she was listening to this conversation from an echoing chamber.

He nodded. "And that is why I wanted you to go. If we're going to part, I want to be certain I won't be leaving you with—with child."

Anne flinched. Although she wanted some time alone with her husband before they had children, time to make him see that they could share a love match, she did long to be a mother. Now Rhys was saying he would deny her that pleasure, as well as the beauty of knowing he cared for her.

Desperation clawed at her at that horrible thought.

"You've told me on numerous occasions that you must produce an heir," she choked, hating herself for sounding so plaintive. "You owe your bloodline, do you not?"

Rhys turned away so she couldn't see his reaction to her charge, but his voice was thick when he replied, "I do indeed, which is why I cannot bring a child, any child, into this world. I'm sorry, Anne, but this is how it must be."

Anne had heard that tone from her husband before. It was one that said he wouldn't bend. And she was too stunned, too heartbroken to argue. Instead she whispered, "We have only lain together a few times."

"Once is enough," Rhys said, and finally looked at her again. "We can only pray the damage hasn't already been done. But making love isn't something we can do again. Do you understand? That is why I have concerns over the sleeping arrangements."

Anne let out a snort of angry laughter. "Because you can scarce control yourself with me?"

He moved toward her a step, and for a brief moment she saw something dark and dangerous in his eyes. Not anger, but something with more heat. More purpose.

Of course he took it away, hiding that reaction just as he hid every feeling and thought from her. And now that he was saying he would end their marriage in every way that mattered, it seemed he would *never* give her more.

All her hopes, all her dreams, everything that was of importance to her . . . he was holding those things up and then shredding them with so little feeling that she could almost feel her heart breaking in her chest.

But she didn't cry. That was the one thing she took

pride in. She didn't cry, she didn't rail. All she did was fold her arms across her chest and say, "Trust me, Rhys, I won't make any attempt to seduce you. Even if I knew how, I wouldn't humiliate myself any more than you have already humiliated me. You can safely sleep in this bed with me."

He stared at her a long moment, then his hand lifted. "Anne—"

She wanted to allow him to touch her, to comfort her, but she didn't. She stepped out of his reach and turned toward the bed. "I'm very tired after the excitement of the past week. If you'll allow me privacy, I'll change and go to sleep."

She felt him standing behind her for a long moment, but then he cleared his throat. She didn't look at him.

"Very well," he said quietly. "Then I'll leave you."

She heard him step into the other room and then a quiet click of the door closing behind him. Anne covered her eyes briefly.

"No, Rhys," she murmured to herself as she took her night rail from the drawer and began the awkward business of undressing herself. "You've already left me. You were never with me to begin with."

Chapter 6

Anne lay on her side, snuggled down into the surprisingly comfortable bed. A heavy weight was draped around her arm, pinning her in place, but she didn't mind it. In fact, that heaviness was more than pleasant, though she was still too lost in the area between sleep and waking to determine what caused it. All she knew was that she was relaxed and happy for the first time in a long while.

She let out a contented sigh and wiggled into a more comfortable position. Behind her she felt warm breath against her bare neck and then a groaning grumble just before a hot, hard body arched against hers.

Anne's eyes came open in a flash, wide as she stared around the room in sudden and fully awake awareness. The bedroom was bright because, although they were closed, sunlight peeked around the edges of the thin curtains. Outside, birds were twittering and the distant sound of the sea echoed as it pounded against the rocks below the cliffs.

Nothing that had happened in the last week was a dream. And now Anne was really here with Rhys. She looked down. Through a fold in the coverlet, she could see that the weight she felt against her was Rhys's arm. He was wrapped around her from behind, his body curled about hers like they were two spoons in a drawer.

She shivered at the intimate, sensual feel of his touch. Slowly she peeked over her shoulder and saw that his eyes remained closed, his breathing heavy and even. He was asleep, his actions now uncontrolled by his rational mind, but by whatever instinct it was that made a man touch a woman.

He arched against her again with a guttural grunt, and Anne sucked in a breath through her teeth. The hard press of his erection stroked against her backside. And while they hadn't made love all that often since their marriage, Anne already knew what would happen if things continued down this path. He would fit himself inside her body, he would claim her.

She thought of the night before. She'd been hurt by his unfathomable desire to end their marriage, and was embarrassed by the situation created when he ran away from everything in his life. In the charged, emotional moment that she said she didn't intend to seduce him, she had very much meant it.

But now, feeling him stroking against her from behind, his hard body hot even through her night shift and the clothing he still wore, everything was forgotten. Everything but a powerful desire to bring him inside her body. To *force* him to remember, by any means necessary, that she was his and he was hers.

Suddenly his hand, which had been resting against the bed beside her, moved, and Rhys cupped her breast. Anne arched at the unexpected touch, and then she moaned when he began to squeeze and tug her sensitive flesh. What was he doing? Before he had always been gentle, slow, but this, this thing he was doing to her body wasn't gentle. It was passionate and powerful.

And she liked it, even though the rough way he touched her bordered between pleasure and pain. He plucked at her nipple through the thin fabric of her night shift, he squeezed the globe of her breast. With every touch, she found herself more and more mesmerized, more and more alive, and she wanted more than ever for him to take her. To taste her. To fill her with himself in any way she could have him.

As if he read her thoughts, his hand slowly drifted lower, sliding over her stomach and finally to rest on her thigh. For a moment he didn't move. Had he fallen into a deeper sleep? She was about to look when he began to fist her night shift into his hand, lifting the fabric until it was bunched awkwardly around her waist and she was bared from there down.

Anne could hardly think, hardly breathe as his fingers moved to touch her naked hip. His skin felt so hot against hers, so rough. Her eyes fluttered shut and she moaned softly. A moan that turned to a cry when his hand slipped away from her hip and he found the tender flesh between her thighs.

She trembled as his long fingers brushed gently at the swollen lips of her sex, coaxing, pleading for her to part her legs. In a trance, she did so, allowing him greater access to that one aching part of her that wanted him so badly.

He didn't disappoint. Gently he parted her flesh, opening her with a finger and thumb. She tensed, grinding back against him when he finally stroked along the wet entrance to her body.

Rhys stared at the cascade of his wife's hair along the pillow beside him. He had been awake for a few moments, probably since Anne moaned when he squeezed her breast. It had been shocking to come awake and find his wife writhing in the pleasure he had sworn to deny them both less than twelve hours before. But her soft cries, her unexpected reactions to his rough touch, had aroused him to a point that almost defied control.

And he had to continue. Even if he didn't take her, even if he denied himself pleasure, he wanted to see hers. He wanted to drown himself in hers, just for a while.

She was bucking back now, her hips arching in time as he slid his fingers over her heated sex again and again and again. The pearl of her clitoris seemed to swell every time he brushed it, and Anne's breath was coming faster and more erratically.

He pressed his mouth to the side of her throat, tasting her flesh at the very moment that he let one finger breach her body. Her inner walls pulsed around him, squeezing him in a hot, wet heaven that he longed to feel around his cock.

"Rhys," she groaned, her voice muffled by her arm, by the pillow as she rolled her head from side to side in pure bliss.

Anne had said his name a hundred times before, but it had never moved him like this, when it was said in pleasure. When it was whispered as a plea for more.

He gave it to her without thinking, delving deep into her clenching sheath with that one finger, driving over and over again with gentle precision until her cries were wild and her hips bucked out of control against his hand.

His own breath was ragged now and he felt his

excitement and needs mounting as he added a second finger to her wet and ready body. Gently he moved her onto her back and hovered over her, holding her gaze so he could see her expression as he drove into her.

Her back arched, her cheeks flushing with pleasure and probably a little embarrassment at being observed so closely in such a state.

But it wasn't enough. Rhys wanted more. To be truthful, he *needed* more, and for once in his tight, controlled life he let himself take what he wanted. There would be consequences, but they would come later, and for now he reveled in her body, in forgetting all his pain.

Anne groaned as Rhys suddenly withdrew his magical fingers. She felt empty, bereft and, ultimately unsatisfied as he pulled back. Enough so that tears filled her eyes and she found herself clenching at his arm frantically.

He looked down at her, his dark brown eyes dilated, and smiled. "I just want to make this easier. I'm not leaving."

Anne tilted her head, surprised by how gentle he sounded. How warm. But then she forgot all that as he pulled her to a seated position and tugged her wrinkled night shift over her head, baring her body to him before he eased her back against the pillows and pulled the covers away.

Although her husband had seen her naked before, Anne couldn't help but blush. As a lady, she had been taught by so many people that her body was a source of shame, something to be hidden and avoided. It was difficult to forget those words that had been whispered to her since her mother's death by elderly relatives and stern governesses. Especially when Rhys was staring at her.

His expression was unlike any she had ever seen before. Oh yes, he had seen her naked, but he had always looked over her with a fleeting gaze, then covered her body with his. A few times he had simply lifted her night rail and not revealed her at all.

But this . . . this was different. He was *staring* at her now, his gaze moving over her with a lazy, heated expression that even he, with all his experience at blocking emotion from his face, couldn't hide. He was drinking her in, memorizing her, and it shocked Anne to her core, as well as pleased her.

This was what she had always wanted: to capture Rhys's interest for more than a fleeting moment. She wanted him to want her, to need her, to love her in every way a man could.

"Rhys," she whispered, reaching for him.

He shook his head as if waking from a dream, and his eyes caught hers the same moment he took her questing hand in his own. His fingers tangled with hers seductively, slowly, and then he lifted her palm to his lips and pressed a searing, openmouthed kiss to her flesh.

Anne's eyes fluttered shut and she let out a low moan. It seemed that his touch had awakened her body in new ways, for every kiss, every brush of skin could now be felt all over her body, but especially in that place between her thighs where he had touched her so intimately earlier. That place that tingled and longed to be touched again and again.

Rhys's head descended just as Anne opened her eyes and then he was kissing her. It wasn't like any kiss they had shared before. Their first kisses as man and wife had been warm, but proper. The kiss in the cottage the day before had been angry and passionate. This was something different. There was possessiveness in his touch that hadn't existed before. There was desire and need and longing that mirrored the feelings that had long been in her own heart.

As Rhys parted his lips and gently tasted hers, Anne sighed and allowed him in. He delved into her, stroking her mouth as she longed for his body to stroke hers. It was as if he couldn't get enough of her now, that he had to taste her so deeply that he wouldn't forget.

Her arms came around him and she clung to his

shoulders, lifting herself to meet his kiss, praying he wouldn't pull away.

But of course he did. Except for once he didn't leave her. No, he did something quite unexpected. He let his mouth come to her throat and then he glided down her body, tasting her flesh all along the way.

Rhys had kissed her breasts before, to prepare her for their joining, but this time, when he drew one erect nipple between his lips, Anne let out a cry that echoed in the quiet room. She felt the wet tug of his tongue shoot like lightning down her body, the sensation alive between her legs as if he had touched her there in the same way.

Rhys let his mouth move lower, gliding with laziness down the apex of her body. He tasted the flat expanse of her stomach, even dipping his tongue into her belly button. He suckled and kissed his way to her hip, forcing her to feel just how sensitive that area was. And finally his tongue traced the flesh of her inner thigh.

Anne struggled to sit up and stared wide-eyed at the image of Rhys lying between her trembling legs. He lifted his head and met her gaze with an even one of his own.

"Rhys?" she asked, uncertain of even what she was trying to express.

"Lie back," he said softly, the order undeniable, but also gentle. "Let me do this for you, Anne. Let me give you *something*."

She froze. In his voice, she heard regret and pain, sorrow unlike any he had ever shown her before. And there was also need there. A need to do this strange thing to her body. And his mouth felt so good, who was she to deny him?

"Yes," she murmured as she lay back against the pillows, only this time she bunched two together so she could look down her body and see what he was doing. She wanted to see.

He lowered his head again, and she felt the steam of his breath against her wet body. Without meaning to, she parted her legs a little farther and arched just a touch toward him. Her action elicited a deep chuckle from her husband, and then he touched her.

His palms flattened against her thighs and he pressed her open even farther so he could seat himself there. His fingers glided inward, gentle in their quest until he parted her nether lips a second time and revealed her gleaming sex. Anne squeezed her eyes shut for a moment, unaccustomed to having her most intimate areas examined so closely. But even so, she felt the intensity of his stare on her. She felt the heat of his breath and the pressure of his fingers.

And then, most unexpectedly, his wet tongue

stroked over her. Her eyes flew open and she stared down to find Rhys, his head angled, licking her wet body with long, languid strokes. As shocking as that image was, what was more shocking was how good it felt. Every nerve ending in that sensitive place fired at once, her hips lifted into his touch, and she thrashed with pleasure.

"Rhys, Rhys," she moaned, unable to stop herself.

He lifted his head briefly and held her gaze. "Just hold on, angel, it will only get better."

She bunched the coverlet in her fingers, her nails scraping over the fabric. Better? How could anything get better than this powerful, wonderful feeling of him tasting her?

He gave her the answer she sought in that moment when he sucked between his lips the hidden pearl of nerves at the top of her sheath. A flood of new sensations instantly bombarded her. She cried out as he rolled that little nub of flesh around with his tongue, sucking it, scraping it gently with his teeth until suddenly a dam of pleasure within her broke and she screamed out with a feeling so intense that her vision blurred.

She bucked her hips, her body no longer in her control, but he never stopped his torment. He continued the stroking of his tongue, drawing her through the intensity of the pleasure, pulling more and more from her even when she thought she had no more to give.

And finally, when her tremors had ended and she flopped, boneless and weak, on the pillows, he rose up to his knees above her.

With effort, Anne opened her eyes. Rhys was blocking the sunlight with his body now, so all he was to her was shadow. But she could see when he moved his hands to his trouser waistband and began to jerk at the buttons there. Her heart rate increased and she opened her legs wider, ready for him, ready to take what he had recently claimed he would deny her.

He had three buttons open when he stopped. Through the shadows, she saw the tension in his face, the lines around his mouth that said he was gritting his teeth, fighting with his inner emotions and thoughts.

"Fuck!" he finally cried out as he turned away and refastened his waistband.

Anne recoiled in surprise. He had never used such a vulgar term in front of her before, but the vile word wasn't what made her cringe. It was the pain behind it. The battle she had witnessed and somehow lost.

"Rhys," she said softly, reaching for him.

He yanked away from her hand and got up from the bed, pacing to the window and pulling the curtain back to look outside. In profile, she saw his scowl, though all his angry emotions seemed to be self-directed.

"I can't, Anne. I already told you I can't make love to you," he said, his voice strained with tension and emotions he normally hid.

She sat up, covering her breasts with the tangled bedcovers.

"Because you don't want me?" she asked, unable to mask her hurt as easily as he seemed to mask his own.

He spun on her, and now she felt some of the anger in his stare. In a long stride, he came to the edge of the bed and caught her hand. He jerked her fingers to his pant front and pressed them against the hard length of his erection that remained outlined there.

"I *want* you," he whispered, his voice harsh. "But I can't have you. I've told you why."

Anne squeezed her eyes shut, fighting tears, fighting frustration and resentment at his repeated denials of the future she had so carefully planned.

Finally he sighed. "I need to leave you now."

Anne's eyes flew open and she stared at him in terror. "Leave me?" she repeated, thinking of the horrible days she had spent searching for him.

He shook his head. "Just for a while. I'll return, Anne, I promise you that."

She opened her mouth to answer, but he turned his back on her and left the cottage before she could speak, slamming the door behind him.

Anne flopped back on the bed. With violence, she suddenly pulled the pillow over her face and did what she had been wanting to do since the day Rhys departed London. She screamed. She screamed into the pillow until her throat hurt and then she screamed some more, pouring all the emotions in her heart into the soft feathers.

Finally she pushed the pillow aside and stared up at the cracked ceiling above her. With some of the emotions she'd had trapped inside her vented by her admittedly childish outburst, Anne could think again. And her mind kept returning, traitorously, to the way Rhys had touched her, pleasured her . . . loved her in this bed.

There was no denying he had felt passionately toward her. Even *he* had admitted he wanted her, which wasn't something he'd ever said to her before. Her body tingled just thinking about it.

Still, Rhys believed he had to leave her, for whatever mysterious reason he refused to share. Only he didn't want to leave her with child . . .

Anne sat up as a sudden thought flashed through her. If she became with child, Rhys *wouldn't* leave her. Whatever else was driving him in these desperate hours, he had too much honor for that. She had come here to help him, but he thwarted her plans at every turn. Well, she could thwart his, too.

If only she could do the one thing she'd sworn she would not. Seduce him. Make him want her so much that he couldn't stop himself from making love to her as he had stopped himself today.

Despite her claims of being uneducated in such matters the night before, it seemed Anne would have to learn the ways of seduction, and quickly.

After all, it might be the only way to keep her husband by her side.

Chapter 7

Rhys stormed down the hillside, away from the cottage, away from the cliffs and toward the stable. Eventually he planned to walk the green expanse of hilly country that seemed to go on forever.

Not that the beauty of his surroundings mattered even a bit to Rhys. He was too frustrated, both physically and emotionally, to notice such things.

Waking up beside Anne, his body curled around hers, his hands touching her in such intimate ways, was not in his plan. He had run here to escape *everyone* in his life, including his wife. He didn't want any of them to see him as he struggled with the truth of his parentage. His vulnerability at this time was unconscionable and he needed peace to overcome it and hide it away before he saw to the business of the blackmail awaiting him in London.

But with Anne here there was no peace. She forced him to face his emotions. She made those emotions merge and twist with the desires he had always fought to control and the feelings she demanded he know.

So instead of respite, now he found himself tormented by and unable to escape the scent of Anne's skin, which still hung on him like perfumed heaven.

He wanted her. He wanted to turn around, go back to the cottage, lock the door, and simply drown in her body for a few days. He wanted to make love to her, to claim her in every way he had ever imagined but suppressed out of a need for propriety and control.

But he couldn't. He knew what awaited him when he returned to London. He had seen the horror of blackmail play out with other men and it never failed to destroy them. Their secrets were always laid bare in the end, no matter how valiantly they had struggled to protect them. Once that happened to Rhys, the scandal would tear through his life, his mother's life, even his married sisters would not be left untouched, though he could at least hope that the superior reputations of their respective husbands would offer some refuge.

But Anne . . . Rhys still clung to the idea that he could keep her from all this. Shield her, at least, from the very worst of what was bound to come. If he could keep her from the truth and make her see that separate lives were the best and only option, there might be hope for her.

But that wasn't his only reason to stay away from the temptation of his wife. Even if he could never be stripped of the title of duke in the eyes of the law, even if the world continued to "Your Grace" him until he went mad from hearing it, *he* knew the truth.

His father had pounded into him the sanctity of his blood and the proud history of his line. And with Rhys, that line had been broken. Intruded upon. If he gave in to his desires, if he drowned himself in pleasure with Anne, he could very well have a child, a son who would inherit Rhys's false title.

But if he had no children, there was still a chance that some distant cousin, some *true* Waverly heir could be found and the line would thus be repaired and carried forward upon Rhys's death.

But for that to happen, he had to stay as far away from his wife as he could. It meant summoning up all the control he had long been proud of and making sure he didn't impregnate her or bind her to him in any other permanent way.

"Damn it!" he cried out to the heavens in general as he raked a hand through his hair.

"It appears *you* are in good spirits this morning."

Rhys froze at the voice that echoed from behind him. Slowly he turned and found a man standing beside the path, an axe over his shoulder and a friendly smile on his face.

"And just who the hell are you to comment on my mood?" Rhys snapped, reaching blindly for the arrogant superiority that had long been his protective mantle.

A smile tilted one corner of the man's lips, a knowing expression that raked across Rhys's already ragged emotions.

"Speak, stranger," he commanded. "If you know what's good for you."

"You really don't recognize me, Your Grace?" the man asked, his smile fading in the face of Rhys's judgment and anger. "Well, I'm not surprised. It's been many years since I could call you friend."

"Friend?" Rhys repeated, sarcasm dripping from every letter. "You must be mistaken. I don't have friends who are—"

He stopped mid-sentence and looked all the closer at his companion's face. It appeared remarkably like the friendly countenance of Mrs. Parks, the village woman who brought him food. And that meant this man was likely . . .

"Stuart?" Rhys said, all the anger leaving his voice and his body. "Is that you?"

Another smile widened across the other man's face, open and friendly, even after Rhys's cruelty.

"Indeed it is, Your Grace. When I arrived late last night, Mother said you had come for a visit. I thought to accompany her here this morning and chop you some wood for your fire."

Rhys blinked, staring at the man who had once been a boy Rhys played with on the cliffs. The boy who had taught him the right place to jump into the sea. The boy who had been his first friend who wasn't of rank or importance to the *ton*.

"Great God, Stuart," Rhys said, reaching out a hand slowly. "I hardly recognize you."

The other man seemed surprised by the offering, but shook Rhys's hand regardless. It was a strong handshake, much stronger than those of some of the so-called powerful men Rhys spent his time with at home.

"Well, it has been many years since we last met, Your Grace," Stuart said. "You have changed much yourself."

Rhys lowered his chin to avoid Stuart's gaze. He could well imagine what he looked like, disheveled from sleeping in the same clothing he had worn yesterday, unshaven, hair a mess. He likely didn't look much like a duke.

But then he wasn't. In truth, he was scarcely better than the man before him. A man he had spoken to in such a dismissive tone not two minutes before.

"But it seems I've interrupted you in the midst of some kind of upset," Stuart said. "I *could* leave you to it . . ."

Rhys frowned at the implication that there was another option. "Or?"

Stuart grinned. "*Or* you could work out some of that frustration with me."

He held up the axe and gave it a wiggle as he laughed. Rhys stared. Was this man actually implying that he should go chop wood? Like a common servant? Like a common . . .

Well, a common person in general. Which was, in truth, what Rhys now was, at least in his heart.

"Why not?" Rhys said as he fell into step beside the man who had once been a friend. "I couldn't feel any bloody worse."

Rhys choked out another deep belly laugh as he leaned against the pile of wood behind him. Stuart let the axe blade split through another log and continued with his story.

"So then the woman says, 'That's not a hat, sir. That's my little doggie.'"

Both men dissolved into shaking laughter. Rhys leaned over, clutching his aching stomach as he slapped a palm against the woodpile a few times. God, it felt good to laugh. How long had it been since he truly laughed like this? He could scarce recall.

Before he could ponder that much more, he heard a feminine voice say, "Goodness, that must have been a bawdy joke indeed, to inspire such hysterics."

The laughter on Rhys's lips died instantly and he turned to see Anne coming down the hill toward them. She was smiling and had a small basket draped over her arm. But as she drew closer, Rhys saw the anxiety in her gaze, especially when it briefly fell on him and then darted away.

"Good afternoon, Your Grace," Stuart said, straightening up from his leaning position on the axe handle and giving Anne a deferent bow.

"Good afternoon . . . Mr. Parks, is it? Your mother said you accompanied her today in order to chop some wood for our hearth." She smiled her thanks. "When I couldn't find His Grace, I thought to look for you here."

"A very smart thought, as here we are," Stuart said.

Rhys stared as Anne gave a light laugh. She was smiling at the other man with a warmth and friendliness that seemed to be at the very core of her nature. Even with an elevated life, an exalted title, Anne had never resorted to the superiority or cutting cruelty that was so often a part of the *ton*.

It was most definitely a part of him. And he had never regretted it until these last few days when he realized he hadn't deserved to see himself as better than anyone, no matter what his so-called father said about it.

"I've brought some of your mother's delightful food," she said, lifting the basket delicately. "You two must be hungry after so much hard work."

Stuart shot a quick look toward Rhys and then shook his head with a smile. "I much appreciate the offer, Your Grace, but I should likely return to your cottage and help my mother back to the village. And then I have a full day of work ahead of me."

Anne nodded, but Rhys thought he saw her gaze slide to him once more. "Very well. It was nice to meet you, and please give your mother my thanks. I much enjoyed the time I spent with her this morning."

Stuart nodded briefly, said his good-byes, and then left Anne and Rhys alone. There was a silence that rose up between them when Stuart was no longer a buffer. Uncomfortable, just as it had been the day before.

Finally Anne stepped a bit closer. Rhys found himself holding his breath as she raised a hand and reached for him. She hesitated a fraction of a second, then brushed at his shirt instead of touching him in any intimate way.

She didn't meet his gaze. "You are filthy, my lord. Whatever have you been doing?"

He smiled. "A bit of wood chopping."

Her eyes widened and she actually took a step backward. "*You?*"

He nodded once and made no further explanation. Of course it was shocking, the work was far beneath him. But once he had gotten the hang of it, he had to admit it felt good to do something so physical. To pour his bitter emotions and frustrations into every swing of the axe and be rewarded by the cleaving of each log.

"Well, I have a flask of tea here," Anne said, setting the basket on the wall of wood beside her. She handed the item over. "You must be thirsty after such hard work."

Rhys nodded his thanks and opened the flask. He was greeted by the rich scent of the tea, and when he took a sip he smiled. It was the most delicious brew he had ever tasted. And it was prepared just as he liked it.

But of course Anne *would* make his tea as he liked it, wouldn't she? After all, she had studied to be his bride for a long time. And there was also the fact that she claimed to love him. Knowing that shocking fact colored the simple gesture of her bringing him tea. It made it an act of love, not just duty or politeness.

He swallowed and motioned to the basket. "Did Mrs. Parks bring this to the cottage?"

Anne nodded. "Yes. And she stayed to tidy up a bit and offered to do any laundering we had. She's a lovely woman, we had a nice talk."

Rhys took another long swig of tea, but kept his gaze focused on his wife as he did so.

"I can well imagine she had stories for you about my past," he said, though the idea somehow made him uncomfortable.

Anne nodded and her smile widened. "Yes. She told me a little about your time here. How much she enjoyed your family visits. Her stories reminded me of how carefree you were when we were children."

Rhys found his jaw clenching and said nothing in response. When a moment had passed, Anne shifted uncomfortably.

"At any rate, I brought this down in the hopes we might picnic if you're hungry."

Rhys hesitated. Sharing a meal with his wife was a perfectly natural gesture, and given their surroundings, a very pleasant idea. But hadn't he just told himself he had to separate more from her?

"Come," Anne said when his hesitation stretched out between them. "You must eat, mustn't you?"

Rhys's stomach replied by growling, and he shrugged before he reached out and took the basket and the blanket she had placed beneath it.

"Very well. Follow me, I'll take you to the best picnic spot on the property."

Anne smiled as she fell into step beside him. As they walked, Rhys waited, ready for her to talk to him about what had transpired in their bed that morning. Or to press him about his intentions to end their marriage.

But she did neither of those things. Their walk was quiet, even comfortable. Anne said nothing until they moved over a hill and she gasped.

Rhys couldn't help but smile, for her reaction was exactly what he had hoped for when he decided to bring her here to this spot that had been a favorite of his as a boy.

A flowing field stretched out before them, awash in color from the many blooming wildflowers. Cutting through the green and rainbow-colored expanse, a stream bubbled toward the unseen but angry sea in a winding path. Just beyond the field, a cluster of untamed trees marked the beginning of wild country where no one had ever planted or marred with human elements beyond footsteps or hoof falls.

"My God, Rhys," Anne breathed as she followed him to a spot beside the brook where he spread out the blanket for their picnic luncheon. "This is magnificent."

Rhys couldn't help but smile at her wide-eyed enjoyment. "Indeed it is. I loved to come here as a boy."

Her gaze darted to his, but she made no comment. Instead she dropped down on her knees on the blanket and began to unpack the delicious foods Mrs. Parks had prepared for them. Rhys joined her, taking the plate she ultimately prepared.

They had eaten quietly for a little while when Anne looked out around her. She took in a deep breath and Rhys knew what she felt and smelled. Sea salt air with a gentle softness of summer to it. There was nothing better.

"This place is so wild," she murmured, then looked at him briefly. "Not at all like you."

Rhys found himself smiling and then, utterly unexpectedly, a burst of laughter escaped his lips. Laughter just as real as what he had expressed when Stuart told him that joke. Anne stared at him, almost like he had gone a little mad.

"Is this an insult, wife?" Rhys finally asked when he regained his composure.

"No!" Anne raised her hands, almost in a plea, and started to speak again. But then she stopped, tilting her face and examining his so closely that Rhys almost turned away. Finally she smiled. "*You are teasing me?*"

He shrugged as he set aside his now-empty plate. "You're surprised?"

Anne wiped her hands on the linen napkin in her lap and nodded. "It isn't your normal demeanor, I admit."

Rhys turned his face. His *normal* demeanor. How often he had found himself pondering that very thing over the last week. Being here, knowing the truth about himself, it made every moment of his life run through his mind in a constant stream. And so often he saw images of how dismissive he had been of others, just as he had initially been with Stuart just that morning. He recalled times when he had been cold, unfeeling . . . even cruel.

Had the victims of his actions really deserved what he said or did? Was his coldness and distantness truly warranted?

"I suppose I am . . ." He hesitated, uncertain of how to describe his behavior. "I am *stiff* under normal circumstances."

Anne frowned, and he saw that she was thinking of his past as well. She claimed to love him, and perhaps that blinded her in some things, but she was an intelligent woman and she had to see his lesser qualities. What did she think of him then?

"Formal. You are formal." She shrugged. "But that comes with your title, doesn't it?"

Rhys couldn't help but cringe at that reminder.

His behavior had been caused by the assumption that he held one of the highest titles in the land. That somehow his birthright had given him more cause to behave in a prideful and superior manner. He had called that propriety and convinced himself it was the way to command the utter respect the Waverly name deserved.

"My title," he said softly. He sounded raw, his voice empty.

She nodded, unaware of the undertones to the path of this conversation. "Yes. Being a duke comes with great responsibility. Even before your father's passing, I saw you transform from the boy you once were and shoulder those things with enormous seriousness."

Rhys rubbed his eyes. He hadn't always been serious. He could remember running through the countryside here with not a care in the world. It was only when his mother stopped bringing him to this place, when his father . . . when the *duke* had become the main guiding force in his life, that he had stopped laughing and started feeling the disdain his birth allowed him.

"But," he said, almost more to himself than to her, "there are many of my rank who are not so . . . *formal*, as you put it. Like Simon. Simon is a duke and he is . . . different."

Anne leaned back, looking at him for a long time

before she spoke. "You know, I cannot recollect the last time you called him Simon. I've not heard you refer to him as anything but Billingham for years."

Rhys nodded. Yes, he had always called those of rank by their titles and insisted others do the same with him, even close friends. But now it was different. Simon was more than a friend. As the days went on, Rhys was beginning to accept that Simon was his brother.

"I-I'm beginning to see him in a different light, I suppose," he answered.

"You see him differently because of whatever happened between you in London. Whatever drove you here," Anne said.

She kept her eyes on the blanket beneath them, plucking at a loose thread absently, but there was no denying her tone. Once again she was pressing him for the truth, though perhaps more subtly than before.

Rhys almost smiled. Anne was tenacious, he had to give her that.

"I cannot speak to you about that, Anne," he said softly. "Someday soon you will understand why. But not now."

She didn't look up from the blanket, but Rhys saw the muscle in her jaw twitch ever so slightly. His answer was unsatisfactory to her and for that he found he was truly sorry, but he couldn't give her more. He had to keep her in the dark about his reasons for running. To shield her, even in the smallest way. If he didn't, she would try to protect him and damn herself in the process.

"Well, then I suppose, yes," Anne said. She glanced at him briefly. "I suppose Simon is less formal than you are."

Rhys leaned back on his elbows on the blanket, crossing his ankles as he looked up at the passing clouds. He thought about why he was so different from the man who shared his blood.

"We were raised differently," he finally mused out loud. "My father . . . the duke, he insisted on my showing no emotion. I was punished when I did. And he drilled me endlessly about the sanctity of rank and the exalted history of the Waverly line."

Anne moved into a similar position as he on the blanket, only she lay on her side facing him. Dark locks of hair fell across her face and he found he wanted to brush them away. Instead he fisted his hands at his sides and fought the inclination.

"Your father was quite intimidating." Anne shivered. "I imagine he must have been as much so to you, especially as a child."

Rhys nodded. Just as images of his own life had been sweeping through his mind, now pictures of his father's behavior crowded his thoughts.

"He was," he said softly. "He was a stern man, he could even be spiteful when it suited him. Any hint of kindness or empathy I showed to others was discouraged by him."

Anne's forehead wrinkled, and a deep sadness entered her stare. "Because he believed empathy and kindness were a weakness."

Rhys nodded, but found himself exploring his wife's face. "And yet you are filled with both and no one could call you weak."

To his surprise, pink colored Anne's cheeks and she dipped her chin with a smile that was filled with pleasure at his compliment.

"I suppose that is how *I* was raised." Anne shrugged one shoulder. "And perhaps our upbringing decides all about us."

Rhys shut his eyes, blocking out the beautiful scenery, blocking out Anne's open and kind face. He wished he could block out everything else. Forget what he knew and what he was.

"That is what I thought, too," he said softly. "But now . . ."

He trailed off, but his eyes came open when he felt the soft touch of Anne's fingers on his cheek. She had moved closer, her body touching his and her palm gentle as she cupped his chin.

"Now?" she whispered in soft encouragement.

Once again he felt a strange and powerful longing to confess his secret to her. To ask her to be a friend to him as she had been a friend to so many others. To let the love she claimed to feel for him soothe and comfort him.

"Now I don't know anything anymore," he said, his voice barely carrying as he kept his gaze locked on her.

Tears filled her eyes, and Rhys stared. They weren't tears for her own broken heart. They were for him. Not out of pity, but a genuine desire to end his pain.

So when she leaned down and wrapped her arms around him, holding him gently and offering the comfort he refused to ask for, he allowed it. And when she drew back and pressed her mouth to his, he didn't pull away from her kiss.

He couldn't have. At that moment he needed her as much as he needed breath, and he was too weak to keep up the pretense of anything else.

Chapter 8

Despite her decision to seduce him, Anne hadn't made plans to kiss Rhys during their picnic. Seduction was best left to nighttime in a bed, not in full daylight and outside!

However, when she stared down at him, she had seen all the pain he normally kept inside. The loneliness he might not even recognize he carried with him. Her first and best instinct was to offer him comfort.

But now, with his arms tightening around her back and his mouth demanding more and more from her kisses, she was beginning to see that this moment was the perfect one for temptation.

She angled her head and relaxed into the kiss, meeting Rhys's questing tongue with her own. He let out a low groan beneath her and his fingers fisted against her back. His reaction emboldened her and she sucked his tongue gently, drawing him into her mouth the way she wanted his body to come into her own.

He allowed it for a long moment, exploring her and tasting her, but just as she felt the wire of his control fray, he pulled his head back. He shifted her away from him as he pushed to his feet. As he turned, she saw the evidence of his desire, but still he shook his head.

"I'm sorry, Anne," he murmured, his breath coming as sharp and hard as her own. "I can't do this."

She squeezed her eyes shut, this utter rejection hurting and embarrassing her all over again. But then she straightened her shoulders. Rhys had already admitted he wanted her. She could see that was true. This refusal to make love to her had nothing to do with her desirability.

It was evident the time had come to fight, truly fight, not just for the right to make love to her husband, but to keep him. To love him.

"Please," she whispered, her hands shaking as she lifted them to the scooped neckline of her gown. One by one she released the buttons there and finally tugged her dress open. Her breasts bounced free.

Anne flushed as he slowly turned and stared at her. How in the world had it come to this? She was *outside* in the bright, unyielding sunshine, her body bared like she was selling it along Fleet Street in

London. Anyone could come upon them and see how desperate she had become, but it didn't matter. Not anymore.

"Please," she repeated, and hated that her voice cracked slightly.

He let out a low curse beneath his breath and she thought he would walk away, but to her shock he instead dropped to his knees on the blanket before her. He drew in a breath and it shuddered out as he looked at her. Then one big hand came out so slowly that it was almost like it wasn't in his control, and he reverently cupped one of her bare breasts.

Anne couldn't help but shiver at the feel of Rhys's slightly rough, but warm hands on her skin. Her body came alive at the feel of them, of him so close to her after having been denied so long. Just like that morning when he had curled himself around her and touched her, then shockingly tasted her until she shattered, her body instantly readied itself for his invasion.

"Rhys," she whispered, her voice shaking with desire and anticipation.

He had been staring at her naked breasts, but the sound of her voice seemed to shake him from that trance. His gaze shifted until their eyes met, and for a long, charged moment they held there. His hand remained on her bare flesh, but Anne could read nothing in his eyes about what he would do next. Rhys had returned to his expert ability to hide himself, hide his heart, from everyone near him. If he was warring within over whether to move forward or to once again back away, she could see none of it.

Finally he shook his head, and her heart sank.

"When I married you, I had no idea you would become an embodiment of all temptation to me," he whispered without breaking the contact of their gazes.

Anne started, lifting her hand to cover her lips. He had never been so bold with her. Even his admission that morning that he wanted her had been made reluctantly, but this was different.

"Anne—" He released her breast and gently cupped her cheeks with both hands. Tilting her face, he whispered, "One fact has not changed: I can't make love to you."

She moaned in pain, but when she tried to turn from him, he wouldn't allow it.

"But there are *other* things we can do. Other ways to please each other, to put out the fire that torments me every moment I'm near you. Normally I wouldn't ask you, a lady, my wife, to do these things, but now—"

Before he could finish, Anne shifted. She pushed herself up on her knees, dragging her body against his before she pressed her lips to his. The kiss was desperate, it was sloppy and had little finesse, but she poured herself into it. She poured her desire, her fear, her love into it as she claimed his mouth and accepted his offer with her body.

Then she drew back. "You can't break me with your passion, Rhys. I long for it as much as I long for your heart."

His lips pursed and she hurried to keep him from denying her love again.

"I know you believe you can't give me that heart," she said. "But I'll take whatever you *can* give. Just teach me how."

She said the words and she meant them, but she hated herself for baring her soul even more than she had bared her body. For revealing, once again, just how lopsided their connection was. Rhys knew she loved him, that she needed him, that she longed for him. And she knew nothing except that he desired her despite himself.

But before she could dwell on that too much, Rhys kissed her once again, stealing her breath and her thoughts with an ardor and desperate passion she had never before felt from him. It was as if he had been waiting, holding back, and now he had some kind of permission to let loose his need on her.

His mouth was rough, but she didn't care about that.

She relished the way he claimed her, driving his tongue into her with hard, harsh, driving thrusts that made her blood boil and her limbs weak and boneless. She made no protest when he pushed her backward, laying her down against their picnic blanket and covering her body with the hard length of his own. She certainly didn't refuse him when he moved his lips from hers and began to suck and taste the column of her throat.

He feasted on her, his tongue moving over her in the same rhythm as his gently flexing hips and she felt both movements pulse between her thighs. Just like that morning, her body grew wet, tingling as she became overwhelmed with the urge to open her legs to him. She wanted to feel them joined as one, to be his wife in every way.

But Rhys had her pinned and she couldn't open herself. Yet somehow that only increased the throbbing, urgent pressure between her legs. She moaned softly as Rhys glided away from her throat and tasted the delicate frame of her collarbone, then lower, lower until his breath steamed over her bare breasts.

There he stopped, and when her eyes came open she saw he was staring at her naked skin again, his gaze dark and dangerous. He pinched one nipple gently and Anne arched beneath him, crying out as she turned her face away. Her breath was difficult to find now, she panted it out in heaving gasps as he toyed with her nipples and sent great bursts of pleasure to ricochet throughout her body.

But that feeling was nothing compared to when he dropped his head and gently sucked one hard peak between his lips. Anne fisted her hands in the blanket beneath her, arching her hips as her breath left her, her voice left her, and all that was left was Rhys and his mouth and his tongue as he swirled it around and around the sensitive tip of her breast.

She had never felt such a thing before, never been so swept away by feeling and desire and need for more. She no longer cared that they were lying out in the open on a blanket. In fact, as Rhys moved his mouth to her opposite breast, she found she liked the gentle swish of the breeze on her bare skin. She only wanted more.

And like a mind reader, he gave her more. More tugging of her sensitive nipples with his lips, his tongue, even his teeth. More stroking against her with his hard body. More of his hands sliding along her flesh, opening her gown farther, pulling it away to reveal her body to him and his passionate ministrations that took her to places she had never imagined, even in her most vivid fantasies.

Finally she was naked, splayed out beneath him like a wanton on the blanket. Yet Anne felt no need to cover herself or turn away from Rhys's blatant stare.

Instead she shifted, moving into the light, showing herself to better advantage and reveling in the way he caught his breath. In the way he wet his lips and trembled as he reached for her.

"I want to taste you again," he murmured before he kissed her. "Even as you taste me."

Her eyes went wide even as his tongue breached her lips. Rhys had never been a vocal lover. Oh, he had been gentle, he had softly explained and soothed the first time they made love on their wedding night, but that was different. This statement, "I want to taste you, even as you taste me," was a sensual promise. A wicked threat that made her body pulse wildly and the intense sensations throbbing through her all the more powerful.

And it made her think of his actions earlier in the day, when he had licked and sucked her until she lost all control and sense. Could she do the same to him? Could she take his power and give him plea-sure in return just by touching him with her mouth? The idea of such an act was a foreign thing, but not unpleasant.

He pulled away and cupped her face, looking down at her with an intensity in his stare she had never before seen.

"I'm sorry, it's too much," he groaned. "I shouldn't have asked for something so bold."

Anne stared at him. What he wanted implied passion. This was an act that he put outside the bounds of a "perfect wife" or a "perfect duchess."

She didn't want to be those things. She wanted to be his woman. In every way. Even if it meant doing something that made her belly stir with nerves.

"I want to be bold," she breathed. "I *want* what you have asked me for."

He stared at her for a long time, the struggle between desire and propriety on his face. She waited for propriety to win, as it had for so long, but for once it didn't.

"You must promise me that if you don't like this, you'll tell me," he said, brushing her cheek with the back of his hand gently. "I'll stop immediately, no matter how far we've gone."

She was taken aback, once again, by his deference to her and her desires, but she managed to jerk out a nod. "Yes."

No sooner had the word left her lips then he dropped his mouth back to her skin. Once more he stroked his tongue along a languid path down her body, pausing to suckle her breasts until she was weak, then gliding down to tease the sensitive, ticklish skin of her belly.

She tensed as he glided lower, lower, and she felt the rough brush of his stubbly chin against her inner thigh. She shivered as she waited for him to kiss her there in that sensitive, private place where she ached so keenly. But instead he rolled away onto his back.

Rhys shook his head as he stared up at the sky. Although she had said yes, had promised to tell him to stop if she didn't want this, his hesitation remained. He had compartmentalized *lady* away from *lover* for so long that he wasn't certain he could bring the two together. And he feared when Anne fully realized he wanted her to place his cock into her mouth, she would recoil.

"Rhys?" she asked, her voice shaking as she struggled to sit up and stared down at him.

God, she was a vision. The sunlight danced off her pale, naked flesh, making her like a goddess in some classic painting. And he ached to claim her. Not just pleasure her, but take her. Bury himself deep within her until she sobbed with pleasure and swore she would never love any other man.

But that was selfish. And so was this.

"I promise you," she murmured. "I want you so much that my body aches for it. And I don't just want to receive pleasure, Rhys. I want to give it. If you'll deny me everything else, please don't deny me that."

His lips parted in surprise. Surprise that shifted to

shock when his wife moved down the blanket until she sat beside him. Then she reached out and delicately cupped his hard cock through his trousers.

Rhys's eyes came shut. He hadn't been touched by anyone but himself since their honeymoon, which seemed like an eternity ago. That morning just the brush of her backside against him had nearly unmanned him, but this . . . this was something entirely different. Even through the heavy fabric of his pants, her touch was like fire. And he arched his hips against her hand almost without the ability to control himself.

"This is right," she whispered, her voice soft and seductive as she unbuttoned the top of his fly and parted the fabric.

Her fingers slid along the skin she had revealed and Rhys clenched at the blanket beneath him as he let out a curse. She smiled before she repeated the action again and again until she freed his cock from its confines.

"I'm your wife and there is nothing more *right* than this."

He could have protested, but when her soft fist closed around his tight, throbbing flesh, he lost all ability to speak. To reason. This felt too good and he let out a guttural moan as she stroked down over him once, twice.

Rhys surrendered, too weak from pleasure to do anything else. He squeezed his eyes shut and let her brush down over him, without argument, without direction. And though she wasn't experienced, with each stroke she grew bolder and more accurate in her touch. She seemed naturally attuned to his body, giving him more when he needed it and less when he danced too close to the edge of release.

The pleasure stirring in his loins boiled hotter and hotter, stealing his breath and making him growl ever louder with desire. But just as he thought it all might be too much, he felt the heat of her breath against his cock, and then the wetness of her tongue shocked his eyes open.

He stared, wide-eyed, down his body and watched as his wife, the woman he had always thought of as the "perfect lady," closed her lips around him and sucked him into a heated heaven.

"Anne," he gasped out.

She looked up at him, but didn't withdraw him from her lips. The image of her, green-blue eyes dilated with desire and pleasure while her mouth covered him in such a wicked and sensual way, nearly made him come, but somehow he maintained control.

"You don't have to do this," he insisted.

She withdrew gently, but kept her fist around him.

"Am I doing it wrong?" she asked, pink flooding her cheeks. "Doesn't it feel good?"

He struggled to speak, to think, to do anything except beg her to repeat that action again and again. "It feels very good," he said, "but—"

She didn't allow further protest, but returned her mouth to cover his erection once more.

He felt her smile against his cock and then her tongue moved, gliding around him in a tight, hot circle that brought his balls up tight against his body and made his seed shift within him.

He was close to the edge and he had yet to give her the same pleasure she was giving him. He thought of what he had originally asked of her. To taste her as she tasted him. He had convinced himself that was wrong, but she was correct when she said it felt right. He had half of that fantasy already. It wouldn't take much to experience it all.

"Anne," he groaned as she glided her mouth down his shaft once again. "Anne, move over me. Place yourself over my mouth and let me taste you."

That stopped her movement. She slowly withdrew his cock from her lips. The soft breeze moved over his hard, wet member and his eyes rolled back in his head from the shocking and pleasurable sensation.

"Is that what you meant by tasting each other?" she asked, her voice shaking.

He jerked out a nod. "Yes. If you straddle me, you can continue to suckle me, but allow me to pleasure you at the same time."

A flush filled Anne's cheeks, but then she nodded. Slowly she positioned herself over him. He scented the heady perfume of her desire, felt the brush of wetness against his chest when she straddled him. He caught her hips and dragged her up, presenting her already trembling sex for his pleasure. She groaned as he did so and he realized she had been aroused by pleasuring him. She was just as much on the edge as he was.

He wet a finger and slowly traced the entrance to her body. She cried out from above him, her gaze peeking over her shoulder. He locked eyes with her and leaned up to press a gentle kiss against her wet and waiting flesh.

Anne bucked backward, her moans echoing in the quiet around them. He licked her, tasting her, treasuring every soft cry and sigh that left her lips.

Anne still held Rhys's cock in her hand and when he twitched, she looked down at it. Slowly she lowered her mouth and took him back inside. She wasn't sure if what she was doing was right, but she did her best to mimic his actions when he made love to her. She drew him in, she eased him out, she took and then retreated over and over again.

Although he had protested, Anne felt no shame in what she was doing. It was giving her husband pleasure, and that excited her almost as much as his touch.

His breath increased against her aching sheath and the stroking of his tongue increased in time with her. She was spiraling close to the edge of madness, close to a release she craved to her very core. And then, without warning, it hit her.

She arched back, crying out through the pulsating pleasure briefly before she took Rhys back into her mouth and continued to suck and lick him. He groaned, the sound vibrating against her soaked body. But before she could continue, he pulled himself from her mouth. His member pumped and he spent his seed away from her.

Anne collapsed over his body, weak and satisfied. Slowly he shifted her until they lay pressed together on the blanket where they had shared a picnic and so much more.

To her surprise and delight, Rhys didn't push her away, he didn't try to separate. There was no discomfort this time, only a sense of peace that allowed Anne to close her eyes and listen to the pounding of her husband's heart. Little by little it slowed until it matched her own.

She smiled as she felt the sun over her drowsy body.

If their hearts could match, couldn't they match in other ways? She looked at him to find he was smiling down at her with a lazy, satisfied expression that spoke of comfort and ease. They had made a connection today, not just of body, but of spirit. And even though they hadn't fully made love, that connection of souls was proof to Anne that there could be more between them.

More than ever she believed she could win this man's heart. One day he would love her and all of this would be a distant memory.

Chapter 9

"**W**ill you help me?"

Rhys turned from the place where he stood at the window and caught his breath as his wife entered the main room of the small cottage.

She wore a yellow gown with pretty flowers hand-stitched across the silk in a fall of green and white. The warm summer color brought out the pretty golden highlights of her otherwise dark hair and brightened the green-blue of her sparkling eyes. Just the sight of her made Rhys smile and simply long to be near her, touch her, drink in her light and joy and pray he could make even a fraction of it his own.

"My God," he breathed as he crossed the room toward her. "You are beautiful."

Anne blushed as she pressed a hand to his chest briefly. "*You* are blind. Without a servant, I know I look a wreck. Will you button me in back?"

She turned and Rhys swallowed. Her gown gaped,

revealing the silky fabric of her chemise and the soft, bare skin along her shoulders.

It had been two days since their unexpected and most pleasurable encounter on the picnic blanket. Even though it went against everything he had vowed, he couldn't seem to deny himself the pleasure of being with her. Rhys had enjoyed every moment he had with his wife since then.

He had spent years telling himself that a lady like Anne couldn't and even *shouldn't* be exposed to the full force of his desire, but she proved him wrong at every turn. She was a passionate lover, letting him teach her how to touch him, how to pleasure him, without ever recoiling or simpering. And she was as responsive as any woman he had taken to his bed. He'd begun to learn where to touch her to bring her almost immediate release, or how to tease her and draw out that pleasure for hours.

In fact, he would have said he was utterly satisfied, except that he hadn't claimed her body. And he wanted to. He dreamed of it nightly. He ached for it. A few times he'd even come dangerously close to submitting to that craving for full possession.

But it was the one thing he couldn't have.

Now, staring at her bare skin, smelling the fragrance of her freshly washed hair . . . he wanted nothing more than to fall into the narrow bed they shared and make her cry out his name again and again.

"This is only a village gathering," he said, fumbling with the buttons. His fingers suddenly felt thick and useless. "You shall certainly outshine everyone there."

Anne turned and her smile brightened her face. "Thank you, Rhys. Now let me straighten your cravat."

Her delicate fingers lifted and he watched, mesmerized as she fiddled with the restraining neckwear. He had gone so long without such finery that it felt odd.

"We are a mess, you and I." She laughed as she flicked lint from his jacket. "It has been such an eye-opening experience to realize one is not capable of taking care of oneself. I never knew how much I depended on Mally and the other servants until I no longer possessed the ability to call on them."

Rhys frowned. He, too, had been rather shocked by how much he needed the help of others. The people he had so easily dismissed and looked down upon in his life had evidently been much more important than he had ever realized.

"Rhys?"

He shook away the troubling thoughts and looked at his wife a second time. She was staring up at him with a smile tilting her lips, though it did not entirely reach her troubled eyes.

"I'm sorry," he murmured as he reached down to stroke her cheek with one finger. "I was woolgathering."

"It appears to be more than woolgathering that troubles you," she whispered.

He stared at her. Over the days she had been here, he'd wanted to tell her the truth so often. In fact, the feeling seemed to grow with each moment they spent in each other's company. Anne, just by her very nature, offered him a respite from his pain, an oasis in the desert of the consequences he'd soon face.

But he couldn't, so he did the one thing that always distracted him from such foolish desires. He cupped her face gently and kissed her. The moment he touched her, she melted, parting her lips, letting him in without hesitation or manipulation.

But this time, as the kiss deepened, she drew away. Her mouth was swollen and she lifted her hands to cover her lips briefly.

"As much as I'd like to do exactly what your mouth offers me," she whispered, "I think we need to be around other people. *You* need it. You've been hiding far too long."

Rhys frowned. He'd always prided himself on being able to hide his emotions, but Anne saw through him and managed to say exactly what he needed to hear, though often not what he wanted her to say.

"No," he snapped, more sharply than he intended. "What I need is—"

He broke off the sentence as he turned away. It wasn't fair to say what he *needed*. He was already being desperately unfair to the woman he had married. Slowly he drew a few breaths to calm himself and then he returned his gaze to her evenly.

"Very well," he said through clenched teeth. "We'll go to the village fair as originally planned."

She smiled as she held out an arm. He took it and led her outside. The walk to the village wasn't a long one. Twenty minutes perhaps, down golden paths that seemed to sparkle in the setting sun. Rhys breathed in the salt-tinged air and couldn't help but smile as the tension left his body. It seemed his wife was right, as always. Being away from the cottage was good for him.

They heard the music before they saw the crowd, and Anne laughed as she turned toward him with excitement. He was captivated by her expression, drawn in by how his wife could live her life with such vivacity and verve.

He wasn't capable of living up to her example. Even tonight, as they crested the hill and found a village full of people dancing, laughing, and indulging in a good time, he bristled. He couldn't help but notice the dirty bare feet of a pair of frolicking children as they raced by with giggles echoing behind them. The sight of a woman, her hair down around her shoulders, lifting a bottle and slurring loudly about the music, made him wince.

All this was so far removed from the calm, regulated, utterly ordered and ranked life he had created for himself that he scarcely knew where to look or what to think.

He sniffed his disapproval even as Anne snuggled closer to his arm, her soft breasts pushing into his side in a most pleasant manner.

"Is it truly *so* awful?" she asked, her voice filled with both faint amusement and a twinge of annoyance.

He shrugged one shoulder as they moved even closer to the merriment. "It is entertaining in a rather base way, I suppose. But not what I'm accustomed to."

She arched a brow. "No, I assume not. I cannot picture you and your stuffy friends pounding each other on the back while drinking fresh cider like those men over there are. Or any in our circles joining hands in the middle of a field and dancing with the raucous abandon that group there is."

"Would you *wish* for that?" Rhys asked, turning on her. "You could not in seriousness want such an utter lack of decorum or the neglect of the behaviors that separate our class from theirs."

In the rapidly dimming light, Rhys was surprised to see that the expression on Anne's face was one of pity. As if he was missing or lacking something and she felt sorry for him because of it.

"I wouldn't wish to forever play and run and behave in such a way, no," she finally said softly. "But from time to time, it is worthwhile to forget rank and position and simply *be*."

"Be," he repeated with uncertainty.

She nodded. "I'm defined by more than just my position as your wife, your duchess, my father's daughter, the amount of money in my pocketbook, and the size of my home in Town. The person who I am is certainly changed by those things, but there are parts of me that are entirely separate from them. And I *like* those parts of me."

Rhys stared. He had so long defined himself by only the very things Anne described that he wasn't certain he could say, with such conviction, that there was anything else to him beyond them.

Before he could speak, Stuart Parks broke from the group and moved their way. The other man had a pleasant smile on his face as he stepped in their path.

"Good evening, my lord, my lady," he said. "How

wonderful you could join our gathering!"

"Good evening, Mr. Parks," Anne said with another of those warm and welcoming smiles that made Rhys's gut clench with desire and wonder. "Is your family here as well?"

Stuart nodded. "Indeed they are. Mother is gossiping with some of the ladies of the village, my father is likely seriously discussing the politics of the day and prices for crops with his cronies. I believe my sister is desperately trying to catch a husband."

He laughed and Anne joined in it. "And are you being pursued by a gaggle of young ladies who consider you husband material?" she asked.

Stuart blushed ever so slightly and gave a sheepish nod. "Indeed. It seems once one reaches the age of thirty, it is open season."

Anne laughed again. "Then it seems this gathering is very like the ones we have in London. Only the costuming and the music are slightly changed."

She said it to Stuart and he responded briefly, but Rhys hardly heard his once-friend's response. He was staring at his wife in bewilderment. Had she just handily put him in his place once again? It seemed she was quite good at it.

He looked around him once more, and this time he made an effort to see the party through her eyes. Indeed, it was not unlike a rout hosted by someone of rank in the *ton*. And when he saw it in that light, he saw people, not bare feet or inappropriate behavior or a lack of refinement.

"Your Grace, perhaps this is too bold, but would you care to dance with our group?" Stuart asked, motioning over his shoulder toward where the musicians played.

Rhys started and shook away his reverie. He stared at Anne. Certainly she wouldn't go so far . . . would she? But it seemed she would, for she smiled brightly in response to the question.

"I would greatly love to join you," she said as she began to follow Stuart away from Rhys's side.

He caught her arm and pulled her to a stop. "Whatever are you doing?"

"Your mother brought you here, so I assume these are lands that belong to your family in some way?" she asked, meeting his gaze evenly.

He nodded. "Yes."

"Then we hold some responsibility to these people?"

"I-I suppose," he stammered, wrinkling his brow in confusion.

"Then it's my duty to show them courtesy," she said. Then she flashed him a brief smile. "Aside from which, I haven't danced in an age and this music is lifting my spirits. Fare thee well, husband. I promise not to fall in love with any fairy spirits."

With a laugh, she extracted herself from his grip and hurried to catch up with Stuart as the other man joined a small group of villagers in the field near the musicians.

Rhys stared, too stunned and frankly curious to stop his wife. He could see, even from this distance, that Stuart was introducing Anne to the strangers around them. From their reactions and bows and curtsies, the villagers were surprised to see a lady of such power and influence in their dance circle, but Anne was . . . well, Anne. And soon they were laughing and smiling together like they were all old friends.

The music lifted and Anne fell into a line of women on one side of the field. It took her a moment to learn the steps of the unfamiliar country dance, but she had always been a graceful dancer. During their long betrothal, Rhys had always enjoyed taking the floor with her. But he had never really *watched* her when she moved. Her eyes were bright in the lamp and firelight, her cheeks flushed as she made a quick circle around the men with the other women.

She looked alive and happy and much like the fairies she had teased him about before she departed. Unable to resist, he found himself moving closer to her. The pounding rhythm of the music had him tapping his toe as he reached a crowd that had gathered to observe the dancers.

He looked at their faces. A loving mother held her child, swinging to the beat of the music with a wide and generous smile. In her face, he saw his own mother holding him as a boy. And he also saw Anne, only with *his* son in her arms. He flinched at that image, knowing it was impossible.

He saw friends, a bottle passed between them, grinning and pointing at the pretty girls in the group. They put him to mind of Simon and himself, in those last wild days at school when they'd played pranks together.

The music picked up in tempo and Rhys's attention was now drawn to the circle. The group there had begun to disperse, each person grabbing another to draw them into the dance and widen the effect of the fun and frolic. Anne met his gaze, laughing as she held out her hands and came toward him.

He didn't resist as she drew him to the center of the circle. He clasped her hands and they spun together as he abandoned himself to the music and the ample charms of his wife.

Chapter 10

Rhys moved through the milling crowd, smiling and greeting those who looked his way, dodging the elbows of the exuberantly drunk and weaving bodies weary from exercise and excess. The night was in full swing now, and after several dances, he was thirsty and so was Anne.

He saw a table a short distance ahead, laden with ales and a heady punch with some enormous level of spirits. His mouth watered just thinking of its sweet and tart flavor.

When he reached the table, another man stood before him, back to Rhys, filling his own cup. Rhys waited, trying to maintain patience and not snap out an order as was his usual mode of getting what he wanted in this world.

Finally the man turned, and all thoughts of drinks and irritations fled Rhys's mind. Before him stood a person he knew. Someone he had grown up with. A man who belonged at this common village gathering no more than he did.

"Caleb Talbot?" Rhys took a step back and stared.

The other man looked at him for a long moment, almost with no recognition in his pale blue eyes. Rhys frowned. From all appearances, Talbot was well on his way to being drunk, and not in the playful way of others around him. From the looks of his sallow skin and haunted expression, he wasn't enjoying the state.

"Great God, if it isn't the Duke of Arrogance," Caleb finally drawled, if only briefly. "Have you come here to laugh at my sorry state, or tell me you knew I'd come to this, having no rank and all?"

Rhys's brow wrinkled. Caleb was right, as the second son of the Marquis of Stratfield, the other man had no rank, though he did have standing in Society due to the highness of his family and the respect with which others regarded his brother, Justin, who was currently Earl of Baybary, and his father. Still, as children, that hadn't been enough for Rhys. Once he formed his "Duke Club," he had actively shunned men like Caleb Talbot.

Now he truly looked at the man. There had been rumors he had been out of good Society for nearly a year after some kind of falling-out with his brother. He was disheveled, but his clothing was still of the highest quality and cut, and there was something in his air that elevated him from a servant or villager. It was evident he didn't belong amongst the happy peasants around them.

But when Rhys looked at the other man's eyes, he saw something that made him step back. Something he felt deep within his own soul now that he knew the truth about his birth.

Caleb didn't seem to belong amongst their upper rank, either. There was a lost, painful expression in his eyes. One Rhys felt a strong connection to and empathy for. Those unexpected feelings gentled his tone when he spoke again.

"Talbot," he said softly, "I had no idea you were here at all, actually. This area is connected to my family and I'm in attendance with my new wife."

Caleb's nostrils flared and he made a quick glance over the group until he found Anne. She was standing across the courtyard, watching the two of them, though in the darkness Rhys couldn't make out her expression.

"I heard you married Lady Anne at last." Caleb snorted. "Don't deserve that one. But then, men like you rarely deserve what you get. Bastard."

That barb came quite a bit closer to the mark than perhaps Caleb knew and it stung Rhys. In other circumstances, he would have lashed out at Caleb for daring to speak to him in such a fashion, but tonight . . . tonight he didn't feel a desire to do so. In some way, he recognized he deserved the slur.

He tilted his head. "Talbot, I realize I've been . . . difficult in the past."

Caleb snorted out a harsh burst of unhappy laughter before he swigged an entire glass of punch in one gulp. "That would be one way to put how you've behaved toward me and many other perfectly decent men."

Rhys nodded. "Yes, I know, and I have regrets for my actions."

"You?" the other man said with a shake of his head. "Regret anything? I don't believe it. What could have brought on such an earth-shattering change, *Your Grace?*"

Rhys shook his head. Perhaps he owed this man no explanation, but he did want him to believe his apology. For some reason, it mattered.

"Recently things have happened," he began, "which have turned my world upside down, and it has made me reevaluate my life."

Caleb suddenly stared at him, and the sarcastic, heated hatred that had bubbled in his stare faded, replaced by a surprised understanding that Rhys hadn't expected any more than his own uncharacteristic candor.

"Well, I know a bit about that," Caleb murmured as he stared at his empty cup.

Rhys frowned. "In the past I wasn't gracious. And I-I . . ." He trailed off, uncertain of how to proceed in these uncharted waters. "I *apologize* for it."

He blinked, realizing in that odd moment that he couldn't recall the last time he had apologized for his behavior and actually meant the sentiment.

Talbot slowly shook his head. "This has been the strangest year of my life, so this fits into that entirely," he murmured, almost more to himself than to Rhys.

Rhys was about to smile, but then Caleb looked at him and he could see there was no forgiveness in the other man's stare. There was nothingness.

"I suppose I should appreciate your attempt at amends," Talbot said with a shrug. "I should ignore everything in me that says you have an ulterior motive and simply accept your words with the grace you claim you've lacked. That would make me the bigger man, after all. But in truth, I'm too exhausted to pretend that I give a damn, or that a few empty words could alter a lifetime of pompous superiority."

Rhys clenched his teeth, but remained silent.

"*You* are one of the worst individuals I've ever known in my lifetime," Caleb finished as he set his empty cup down. "And you can't take that back with words, Waverly. Perhaps you can't take it back at all."

With that, the other man turned and walked away, leaving Rhys to watch after him with a frown. And a sinking feeling that perhaps Caleb Talbot was correct. Perhaps there was no way he could ever change who and what he'd been.

Anne slipped up beside her husband, feeling like she was approaching a skittish colt. With a smile for him, she took his hand and squeezed it gently. He glanced down at her, but the brief upturn of his lips could hardly be described as a smile.

In the hour since she had seen him speaking to Caleb Talbot, Rhys had been distant. Oh, he had remained by her side, he had even continued to partake in conversation with those around them, but he seemed troubled, aloof. She had no idea what the two men had spoken about, but it had apparently been quite serious.

"You remain troubled," she said, not a question, but a statement. She hesitated as another couple weaved close to them, talking softly in the darkness.

Rhys shrugged one shoulder and gently extracted his fingers from hers.

"It's been an odd night," he admitted, looking around him at the fading party. The musicians were packing away their things, leaving only a lonely lute player to strum his instrument softly, the forlorn sound carrying in the still night air.

"Because you saw Caleb Talbot?" she asked, retaking the hand he had removed. This time he allowed her to hold it. "Would you like to tell me now what you spoke of?"

He glanced at her from the corner of his eye briefly, then he lifted his free hand to scrub it over his face.

"It isn't really a question of what was said between us," he admitted. "It's just . . . being here, Anne . . . it's like looking into some stark, cold mirror. I am now seeing myself for the first time. I see the things I've done . . . the things I've said and been."

Anne tilted her head at the unhappy expression in her husband's eyes. His regret was unexpected and painful, but it sparked hope in her, just as all the changes she had seen in him since her arrival had.

"We aren't static beings, my love," she whispered. "The wonderful thing in life is that we can change our behaviors, our identities. If you truly wish to be a different man, you can be. I-I'd help you if you'd allow it."

He started, and suddenly his dark eyes turned on her, fully taking in her face, really seeing her. And there was such sadness in their depths that she almost turned away from it because it showed how hopeless he felt the situation was, and that broke her heart.

"A different man," Rhys murmured, then he turned his face away. "Yes, I fear that is inevitable. But who will that man be? Who am I?"

She reached for him, her hand trembling as she cupped his cheek and forced him to look at her.

"You are my husband," she whispered. "And it is late. Let me take you home."

He didn't move away from her touch, but the distant smile that tilted his lips gave her no comfort. Even though they were closer than ever, even though she felt the shift in Rhys's behavior every day, he continued to withdraw from her. There seemed to be no way to keep him by her side.

"Home. What is home?" he asked.

She hesitated. The cottage just a short walk away was beginning to feel like a home to her, no matter how different it was from the life she'd come to know and expect. Their estate in London was also home, though a much colder and more proper one.

But those weren't the answers that would comfort Rhys in this odd moment of rare self-reflection. He needed more. He wanted more. For once she thought he might accept what she could give him.

"Let *me* be home," she said, her breath and words catching on the lump that filled her throat.

He drew back and opened his mouth. She saw the protest in his eyes, the denial, once again, of the love she felt for him, of the future she wanted to share with him with such desperation. She couldn't allow him to say those things. She couldn't hear, once again, that he felt nothing for her but a desire he regretted.

"Rhys." She lifted on her tiptoes and pressed her fingers to his mouth. "Please. Just for tonight."

He didn't respond for a long moment, but then she felt his lips shift against her fingers. Slowly he kissed them, then he lifted his hand to take hers. He turned her hand over and kissed the top, gentle but also seductive as he tasted her flesh.

She sucked in a breath, almost against her will, and her knees went weak. He smiled, and for the first time since they danced together, since he left her side to fetch her drink, it was a real expression, laced with sensual promise and a longing and passion that rivaled her own.

He bent his head and then his mouth was on hers. For a moment, Anne was too shocked to respond. Here they were, in the midst of the village square, lingering strangers still milling about, and Rhys was kissing her with abandon under the light of the lamps like he didn't care who saw them.

It was delightful.

The shock at the situation faded and Anne put her arms around him, holding him close as she opened her lips to allow him access and melted into the kiss.

Before it could go too far, Rhys drew away and looked down at her with another smile.

"Come, before we shock the neighbors," he whispered, then he grabbed her hand and they ran toward the cottage, laughing like naughty children.

The moment the cottage door closed behind them, Rhys's mouth was on hers again, and he backed Anne toward the bed with a purposeful, driving motion. She offered no resistance, she felt no need to do so. Of course little was resolved between them, of course she felt the drive within him to banish his unhappiness in the cradle of her body.

But she didn't care. She didn't even care, in that moment, if this was only temporary. What mattered was that they were here, *Rhys* was here, and perhaps tonight would be the night he wouldn't be able to resist the desire to drive his body into hers and claim her as his bride once again.

She ached for that, not only because it would force their union to go on a little longer as they waited to see if she would breed, but also because even as an innocent, Anne recognized she was missing something by not joining her body to his. Now that the feelings between them were deeper, she had no doubt the act of making love would mean more, as well. She ached for that union of body and soul, she craved the intimacy of it that no one could take away.

They fell back on the narrow bed, his body covering hers, his hot mouth moving away from her lips to suckle her throat as he yanked and jerked at the buttons that were pinned between her body and the bed.

He made a sudden sound of frustration and then they rolled and Anne found herself on top of him, her legs splayed open around his hips, her body covering his. She stared down at him as he flicked open the buttons he hadn't been able to free before and her gown gaped. They had never been in this position, but already Anne could see the advantages. Why, if she was on top, perhaps she could have enough control to—

Before she could finish the thought, Rhys tugged her gown around her waist and then flipped her beneath him once more. He brushed hair away from her face as he stared down at her, his ardor apparently slowed by the need to remove her clothing.

"You were so beautiful tonight," he whispered.

Tears leapt to Anne's eyes as she stared up at him. Before the cottage, Rhys had never been loose with his compliments, only giving them sparingly and almost with distraction. Now, with him looking at her with such fascination and desire, she felt that he meant this one, and it warmed her.

"You don't even know what you do to me," he murmured as his mouth came down on her shoulder and his hot breath steamed around the thin strap of her chemise. "What you always did to me."

Her eyes widened at that unexpected admission, but before Anne could respond or question him, he pulled the chemise straps away and bared her from the waist up. Immediately he cupped one breast and took it into his mouth, sucking gently on the nipple. The thoughts Anne might have had dumped from her brain like sand from a child's shovel, and all she could do was arch helplessly against his chest.

The rough fabric of his jacket rubbed her skin and her eyes came open. She looked at him, licking her nipple with little strokes, and smiled.

"Too many clothes," she gasped as she tugged against his jacket.

He glanced at her, sucked one more time on the turgid peak and then pulled away. As he tore his jacket and shirt off and then began to work on removing his trousers, Anne struggled with her wrinkled gown. She had it around her ankles and was kicking it aside when she heard the thump of Rhys's boots and looked at him again. He stood at the foot of the bed, utterly naked.

Only firelight lit the room, for they had been in too much of a hurry to light a lamp or a candle, but the soft glow bounced off his skin and was more than enough to make her mouth go dry.

She would never overcome how arousing she found her husband's body to be. With muscular shoulders, a flat belly slightly textured by the muscles beneath, and hips that tapered downward to the powerful legs beneath, he was a specimen to behold. And then there was his . . . *cock*, he had called it once, although she had never been so bold as to repeat that harsh and naughty word.

Anne had little experience with such things, but she couldn't help but stare at the hard, ready member that stood at attention against Rhys's belly. Although he hadn't breached her with its stiffness more than a handful of times, she no longer worried when she saw it. In fact, now she ached to feel it deep inside her. She wanted to cradle it within her sex and feel him tremble when he found release.

Her body grew even wetter and hotter in anticipation of that act.

"Why did you stop?" Rhys asked with a smile as he knelt at the bottom of the bed near her feet. "You aren't yet undressed, though you are delightfully close."

He caught up the tangled gown and chemise that

were wrapped around her feet as evidence.

"I was distracted," she retorted. "You have only yourself to blame."

"Did I distract you?" he practically purred as he slipped her gown free from her slippered foot. "I apologize. Let me assist you now as my penance for such a transgression."

Anne lifted up to rest her body on her elbows and watched as he carefully unbuckled her slippers in turn. He tossed each one over his shoulder and they clattered somewhere behind him.

She laughed, but the sound turned to a moan when Rhys cradled her stocking-clad foot in his hand and began to massage it gently, then harder. Her body melted under his touch and she lay back as he massaged away the tension created by dancing and walking.

His fingers danced higher, sliding over her calf as he moved up the bed. Then her thigh, and when he found the bare skin at the top of her stocking he pressed a hot kiss there that made Anne suddenly very aware of her position. Her leg was resting on his shoulder, her body open wide to him.

She opened her heavy lids and they locked stares. It seemed he was as aware as she of how vulnerable she was. How easily he could do whatever he wished to her and she wouldn't protest. Silently she dared him to take her. He held her gaze evenly, but she saw the fight in him. The desire to do what she hadn't stated out loud.

But of course he had more control than that. To her utter frustration, he always had. He caught the edge of her stocking and drew it away, rolling it back on the path he had taken. He repeated the same slow action on her other leg until both her stockings were gone and she lay naked across the bed, ready for him, even though he would never take full advantage of that situation.

Still, she opened her arms, beckoning him to her, praying he would forget whatever strange logic it was that dictated he leave her unclaimed. He stared at her, outlined in the firelight, and then to her surprise, he lowered his naked body to cover hers.

They had lain together before, but never like this. Her legs were open, welcoming him to come inside, and she felt the length of his body resting flat against her pelvis as he pressed his mouth to hers with a heated passion that spoke of desperation as much as desire.

It would take only a slight shift for him to breach her. Her heart raced and her breath came short at such an idea. She found herself lifting her hips in the hopes that she would find the right angle to do just that. It didn't work, but it rubbed his hardness against her in a most pleasing way.

Apparently it was equally pleasurable for him, because Rhys stopped kissing her and instead rested his mouth against her shoulder and let out a sighing moan that echoed in the quiet room around them.

He slipped a hand between their bodies, and Anne held her breath. This was the time! He had finally surrendered and now he would take her.

She felt his fingers open her, spreading her wet folds until she was fully exposed, but instead of breaching her, he shifted until his cock rubbed along the outside of her body, lubricated by her juices.

He squeezed his eyes shut and began to arch and thrust his hips. His member glided along her wet slit, stroking her clit with each thrust. Anne clung to his bare shoulders, arching to meet him, forgetting everything in that moment except for the pleasurable way he stroked her again and again and again.

As her fingernails dug into his skin, his shoulders trembled, like he was wrestling with a great physical burden. When she drew back to look at him, the lines of his face spoke of his struggle. His jaw was set, his teeth grinding together as he arched his hips against her.

She shimmied, trying once more to force him to breach her. He let out a growling sound of pleasure and displeasure at once and glared at her.

"Anne . . ." His voice was a warning.

She lifted her hips again. "Please."

Rhys's eyes came shut and the veins in his neck swelled with the restraint he seemed compelled to practice.

"I can't," he whispered, but before she could argue, his mouth covered hers. He cupped her backside, holding her close against him so she could no longer make any attempt to force his hand.

His hips jerked faster now, his slick cock stroking the outer lips of her body, stimulating the tingling nerves of her clit with expert precision.

The pleasure mounted deep within her and her sheath clenched at emptiness, teased by having him so close. Her body could no longer deny its release and she cried out, burying her face into his shoulder and rising to meet him as she quaked with intense pleasure. Her release seemed to spur him forward as well, for he let out a guttural groan and then rose up and turned away, spilling his seed into his hand as his shoulders shook.

She watched as he rose and found a clean cloth with which to wipe his essence away. He remained silent as he tidied himself, as did she. Now that it was over, the pleasure she had felt faded and was replaced by that lonely emptiness that had so long been her companion. Her pleasures at his hands since she came here had been wonderful, of course. But they had never been enough to satisfy her beyond the moment of release. They were empty, just as she remained empty.

The bed sagged as Rhys took his place beside her. They faced each other, still silent in the growing darkness. His frown spoke his displeasure with the situation, and it was as powerful as her own.

He watched her face, gently brushing away tangled hair from her mouth and eyes.

"I realized something tonight," he finally said after the silence seemed to stretch forever.

Anne tensed, seeing the determination on his face. Whatever he had "realized," it was likely not something she was going to enjoy hearing.

"And what is that?" she asked, fighting to keep the tremor from her voice, fighting to keep a fraction of what little dignity she had left.

He cupped her cheek. "Anne, it's time to go home . . . to London."

In the dying firelight, Rhys saw the flash of hurt, of fear that lit Anne's eyes. When he said it was time to return to London, it was clear they both understood what he meant. He had already told her once they returned, he would end this marriage.

And that was better for her. Once she understood why, once the scandal broke . . . she would thank him for distancing her from his disgrace. Eventually, when the first round of whispers faded and Anne found acceptance in Society again, she might even think of him warmly for sparing her the utter shunning he would receive.

Because after his encounter with Caleb Talbot, Rhys was more certain than ever that shunning was exactly what he could expect. It was evident he had burned too many bridges, said and done too many things to expect any kind of forgiveness or kindness from those around him once they knew of his shame.

There would be many people who would revel in his fall and make his life a living hell to repay him for his behavior over the years.

"I suppose we couldn't stay here forever," Anne said, rolling on her back to stare at the ceiling above. "It was foolish to think we could."

Rhys nodded, but she had struck upon a desire he'd hardly allowed himself to have. Staying here forever sounded like paradise to him. Eden.

But even Eden had fallen in the end. And Rhys had more sins to face than Adam and Eve combined.

Rhys looked at Anne once more. Her expression was troubled and pained. He hated that he had done that to her. That he had hurt her like this. Especially after she'd offered him such comfort and friendship and love.

Tonight she had asked him to allow *her* to be his home when he feared he had none. She had meant for tonight, but these feelings he was beginning to experience, these desires and regrets that tormented him when he looked into her eyes . . . they seemed like they would last beyond a night or a month or a year. He feared he would feel this way forever.

And that was so unfair when Anne was bound to be snatched away from him. Perhaps, in this entirely appalling situation, it was the biggest injustice of all.

Chapter 11

Anne peeked past the fraying curtains and out the window with a sigh. A carriage was parked in the drive. A hateful, horrible carriage that Rhys had walked into the village that very morning to let. And the moment she stepped into that vehicle, her war for Rhys's heart, for her life as she knew it, would very likely be over.

Back in London, her husband's attention would be drawn by other things, other people. She would have far fewer chances to seduce or convince him to remain with her. For all she knew, he intended to take her directly to her father the moment they reached Town.

She straightened up as Rhys came around a corner and began to direct the men he'd paid to load their items. The glass was thick enough that she couldn't hear his words, but that didn't mean she couldn't observe his behavior. Once not so long ago, he would have snapped, ordered, yelled at those he considered lessers. But something had changed in him since his arrival here.

Now he spoke with a firm determination on his face, but no disdain. And when they began to lift a bag onto the top of the gig and one of the shorter men lost his grip, Rhys even stepped into his place to assist them without so much as a cross expression.

Anne stepped away from the window and frowned before she shook off her troubled thoughts. There was no time for this. She had duties to perform before she went away with her husband. Lifting her chin, she looked around her for anything they had left behind. But the cottage was all but empty. The only evidence they had stayed there for any length of time was the basket of dirty dishes from their breakfast and the rumpled bedclothes.

Her gaze lingered at the bed. Although he'd never fully taken her, Rhys had claimed her more here than he ever had in their marital bed or on their honeymoon. He had loved her, at least with his body, and finally she understood the giggling whispers of her happily married friends and the long, lingering glances she saw shared between people like Simon and Lillian.

Passion was a powerful thing. She hated to lose it, but feared that was her fate.

Behind her, the door opened and she turned. Rhys leaned in the doorway.

"Stuart has finished loading the carriage and is going to depart back to the village. Would you like to say good-bye to him?" he asked.

Anne didn't answer, but slowly crossed the room to her husband. She drank in the sight of him, slightly disheveled, completely at ease, utterly handsome, and almost hers. When they were back in London, he'd no doubt become proper and distant again, so she wanted to hold this moment in her mind forever.

She could have sworn he caught his breath ever so slightly when she stopped just inches before him. Reaching up, she wiped a smudge of dirt from his cheek, then rose up on her tiptoes. His breath stirred her hair, his skin was warm as she neared him. When she pressed her lips to his, they were firm and welcoming. He released the doorjamb slowly and curled his fingers around her upper arms, holding her to him as their lips parted and the kiss deepened.

Finally she drew back, her heart pounding like butterfly wings against her rib cage and her body crying out for more than a mere kiss. She took a long moment to draw in a few breaths and calm herself before she answered the question.

"Yes."

Rhys blinked down at her, his expression filled with desire, but also utterly confused. "Yes?"

She couldn't help but laugh. "You asked if I'd like to say good-bye to Stuart, and I'm saying yes."

He remained staring at her for a moment more before he nodded. "Yes, Stuart, forgive me. Of course. He is . . . he's beside the carriage."

Anne laughed at Rhys's uncharacteristic distraction, but then took his hand and drew him outside to find the man who had become, in some small way, a friend to them while they stayed here. As she approached the carriage, she saw him there, leaning against the vehicle. He smiled as they approached and straightened up while he swept his battered hat from his head.

"Your Grace," he said with a small bow. "I'm so glad I have a chance to say farewell, both for myself and for my family."

Anne released her husband and approached the other man. "As am I. You've been such help, as has your entire family. I hope you'll pass along my most sincere thanks for all their attempts to keep us comfortable. I've loved meeting them and will very much miss your mother's fine cooking."

Stuart dipped his chin slightly, but Anne thought he blushed with pleasure. "I'll certainly pass along your kind words. And the next time you two decide to visit here, I hope you'll send word ahead of you. We will have the cottage ready."

Anne's smile fell a fraction. How she would love to make a yearly trek to this place, to have a week or two with her husband where they could simply lose themselves in the beauty of the sea and each other. But Rhys had already determined that their marriage would be over. What was awaiting her in London was pain and heartbreak and perhaps ruination. She might never return to this wonderful place.

"My lady?" Stuart asked, his face falling.

She shook her head as she sent a quick glance toward Rhys. He was standing ramrod straight, his mouth a thin, unhappy line. It seemed his thoughts mirrored her own.

"I'm sorry, Mr. Parks," Anne said. "I'm afraid I lost myself in thought."

Stuart nodded, but there was a flash of concern in his gaze as he looked from Rhys to Anne and back. "Well, that is bound to happen when one is about to return home. I wish you both a very good and safe journey. Farewell."

Anne shook his hand, as did Rhys, and Stuart walked away down the path toward the village, leaving them with only their driver and the dreaded carriage.

Rhys turned to the man with a sigh. "We'd like

to take a final short walk around the property. Will you meet us at the top of the road?"

The other man nodded swiftly and got into his rig, urging the horses to drive on and away from sight. Anne glanced up at Rhys.

"One final good-bye, eh?" she said, her voice lined with tension she couldn't conceal no matter how hard she tried.

He nodded, the motion a jerking one. "It seems fitting."

He held out an arm and Anne hesitated before she took it. Awareness crackled between them, desire and also a sense of melancholy as they walked down the short hill toward the cliffs that overlooked the boiling sea.

Anne smiled as they reached the edge.

"Here is where I first saw you," she murmured, thinking of Rhys standing nude at the edge of the cliff.

"You nearly killed me," Rhys said with a low chuckle that seemed to resonate all the way down her spine.

She glanced at him quickly, trying not to relive those horrible moments when she'd thought Rhys was trying to kill himself. "Yes, but I *was* trying to save you, so I suppose I should have some credit for that."

He turned to face her, his expression quite serious now. He cupped her chin gently. "You have the credit and all my thanks for the attempt."

The gentleness in his tone and the true gratefulness touched Anne to her very soul. This version of Rhys, with his ease with others and his attentiveness to her, was everything she'd ever dreamed of, everything she'd known he could be from the first moment she met him as a child. She should have been happy, but she couldn't be, for this was bound to end.

She smiled because she feared if she didn't, she might cry, and that wasn't what she wanted in these last moments here.

"Did you truly jump off these cliffs as a boy?"

He released her face and motioned to their left. "Yes. This rock marked the safe place."

She looked at the oddly shaped rock he indicated, then down the long, sharp drop to the sea below. She shivered. "What is it like, to fall so far?"

He didn't answer for a long moment, and when he did, his voice was strange and distant. "It's like freedom, Anne. Like flying."

She stared down below once more, then turned toward him. "I want to jump, Rhys. I want us to jump together."

Rhys stared at Anne, certain he'd misheard his proper wife. She couldn't *really* desire to hurtle herself over the edge of the cliff.

"I-I beg your pardon?" he stammered.

She smiled at him, but it was a wild expression that brightened her eyes, one born of panic and desperation, not pleasure.

"I said I wish to jump," she repeated in a firm, calm tone.

"Absolutely not." He stepped back from the edge and pulled her along with him.

"Why?"

"It isn't ladylike, for one," he protested, though it was rather weak. No one could ever accuse Anne of being anything but a lady. One moment of frivolity wouldn't change that in anyone's eyes, including his own.

Her hands came to her hips in irritation. "Please don't insult me so. Apparently you think me incapable of handling any kind of truth, but I'm not so stupid or emotional as you seem to believe. And I *know* when you are avoiding a subject."

Rhys flinched, fully aware that they were no longer talking about a cliff dive, but about his refusal to share the truth of his birth with her.

"Anne . . ." he began.

She shook her head. "No. Tell me, what is your real reason for denying my request?"

He struggled for a moment. The real reason was that the idea terrified him. He didn't want to allow her to do anything dangerous that could hurt her. That could make him lose her.

But he couldn't say that because she was already fully aware that he intended to leave her when they returned to London.

"Because it is fifteen feet down!" he finally choked.

Once more, she appeared incredulous. "When I arrived here and thought you were attempting to do yourself a harm, you assured me that the jump was perfectly safe. That you and countless others, including *children*, had managed the feat. Is there something lacking in me, something that makes me physically incapable of the same?"

He stared, blinking. Her jaw was set so tightly that there was no way one could mistake her anger for anything else. Anne was furious as she stood before him and he realized it had little to do with his refusal to allow her to jump the cliff.

She had kept it in check well enough during their time here, but now he saw she hadn't overcome her anger at him. For leaving her so abruptly. For telling her he would end their marriage physically, if not legally. For refusing to tell her why all this was necessary . . . a gift to her, even.

And now this one small rejection, this one tiny refusal as they readied themselves to return home and what would surely be the end of them, it set her off.

She deserved her anger. *He* deserved her anger even though such an unflinching show of emotion still made him uncomfortable.

"Of course there is nothing wrong with you," he said softly.

He found he wanted to reach for her, but was certain that would be incorrect in their current circumstances. Anne might see it as patronizing and placating, rather than soothing.

"Then why not allow me this one simple request, Rhys?" she asked, moving back toward the edge in an act of pure defiance. "You've told me that the jump is like freedom, like flying. When we return to London, I'll have neither of those things, especially if you have your way and separate from me. Can you not give me this *one thing* now?"

Rhys stared. Her statement stung, and the person he'd been even a few weeks ago probably would have lashed out at her or dismissed her as a way of dealing with the pain. Today, though, he took it in. And he realized how fair it was that she doled it out.

Over the years she had been nothing less than the ideal fiancée. She had done as he asked, she had been at his side when he required it. She had loved him, but never asked him for his heart in return, although he now realized just how deeply that must have hurt her.

In contrast, he had been terrible during their betrothal and even in the days of their marriage before he left. Oh, he had never struck her or purposefully embarrassed her as he'd sometimes seen others of his rank treat their women . . . but he had never *given* her anything beyond meaningless baubles and empty compliments.

In truth, until he came here, until she followed him, he had never even thought to ask her what she desired.

And now she told him exactly what she wanted, in no uncertain terms. And although he feared it, he realized the best thing he could do for her was to give her this gift. She deserved it and so much more.

"Yes," he heard himself say.

She parted her lips like she was prepared to argue further, but then she stopped and merely stared at him.

"Yes?" she repeated after her stunned silence had lasted a moment.

He nodded. "Yes, I'll jump with you."

To his utter shock, Anne launched herself into the air with a whoop that any boy would have envied. He stared, seeing her as a girl, seeing her as a *person*, perhaps for the first time since they were young children awkwardly spending time together. Feelings bubbled up from some dark and deep place within him. Emotions that were powerful and unexpected and so varied he couldn't have separated them and named them all.

But one he *could* was a caring he hadn't ever felt for another person. Something different, even, from the warm feelings he experienced for his sisters, his mother, even his stern father. These emotions toward Anne were something deeper and more meaningful, something that touched his very soul.

But all he could do was squash them instantly and pray they would never come back to torture him again.

He cleared his throat. "You must do as I tell you so that you won't injure yourself."

She smoothed her skirt reflexively even as she nodded. "Yes, Rhys. Of course."

He stared over the cliff at the water below. He'd seen people jump in pairs before, even in small groups, so he knew it was safe enough, but nervousness still made his stomach dance. None of those pairs or groups had ever been people he'd given a damn about. This was different.

"First, we must stand at the exact spot," he began. "If I tell you not to jump, you mustn't do it until I give you the word."

Anne nodded, but by her smile and bouncing demeanor, it was clear she was only placating him.

"You forgot one very important rule," she said with a light laugh that seemed to touch the very core of him.

"What is that?" he asked, turning to face her.

She lifted her fingers to the buttons along the front of her gown and began to unfasten them with swift efficiency. He stared at the rapidly revealed expanse of bare, perfumed skin.

"We must be naked when we jump," she said as she shrugged her arms from her dress and chemise at the same time and bared herself from the waist up.

"Great God, woman!" he burst out, leaping to her and lifting the fabric back over her skin, but not before he brushed the back of his hand against her breast. She sucked in air in a *whoosh* and he yanked the hand away to her arm instead, as if burned.

"You'll be seen by half the county!"

She stared at him evenly, her pupils dilated with excitement, and now he saw desire. "That didn't seem to bother you a few days ago when we were picnicking."

Rhys shut his eyes with a low curse as images from that passionate afternoon bombarded him. God, he could still taste Anne's skin and hear her sighs as they floated away on the soft breeze.

He forced himself to look at her. "That day I was . . . carried away. It was not appropriate and I apolo—"

"Don't!" Anne cried, lifting her hand to his lips and pressing there. "Don't you dare say you're sorry and take that day from me, from *us*."

Rhys stared at her, shocked by her passionate response. Finally he nodded slowly, and she lowered her hand. Straightening her spine, she looked at the sea again.

"Be calm, my dear," she said softly. "The driver has gone up the hill as you requested and no one else is around to see. Besides, I must take off my clothing, for I don't relish the idea of being sopping wet all the way to our first stop along the road tonight."

She met his gaze again, her green-blue stare almost daring him to try to stop her. He made no move to do so as she pushed her dress to her ankles, where it pooled at her feet. She toed off her slippers and let the stockings she wore follow and suddenly she was very naked, very close, and Rhys found himself instantly aroused. How perfect would it be to take her on this cliff, in the water, against a tree . . . anywhere that he could feel her body pulse in pleasure around his? He wanted that more than anything.

"Won't you join me, Rhys?" she asked, her eyes all innocence but her demeanor anything but as she stood there, utterly unashamed and on display for him.

"Yes," he managed to push past a dry throat.

He quickly undressed, knowing she would see the evidence of his desire as soon as he straightened up, if she hadn't seen it already, for his cock thrust against the confines of his trousers. By her smile, this time knowing and seductive, she already knew and enjoyed the sight as he stood before her, cock at the ready.

But she made no motion to touch him. Instead she remained focused on the cliff and the idea of jumping over.

"Now what?" she asked, though by the tremble of her voice it was clear she was beginning to grow nervous at the prospect of what they were about to do.

He stood beside her and double-checked the position of the rock near them. "Move a bit to your left," he ordered. "Yes, very good. Now, we jump when I count to three. Unless you've changed your mind."

Anne shook her head swiftly. "No. I cannot."

Rhys took a side stare at her and saw her jaw clenched, as if she had surrendered herself to this. It meant something to her, something greater than the absolute thrill of making it to the sea safely.

And he supposed, as he looked out past the cliff to the gray-blue water that stretched out forever before him, that it meant something more to him as well.

He had always said farewell to this place by jumping off the cliff like this. But today he was saying good-bye to more than just the cottage. He was saying it to the life he'd once known and the person he'd once been. When he arrived in London, he would be forced to face the changes he had not chosen and the person who threatened all he held dear.

"Are you ready?" he asked, his voice seeming very far away to his ears.

"Y-yes," she said beside him.

"One . . . two . . ." Before he said the third word, Anne reached out and took his hand. He stared at their interlocked fingers, wondering at the absolute trust she put in him to get them to the sea safely. Then he uttered, "Three!"

And they jumped. Just as it had always been, the short descent was swift and thrilling. But even more so with his hand tucked in Anne's. As he looked at her, time seemed to slow.

She was smiling, completely enchanted by the flow of air past her hair and face, utterly trusting that he had chosen the correct place on the cliff that would keep them safe.

They hit the water and her trust was proven warranted, for the deep sea enveloped them gently in the one place where the water didn't meet land with violence. He swam for the top, his hand still gripping hers, and they surfaced at once, both dragging in a huge gulp of fresh air.

Anne stared around her, eyes wide. She seemed so stunned he feared she might be in shock from the fright. He reached out to comfort her, but it was in that moment that she began to laugh.

"That was thrilling! Far more exciting than almost anything I've ever known!" She wrapped her arms around his bare neck and floated there as she continued to talk. "The wind on my face, the taste of the salt on my lips as I hit the water! Oh Rhys, no wonder you did this, it is—"

She didn't finish, he couldn't let her. They were so close and had just shared an experience he had never thought to give to her. And it was more powerful than he had ever imagined it could be.

All he could do was kiss her. He pulled her slick, naked body against his in the cool water and their lips met. She tasted of salt from the sea and sweet from her morning tea. The combination burst on his tongue and he delved for more.

She opened to him, her legs moving around his waist in the water and holding tight as they bobbed up and down and kissed and kissed until he felt like he was drowning, only he welcomed it. He didn't want reality, he didn't want duty. In that charged moment, he could have stayed in the water with her for a lifetime and surrendered to all the joy and pleasure and love she offered him just by being here at his side.

He'd almost convinced himself it was possible when Anne pulled away with another smile, this one dazed and shy. She shivered ever so slightly.

"The water is cold."

He nodded. "Come, we'll go up to the shore. It's a warm day, the sun will solve that problem quickly enough."

He swam for the curved swath of beach a few hundred feet away and soon enough they were on shore, the warm sun drying them and taking away the shivers that racked them both from the cool water.

But as they walked up the path to the piles of clothing they had left above, Rhys couldn't help one last glance over his shoulder at the cove behind them. This place had been a fairy tale to him as a child, and a dream during the short time he'd spent here with Anne. But now . . .

Now it was time to return to reality. As much as he dreaded it. As much as he wished he could pretend it wasn't so.

Chapter 12

The rain began just as they arrived on the outskirts of London. It was a hard rain, one that sometimes caused the carriage to tremble and made it stuffy and close during the final hour through twisting city traffic. Anne sat alone in the vehicle, this one the fine ducal carriage that had met them along the road the previous day, and watched the droplets drag down the window like teardrops.

At least the weather matched her mood.

The vehicle shivered to a stop and she wiped at the steamy glass with her sleeve. Outside, Rhys sat on his horse, his greatcoat pulled tightly around his shoulders and his hat low over his eyes to protect them from the rain. She sighed. Even now, sitting at the gate to their London home, her husband already looked more like a duke. It was silly, but he held himself differently somehow.

Would she ever again see the man who had teased

her, pleasured her with such abandon, and jumped over the cliffs with her?

The carriage lurched onto the drive and stopped a second time. Anne looked around her, gathering up the few items she'd carried along the road and tucking them into her reticule in preparation for disembarking. The carriage door opened, but before a servant could come to assist her, Rhys appeared in the doorway. A few droplets of water trickled from his hat and hit his face, trailing along his cheeks like tears. She couldn't help but stare in wonder at the image.

"Anne?" he said softly.

She shook off her thoughts and forced a smile. "You poor thing, you're soaked through."

He shrugged one shoulder as he offered her a hand to exit. "I'll be dry soon enough."

"You could have joined me in the carriage," she said as she stepped onto the drive.

A servant sidled up beside her with an open umbrella to protect her as they all scurried for the front door and the dry foyer within.

Rhys nodded as they crossed the threshold. "I thought of it, but . . ."

He trailed off and Anne pursed her lips in understanding. He hadn't wanted to be alone with her.

She was happy not to have to reply when the servant lowered the umbrella and moved away, leaving Gilmour to close the door and turn toward them with one of his usual bland but pleasant smiles.

"We are very pleased to have you home my lord, my lady," the servant said, though Anne could see there was a slightly curious expression in his eyes as he looked at them.

Surely their sudden departures must have caused quite a stir among the servants, especially with all of Anne's upset and inquiries before she followed Rhys to the countryside. And their curiosity was only a small glimpse of what would follow if Rhys had his way.

Anne sighed before she said, "Yes, thank you, Gilmour. I assume there has been much correspondence during our absence."

He nodded. "Indeed, Your Grace. Both of you have received several items."

First he gave a letter to Rhys and then the butler held out a high pile of notes and invitations that Anne took with another sigh. She would have much explaining to do to those whose parties they had missed without acknowledgment. But by now probably everyone in Society knew she and Rhys had taken off for the country with no explanation. No doubt there had been much speculation about the cause.

She shivered when she thought of what they would

say when Rhys abandoned their marriage entirely.

Shooting a side glance his way, she saw her husband reading the missive that had been addressed to him. She recognized the hand on the outside of the pages as Simon's. Her lips pursed. The note likely had something to do with Rhys's reasons for leaving her.

Rhys folded the note smartly and stuffed it in his wet pocket. To her surprise, he began fidgeting with great discomfort.

He nodded to the butler, and just as any man in his position who had any experience in his work would do, the servant took the hint and slowly backed away.

"I will oversee the unpacking," he said with grace. "Perhaps I could speak to Your Ladyship later about some household matters?"

Anne nodded absently, never taking her eyes from her husband. "Yes, of course."

When they were alone, Rhys let out a breath, as if he had been holding it in waiting. She smiled in some attempt to ease his apparent discomfort. It was odd to see him so, for he had always done the things his title required with effortlessness. Now it was almost as if he didn't quite . . . *fit* anymore.

"I'm sorry, Anne," Rhys said, his low voice hardly carrying, even in the echoing foyer. "I have some urgent business I must attend to."

She opened her mouth, greatly desiring to ask about the letter he'd received. Wanting to inquire, once again, about what so troubled him. But she saw the look on his face and the determination in Rhys's eyes. Whatever respite he had allowed himself at their seaside retreat, that was over now. The separation between them suddenly felt irreversible, and her heart ached.

"Very well," she managed to choke out. "I, too, have much to do now that we've returned. Perhaps . . ."

She hesitated. Perhaps what? Perhaps she would ambush him later when her curiosity overwhelmed her? Perhaps he would run away without word again? Perhaps she would love him for the rest of her life, even though it was an utterly foolish thing?

"Perhaps we'll see each other later," Rhys finished for her, his voice gentle.

She blinked as she stared at him, surprised by how comforting he sounded.

"Perhaps," she whispered, then she gave him a quick smile and turned toward the stairway at the end of the long foyer. Before she had gotten more than a few steps, Rhys caught her arm.

He turned her back, and for a long, charged moment they stood there, eyes locked and so much emotion passing between them that Anne's chest physically hurt.

Finally Rhys bent his head and gently kissed her forehead. It was by no means the most passionate kiss they had ever shared, but it meant a great deal to her. As did his words when he whispered, "Thank you, Anne."

She stared as he pulled away, then headed for the hallway and his office. He didn't look back. She knew that for certain because she watched him until he disappeared from sight. The door opened and shut in the distance, and Anne let out her breath. She stood alone in the foyer for a moment, then moved toward the stairway.

As she dragged herself toward her chamber, she flipped through the letters she had almost forgotten she held. Most could wait, but there was one from Rhys's mother that was rather urgent. Anne flinched.

She liked the dowager duchess a great deal, and apparently Anne's frantic inquiries about Rhys's whereabouts before she left for the cottage had caused the other woman some concern. She would have to write to her new mother-in-law this afternoon and perhaps arrange for a supper so the woman could see her son.

Anne didn't relish the idea of explaining her situation to the woman. The dowager didn't miss much, and Anne feared her own upset, as well as Rhys's, would be very clear.

Stuffing the letter into her pocket, Anne hesitated at her chamber door. Once inside, she would fully return to her life in London. There would be no going back. She almost wanted to run from that. To turn away, get into the carriage, and take flight, just as Rhys had done not so long ago.

But before she could do something so foolish, the door opened of its own accord and Malvina stood inside waiting for her. Her servant's friendly face crumpled as she saw Anne, and suddenly Anne was enveloped in her maid's warm embrace.

She hadn't realized just how exhausted she was, emotionally and physically, until that moment. As her servant and friend held her, Anne almost melted, letting the other woman support her for a long moment as she squeezed her eyes shut and tried very hard not to let fall the tears that she had controlled for so long.

"Oh, my lady," Mally said into her hair, her voice sad and supportive.

That was the last straw. Anne felt a tear trickle down her cheek, then another. She pulled away and rushed into the chamber, slamming the door behind her so no one would see her pain. She tossed the unread letters and invitations on her dressing table and crossed to the window to stare outside and gather herself.

"Here."

Anne turned to find Mally standing behind her, a fresh handkerchief extended. She smiled and took the cloth, wiping her eyes as she drew in several breaths and attempted to control herself. This would not do. She refused to allow it.

Finally the tears stopped and she was able to bring herself back to some semblance of decorum. It was only then that she spoke.

"Hello, Malvina."

Her servant stared. "*Hello?* Is that all you can say to me after you disappeared with hardly an explanation and stayed away for over ten days? I had no word from you, I had no idea where you could have gone."

"I told you before I left that I had to find my husband," Anne said through clenched teeth as she tossed the handkerchief on her dressing table beside the letters and paced away. "I do not need your judgment, I'm a grown woman."

Mally followed after her. "Grown or not, it isn't proper for you to run into the wilds of heavens knows where without a chaperone."

Anne squeezed her eyes shut and clenched her fists at her sides. She was back in a world full of rules and edicts about decorum, but now they seemed rather ridiculous after all she'd been through and seen over the past few weeks. The very notion that her main problem was that her disappearance had been *improper* was ludicrous, considering.

In fact, she couldn't help a rather hysterical giggle that bubbled past her lips and echoed in the chamber.

"My lady?" Malvina said, her tone concerned. "Is this somehow funny to you?"

Anne pivoted to face her old friend. "Funny? Oh no, Malvina, trust me that it isn't funny in the least. I just wonder at your idea that being unchaperoned with Rhys is improper. He is my husband, after all, we don't require a guard to keep us apart anymore." Her smile fell. "But perhaps you're correct, after all. If he . . ."

She trailed off and balled her hand tighter. Rhys wanted to end their marriage in every way but legally. So in his eyes, in her own, she would become a wife in name alone. In that light, it made all those moments they had shared in the country seem as wicked as Mally implied.

"If he what?" her servant asked, tilting her head to examine Anne's face with more focus. "I want to help you. Please, what is going on, my lady?"

Anne looked at her servant. If there was one person in this world whom she trusted more than any other, it was Malvina. She could surely tell this secret to her old friend and know it would never be repeated, even below stairs where gossip ran out of control.

Not to mention that if Rhys fulfilled his vow to separate from her, Malvina's future would be affected as well.

"I-I don't know why my husband disappeared," Anne admitted, never breaking her friend's gaze. "But when I found him, he told me that . . . that . . . he intends to separate from me now that we've returned to London. He even asked if I would consider lying to obtain an annulment, but of course I refused."

Mally blinked, and Anne thought that her friend's blank, confused expression must be quite close to the way her own face looked when Rhys dropped this same unexpected twist on her in the country. She had certainly *felt* numbed and shocked by the words he spoke then.

"How could he say that?" Mally finally asked, voice blank. "Why would he wish to end your union when you've been nothing but a good and steady companion to him? You have dedicated yourself to him, despite his numerous faults!"

Her servant's face had begun to darken as she spoke, and Anne realized that Mally was beginning to shift from shock to anger. Anger that reflected all the same emotion Anne had suppressed and controlled while in the country with Rhys. Now her own rage began to twitch and come to life inside her.

"I don't know why," Anne snapped, folding her arms as she paced away restlessly. "But he continually claims it is a way to 'save' me, though he makes no explanation of why or from what evil. All I know is that if he does this, there will only be ruination and destruction in my future."

Mally moved toward her. "No, my lady!"

"Yes!" Anne spun on her with a frown. "The *ton* will go wild with this. Can you imagine? Rhys is one of the most powerful and feared men in Society, they shall salivate over a scandalous tale of how he abandoned his wife less than a month after we wed. The speculations about my faults will run unchecked, I'm certain."

Mally flinched, but comforted Anne with a light touch on her arm. "Yes, of course they would talk. Such a thing is so unexpected that you couldn't stop their whispers. But you are a well-liked member of Society. If you held your head up and carried on with dignity, I think your reputation, as well as your father's support and that of your friends, could carry you through."

"Yes." Anne sighed. "You have mirrored Rhys's thoughts exactly. But what kind of life is that? Will I be relegated to the pitying acceptance of Society? The whispers? And a life without love, children, or even companionship?"

Mally looked at her, a sly expression lighting her face. "Perhaps not without love, my lady. There were many men who regretted you were betrothed from birth, you know. It is very likely one of them would be happy to step in and offer you something *more* than friendship if you asked."

Anne's eyes widened and she backed away from her friend with a gasp. She hadn't even considered that possibility. The idea of taking another man as her lover . . . it was repugnant to her. Even through her anger and heartbreak, she loved Rhys. She couldn't imagine loving another man in any way, let alone enough to bond herself to him physically or emotionally.

She opened her mouth, trying to find some way to respond to her friend's attempt at comfort, but nothing would come. Mally stared at her, waiting, but before Anne could speak, there was a light knock behind them.

"Anne?"

She pivoted to face the door. That was Rhys's voice. Apparently Malvina recognized that fact as well, for her servant's face darkened with even more anger and her gaze darted to Anne with expectation and question.

"Should I send him away?" Mally asked in crisp, chilly tones.

Anne shook her head. "I'll be right there, Rhys, one moment," she called out to stall her husband. She turned to her servant and caught Mally's hands in her own. "My dearest friend, you must listen to me. I know you have some desire to protect me, to defend me, and I appreciate it, but I do not wish for it."

Mally opened her mouth, but Anne grabbed her harder to silence her.

"Please, Mally! This is *my* problem and I must address it in my own time and my own manner."

Malvina pursed her lips, but finally bobbed out a quick nod and extracted herself from Anne's grip. "Yes, Your Grace. I understand. In this I cannot be your friend, I must only be your servant."

Anne nodded quickly. "Now I must let him in. Can you promise me you'll not do anything rash?"

Mally shifted slightly and then nodded a second time. "I'll bite my tongue."

No sooner had the servant said as much than Anne hurried to the door. She opened it wide and found, just as she had expected, Rhys waiting for her.

But to her surprise, he seemed . . . upset, emotional. His face was pinched and his eyes dark with pain. These glimpses of his soul were so rare that her entire being welled with an empathy that subdued her anger. It was difficult to maintain any kind of rage when faced with such a depth of agony in her husband.

"Rhys?" she said softly, reaching out to touch his face. "What is it?"

He stepped into the room and looked around. When his gaze fell on Mally, standing in the corner of the room, her arms folded and glaring daggers in his direction, he stopped and turned to Anne.

"I apologize, I thought we were alone."

Anne gave Malvina a quick glance. "Mally was just leaving to oversee the laundering, weren't you?"

Mally straightened up and made her way across the room slowly. "I suppose that is true. Good day."

But before her servant could exit the room, Rhys turned toward her. He smiled, and to Anne's surprise it was a genuine expression of kindness and friendliness. She had never seen him look at any servant in such a manner, even Gilmour, whom he seemed to tolerate the most.

"Malvina, isn't it?" he asked. "Or Mally, as my wife calls you. You've been with Her Grace a long time, haven't you?"

Mally stopped, her eyes just as wide with surprise as Anne's. Rhys had never spoken to her before, or even acknowledged her except to scold Anne in private about how close the two women were.

"Y-yes, Your Grace," Mally stammered.

Anne still saw a flash of anger and upset on her servant's face, but it was dulled by surprise and even a touch of fear that she was being singled out in such a fashion.

"Then you must have been responsible for fulfilling my orders about this chamber," Rhys continued as he looked around the large, airy room.

Again Mally nodded. "I was, sir."

"Well, it's lovely. You've done a wonderful job and I thank you. I want Anne . . ." He gave Anne a quick side glance. "I would like for her to be as happy and comfortable as I can make her while she resides in our . . . *this* house. You've helped me do that for her, and I appreciate it more than I could ever express."

Mally stared for a long moment, apparently stunned speechless. Finally she shook away her shock and ducked out a quick curtsy. "Thank you, Your Grace. I'm happy to do anything in the world for Lady Anne. Now I'll leave you. Good day."

The servant scurried from the room and shut the door behind her, leaving Anne and her husband alone. Anne couldn't help but let her gaze flit through the connecting door to the bedchamber a few feet away.

If Rhys had the same thoughts, he controlled them, for he patently avoided looking in that direction as he moved farther into the room and put his back to the beckoning bed she had stared at with such longing.

"Your servant is afraid of me," he said with a somewhat sad smile.

"*All* servants are afraid of you," Anne retorted with a light laugh that she had to force past her suddenly dry lips.

She had no idea why Rhys was here and was almost as terrified as she was curious. He had all but dismissed her not an hour before.

He frowned, as if her playful barb had hit a tender spot. "Yes, I suppose they would be. I deserve that."

Anne's brow wrinkled, for it seemed to be true regret that lined Rhys's face. It reminded her of the night they had danced at the village fair just before they returned to London. He had seemed just as self-reflective now as he had been after he spoke to Caleb Talbot. She'd thought that was a fleeting thing, but now it seemed more lasting.

"Rhys?" she whispered. "Can I help you in some way? Is there something I can do to ease whatever pain you're enduring?"

He flashed a gaze to her with sudden clarity. "You read me so well now."

She reached out to touch his arm, remaining quiet as she prayed he would finally take her into his confidence. He seemed to struggle with words, fighting to find the thing he wished to say to her.

"The note I received upon our arrival was from Simon," he finally said, his tone choked and tight, as if he was forcing the words from his throat.

"I thought it was." She nodded. "I recognized the hand."

"Apparently he has spies watching our home because not half an hour after our arrival, I received a second missive from him, this one asking me to come to his home as soon as I could."

Anne tilted her head. "So you'll go?"

He nodded, the action stiff and as forced as his tone. "I must, I fear. The time has come to face my demons. But I find that it's hard to do so. So I . . . It's unfair to ask this of you, especially considering how much in the dark I've kept you, but I think it might be easier for me if you accompanied me."

Anne drew back, his words settling over her like a thick blanket. She stared at him, his face filled with pain, but also hope. And need. For the first time, possibly in all the years she'd known him, she recognized how much he *needed* her. That need was all she'd ever hoped for, but now she felt no thrill or triumph at it.

But even though she feared what he would do once he had spoken to Simon, even though her anger continued as a dull throb in her chest, she couldn't deny him this need. She couldn't withhold her support. It was what she had promised him in a church not so long ago. And she kept her promises.

She nodded. "I'll go with you, Rhys, of course."

He physically sagged with his relief, and his dark and worried expression lightened a fraction. "Thank you."

Anne touched his arm. "But at some point, I cannot be in the dark about this any longer. I want the truth, Rhys. I think I deserve it."

He slowly reached for her, his long fingers curling around her shoulders with exquisite gentleness.

"You deserve so much more," he whispered. "And I promise you, the truth is coming. For better or worse, this will all be over soon."

Chapter 13

The parlor in Simon's London home was quiet, soothing, or at least it would have been if Rhys wasn't quietly driving himself mad. He clenched his fingers into and out of fists in his lap and stared, once again, at the ticking clock on the mantel. How was it possible that it had been only five minutes since Simon's butler led Anne and him to this room? It felt like an hour and he was growing more and more restless.

Anne reached out and gently placed her fingers over his clenched ones. She stroked lightly and his knuckles relaxed at her touch.

"I'm sure they'll be here momentarily," she said softly, as if reading his mind.

He tilted his head to look at her. He never should have brought her here. It was unfair to encourage her continuing hopes that they could remain together. And he could see from her expression that she still harbored those dreams of a happy marriage.

Beyond that, her presence was dangerous. He'd come to speak to Simon about the truth of his parentage and the blackmailer who was about to force his hand. Since he didn't yet want Anne to know about either of those things, he shouldn't have brought her anywhere near them.

But when he'd entered her chamber, bound to tell her he was going to Simon's, if only so she wouldn't panic and think he had run again, just the sight of her had calmed him. And in that moment of weakness he had wanted her with him during this difficult time.

No, he had *needed* her with him.

It was a shocking revelation, that he needed her. He didn't like it, for soon she wouldn't be there to support him, and he feared being weak without her.

"Rhys?" Anne said softly after he had been staring at her for close to two minutes without speaking a word.

He shook away his thoughts and tried to think of something benign to say, but the opening of the parlor door mercifully saved him.

He and Anne rose in unison as Simon allowed Lillian to enter before him. Lillian smiled first at Anne, but then surprised Rhys by turning that same welcoming, friendly, and even caring expression toward him. He shifted beneath it, for he didn't deserve it. In the short time of their acquaintance, Rhys hadn't been kind to Lillian. He certainly hadn't been welcoming. And yet, without hesitation, she gave him more than he had ever gifted her.

"Rhys, Anne," Simon said as he closed the door behind him firmly. "We're so glad to see you."

He smiled at the couple, but Rhys recognized there was no true happiness or light to the expression. His friend remained worried and tense, and that made Rhys stiffen, too. The reason for his coming here was outlined in every concerned contour of Simon's face.

Anne seemed to recognize the tension that coursed between the two men, for she was the one who answered. "Thank you for having us, Simon. And thank you for your earlier assistance. It was greatly appreciated."

Simon looked at Rhys when he answered her. "Anything for a friend."

Rhys's jaw twitched as he clenched his teeth and stared at his friend . . . his *brother*, which was still a foreign concept to him in so many ways. His reaction was even more so.

All his life he had been taught to control his emotions. Because of the difficulty of that task, he had endeavored not to experience those strong emotions at all, avoiding situations that would create them and even mocking anyone who felt too deeply.

But now, as he stood a few feet from Simon, Rhys's emotions bubbled free from their normally restrained state.

He was *angry* at his friend. Angry that Simon had been the messenger of his destruction. Angry that Simon had sent Anne after him even though Simon must have known it wasn't what Rhys wanted for himself or for her.

But quite shockingly, alongside the anger there existed another feeling. One he had stifled throughout his life just as handily as he had crushed fear or regret or empathy or anger.

There was joy.

Simon Crathorne had been one of Rhys's only true friends, chosen not just for his position in the world, but for his loyalty and decency. And now they were true brothers, in blood not just spirit. Simon was an ally in a different way than he had been before. No matter what came between them, no matter how passionately they argued, Rhys had no doubt that his friend . . . his *brother*, would always be there for him. Even if the world turned against him, Simon would remain true.

"How was your visit to the countryside?" Lillian asked, clearly hoping to cut some of the thick tension that had hung in the quiet room since their entry.

Rhys forced his attention to the woman he had

shunned upon first inspection. She was beautiful, though he had never denied that, with honey-colored locks and remarkable golden hazel eyes that changed color with her moods.

No, her looks hadn't been what put him off. It had been her lack of standing, her deficit of funds, and the whispers that surrounded her family that had made him fight to keep her from Simon's life, even while he watched his friend fall deeply in love with her.

Now those objections seemed laughable when compared to his own hidden past. When he thought of how he had treated Lillian, he was flooded with regret, but also with anxiety. After his encounter with Caleb Talbot, Rhys was beginning to realize that all the ways he'd mistreated others were soon going to be visited on his own head. If and when this secret came out, he would feel the sting of disdain as much as he had doled it out to people like Lillian.

But through it all, Lillian had been so strong, holding her chin up with every whisper and hiss. He admired her for that, for he didn't know if he had the wherewithal to do the same. At some moments, it seemed easier to hide, to run as he had done when his parentage had first been revealed.

He smiled at Lillian, perhaps the first time he had ever done so with genuine warmth.

"That part of the country is very beautiful, Your Grace," he said. "Have you ever been?"

Lillian shifted ever so slightly, and a touch of embarrassed color filled her cheeks. "I'm afraid not. I wasn't widely traveled as a girl and Simon and I have been kept in London since our wedding."

Rhys inwardly cringed. It was odd, he had spent the weeks leading up to Simon's sudden wedding reminding his friend that Lillian was utterly unsuitable, and yet in this moment he had forgotten her once-lowered status. And still managed to hurt her with his blunder.

"I know you and my . . . *friend* have been forced to stay here because of circumstances that involve me. But once this is resolved, I think you'll love seeing more of the world. In fact, if you two would like to go to the countryside, I would happily offer the use of the cottage to you, though I warn you, it is rustic."

From the corner of his eye, Rhys saw Anne flinch. To cover the pained reaction, she paced away to look out the window to the rainy gardens below.

Lillian didn't seem to notice Anne's reaction, but instead looked at him in surprise. "Why, th-thank you. I very much appreciate your offer, Your Grace."

He reached out to touch her hand briefly. "Rhys,

my lady. I would greatly like it if you might call me Rhys from now on."

Lillian's expression softened and she covered his hand with her own. "Rhys."

Behind them, Simon cleared his throat. "Rhys, perhaps you and I should go to my office. I have a few things to discuss with you."

Rhys shook away his thoughts and released Lillian's hand. "Yes, we do have much to talk about."

He turned to Anne and found she had looked away from the window and was staring at him. Her face, which was usually so vibrant and reflective of her emotions, was curiously blank. She didn't move or say anything as they stared at each other across the room.

"Do you mind, Anne?" he asked.

She shook her head briefly. "Of course not. This is why you came, after all. And I'm sure Lillian and I can find something to discuss in your absence."

Her words were friendly enough, but her tone troubled Rhys. Her voice was taut with tension, like she was swallowing back more than she said. But he nodded nonetheless. "Very good. I'll be back."

She took a sharp breath. "I should hope so."

Rhys felt the pain and the anger she had so long withheld while tending to him. It was in the air around them, suddenly palpable and dangerous, but he was helpless to do anything in that moment. So he nodded slightly and instead followed Simon from the room.

As they walked down the hallway toward Simon's office, Rhys found himself pondering not what his friend would say, but his wife. He had hurt her today, though he didn't know exactly how. He had hurt her so many times, perhaps not meaning to, but what consolation was that?

He could only hope she'd understand everything he had done once the truth came out.

They entered the large, tidy room Simon called office, and his friend closed the door behind them. Rhys shifted as he looked around. How many times had he been here? A hundred? But now it seemed ominous and different, though not so much as a stick of furniture had been changed.

But then that wasn't what had been altered, was it? No. *He* was different.

"Would you like a drink?" Simon asked as he opened a box of cigars and offered one to Rhys.

He shook his head to both. "As much as I'd like to numb this unsavory situation, I think it would be better if my mind were clear for what we are about to discuss."

Simon nodded and closed the box without taking

a cigar for himself, either. He sat at his desk, Rhys across from him, and smiled slightly.

"Thank you for what you said to Lillian. She isn't yet comfortable with the role of duchess. I know your acceptance means something to her."

Rhys frowned. "Considering my position now, I think it's foolish that I ever withheld it. I was needlessly cruel to her and I hate myself for it."

Simon met his gaze evenly, not denying Rhys's prior cruelty, but not censuring him for it, either. "Luckily we can always change."

"Can we?" Rhys asked with a hollow laugh.

"Yes, and I sense you *have* in the time since I last saw you."

Rhys looked at his lap, fiddling with a loose thread at his wrist. "Of course I have changed. I'm no longer the man I thought I was."

"That isn't what I meant," Simon said, softer than before. "I found your disappearance troubling. I was worried about you, my friend."

Rhys's gaze snapped up. "And *that* is why you sent my wife after me so recklessly?"

Simon shrugged. "Anne would not be stopped."

Rhys shook his head at that statement. He could well imagine it was true. Certainly she had been a bulldog when it came to her interactions with him in the countryside. Her stubborn devotion was one of the first fascinating things he had never before recognized existed in her. That and the feelings he hadn't known she held inside.

"Because she loves me," Rhys said, his tone dull.

Simon leaned back in his chair as his eyebrow arched. "Yes. That fact became eminently clear to me in the weeks before you married and even more so once you ran away. Anne's feelings run very deep. I must admit, I'm surprised you recognize that fact. You've never been very good at sensing the emotions of others."

"I'm not any clearer of vision than I was before, I'm afraid. She told me her feelings," Rhys all but whispered as he thought of that charged day when she had confessed her love for him.

Simon chuckled low, though there was little humor in his tone when he said, "Yes, *that* I can see. She is direct when she sees the need for it." There was a moment's silence and then Simon asked, "So what do you feel for her?"

There it was in unavoidable terms. Simon had just asked Rhys the one question he'd been trying to avoid at all costs since the first moment he saw Anne racing down the hill to "save" him from himself.

He didn't *want* to analyze his emotions for his wife. He didn't want to feel any particular emotions toward her at all. In the end it didn't matter how he felt or what he wanted, because he couldn't have those things. He couldn't *have* Anne. The situation that had driven her into his arms and his life in a way he had never expected was also the situation that would keep them apart forever.

Rhys shrugged, refusing to torment himself with the answer Simon sought. "There is really no choice in the matter. I must leave her."

Simon pushed to his feet with a sharp intake of air that seemed to echo in the otherwise quiet room. He stared down at Rhys with such a look of shock and dismay that shame filled him.

"You cannot be serious," Simon said as he paced to the sidebar and poured himself a drink, which he downed in one swig without taking his eyes off Rhys.

"I'm afraid I'm as serious as the grave," Rhys said, his voice cracking slightly before he reined in the reaction that so revealed his true feelings on the matter.

"How will that even be possible?" Simon asked. "This union was legal, consummated, and utterly public. You couldn't have it annulled, and divorce is almost an impossibility. Do you think you can just walk away from her? I think she's more than proven she'll make chase."

Rhys nodded. "Yes, perhaps once, but I think now

she might no longer do so. I've made it clear that separation is the only option for us."

"Does that mean you've told her the truth about why you ran, then?" Simon asked.

Rhys shook his head. "To protect her, I have kept her in the dark as to my parentage. That way she can honestly say she had no idea of my birth when she married me."

"But you could still reveal what you know to her now and that fact would remain true," Simon reasoned.

"With a blackmailer lurking in the shadows? This person could reveal the truth before I'm able to handle the situation. If that occurs, it will be best if Anne is as surprised by the revelation of my parentage as everyone else. I can only hope that will offer her some protection."

Simon released an incredulous snort. "You cannot think she won't be touched by this, no matter how much you distance yourself from her."

"Of course she will," Rhys snapped as he got to his feet and paced to the window. "But if we are already living apart I cannot help but believe she has a better chance of survival than if she stayed with me, stood by me as the world discovered I had been masquerading as a duke, looking down on them and making their lives a hell."

Simon took a long step toward him. "Rhys!"

Rhys ignored the interruption. "No, if I set Anne free in this manner, I think Society could see her as a victim of a man many of them already despise. With her father's support, with the assistance of her friends, many of whom are devoted to her, she could weather the storm."

"You are not so hated as you make it out," Simon protested, though his tone was less than convincing.

An incredulous arched brow was Rhys's response. "Do you know who I saw while in the country?"

Simon sighed heavily. "Who?"

"Caleb Talbot. He was at a village fete Anne and I attended."

His friend blinked once. "Somehow I'm having a difficult time picturing you at a village party, but very well. Why was Talbot there? He's been missing from Society for nearly a year."

"I have no idea, but he was right on the edge of an ugly drunk and miserable, so I doubt it was for pleasure. He likely struck upon the gathering by chance. But I spoke to him, Simon. I even tried to apologize for how I acted toward him, for who I was when in his presence."

He swallowed as he spoke, trying to keep his tone even, trying not to let Simon hear and see how much that moment had affected and changed him.

"And what was his answer to your apology?" his friend asked softly.

"Let us just say that his reaction wasn't one of forgiveness." Rhys shook his head. "Most people will offer the same response, I think. I've given them little reason for charity and mercy toward me."

Simon dipped his chin. He drew in a few breaths before he looked at Rhys again. This time there was firm determination in his brother's stare. And a sadness that seemed to be caused by more than just Rhys's situation.

"Have you ever considered simply *not* telling anyone else the truth?" Simon said with the slightest tremble to his voice.

"Of course I have!" With a scowl, Rhys clenched his fists at his sides. "I've contemplated every scenario, and hiding the truth and continuing on as before has always been the first thing to come to mind."

Simon nodded to encourage him. "It would protect your mother, your family, and you could remain with Anne."

Rhys shut his eyes. His brother had to know he was offering him heaven, but there was more at stake here than simply protecting his family reputation.

"All those things are true. And it is easier to believe I could hide it, but perhaps . . ." He trailed off.

"Perhaps it is better that the truth come out."

"You cannot mean that!"

"I very much do. Before I knew I was your brother, when you told me that he was a man of title, I said that the world deserved to know the truth. That even if the law allowed a bastard born within the confines of a legal marriage to keep his title, Society should be made aware and the man should face the consequences." He shrugged. "Why should that not remain true, even if it is myself I condemn?"

"So despite the changes in you, the idea of family blood and history still utterly controls you?" Simon snapped in disgust. "To the point that you would put your own feet and those of your family to the fire."

"My father—" Rhys cut himself off. "The last Duke of Waverly instilled the value of the pureness of our family line and history into me almost daily. The Waverly title has great power, should it not be held by someone who actually has blood from that family? And if it isn't, should the man who is forced to keep that title despite his blood still be revered and held up as an example, as if the truth didn't exist?"

Simon looked at the floor. "One day I'll tell you the whole story I discovered about our father's duplicity. One day. But for now, I'll only say that I understand, somewhat, what you are going through, how you are torn between two worlds. But I'm telling you, Rhys, sometimes it *is* better to live the lie. It may sound strange, but revealing the truth can be more damaging in ways you haven't fully considered."

Rhys cocked his head at the hollow sound of Simon's voice, but didn't press for more details. By the expression on his brother's face, he could see Simon was too raw to discuss whatever troubled him.

"But don't you understand?" he asked. "I still see a way to repair the line by revealing the truth."

"Repair the line?" Simon repeated, shaking his head in confusion.

Rhys nodded. "If the truth were to come out, people would see I don't deserve to continue the line, even if the law recognizes me as duke. And if Anne and I are separated, not only will she be somewhat protected from the scandal, but we won't produce children, more pointedly *heirs* whose birth would force the Waverly line to continue with my blood instead of a real person who shared the Waverly blood and history. Upon my death the line will revert to someone else. A distant cousin will be found who—"

Simon looked at him. "There is no distant cousin, Rhys."

Rhys staggered back in surprise. "What?"

"I did some research while you were away. You are, by all accounting, the last male of the Carlisle line. Whether the truth of your parentage comes out or not, if you don't produce a son of your own to carry on the title, it will revert back to the Crown. Do you know who they'll give it to?"

Rhys shook his head.

"Likely it will go to a common person who has either served or *paid* the Crown well. Someone with *none* of the family ties and likely little of the noble blood you so claim to value. And your family, your mother, your sisters, your *wife* will all live with the stigma your revelation will put on them. For what?"

Rhys clenched his fists at his sides. He had long known there were no close male relatives on his "father's" side of the family, but he hadn't realized there were not even distant relations who could take this title from him.

Suddenly the idea of keeping his silence, of protecting all those he held dear, became a much more viable one again. Only there was one fact that kept him from surrendering to the easy future his brother encouraged him to grasp for.

"But you forget something, Simon. There *is* a blackmailer out there. Coming in a matter of, what . . . a week? Ten days at most? Another person, one with villainous intent, knows this secret and could reveal it at any moment and in the worst way possible. This won't end simply because I decide I wish it to. Until I have dealt with that person, I cannot completely rule out revealing this secret myself, if only to control the manner in which the information is shared."

Simon closed his eyes. He nodded as he scrubbed a hand over his face.

"Very well, let us set aside our argument about you ending or not ending your marriage, about you revealing or not revealing your identity. You are correct. There *is* a blackmailer. And perhaps it is time to talk about that fact and truly decide how we will deal with this. As brothers."

Chapter 14

Rhys's stomach rolled as it always did when he allowed himself to think of some nameless, faceless villain who held the keys to his family's humiliation.

"Do you have more information about this . . . *person?*"

Simon nodded slowly, and the look of disdain on his face was powerful. "Do you remember the name Xavier Warren?"

Rhys blinked as he tried to recall. "It seems familiar. Wait, wasn't he quite involved in politics a number of years ago? And we discovered something about him and your father." He stopped and stared at Simon. "I mean, *our* father."

Simon took a slow step closer and reached out to briefly squeeze Rhys's arm before he released him and gave a short nod.

"Yes. Since I received the initial threat of blackmail,

I've done quite a bit of research, and Warren's name is the one that comes up time and again. It seems the amount of underhanded politicking he and our father partook in was enormous."

Simon broke off suddenly and Rhys saw the deep and abiding pain that briefly darkened his friend's eyes. As excruciating as this situation was for Rhys, it was equally difficult for Simon. He'd been drowning in disappointing truths about the man who raised him for weeks now.

Rhys tilted his head. "Simon, I realize how distressing this is for you," he said softly, wondering at how odd these words of true comfort felt on his tongue. He had said such things so infrequently, even when they were warranted. "I'm so very sorry."

Simon laughed softly. "We both are, my friend. Our father was so revered for his goodness, but the more I learn, the more I realize he had none in him. And now his lies and treacheries are being visited upon us, his children."

Rhys nodded solemnly, and the two men were silent for a moment as they each pondered that fact and its consequences.

Finally Simon shook his head and continued, "At any rate, I believe Warren might be involved in the blackmail. When I delved deeper I discovered he knew the solicitor who held the paperwork about you. Warren had some hand in 'finding' him when the old solicitor died. But it turns out that the new man had no *real* relation to the original. It was all a fraud, meant to gain access to the paperwork being held in his office, and not just the papers regarding our father."

"Damn," Rhys growled as he paced to the window. He scrubbed a hand over his face. "It sounds like this man is quite the villain indeed. But why do you think he allowed us so much time before moving forward with the blackmail?"

"A few years ago, Warren was accused of involvement in some kind of intrigue. There were whispers that he was a traitor to the Crown." Simon frowned. "Warren's arrest was called for and the man bolted from the country. But about a month later, my father's records show he began sending a large monthly payment to an unnamed account on the Continent. It's possible Warren was already blackmailing him. But once he heard the late duke had died and his son had come to the solicitor who held the keys to it all . . ."

Rhys faced his brother. "He thought perhaps he could get more from two live dukes than one dead one. And he decided to take the risk to come here and face us."

Simon nodded, his face grim. "I believe that's why

there was such a long time between the initial letter and when Warren plans to meet with us. Partly it's a game of cat and mouse meant to drive the anxiety we feel to a peak so that we're primed to do whatever he asks when he arrives. But I think part of it may have to do with the time it takes to smuggle oneself into the country when one is a wanted fugitive."

"It makes sense," Rhys said, that sick feeling in his belly growing. "But having an idea who the villain behind this situation could be changes nothing. If it *is* Warren who arrives on our doorstep demanding something for his silence, our choices remain the same. We can either pay him and risk exposure, ruin, and a future filled with ever-increasing demands and threats . . ..or we can allow this information to come out in our own way."

Simon was silent for a long time. He sank into the chair behind his desk and steepled his fingers.

"Then you might reveal this information yourself?"

Rhys looked at his friend. The question had been asked in a calm tone, but he saw the worry in Simon's eyes. In that moment, he had a sudden realization. He had spent all the time since he found out the truth ruminating on the effect revealing what he knew would have on his own life and that of his family.

He had never once considered Simon and the rest

of Simon's family. Now he moved toward his friend with a shake of his head.

"The consequences to you . . ." he began, his voice breaking a second time.

Simon's expression softened. "You've just thought of them, eh?"

Rhys rubbed his eyes. "It seems I am as selfish as my true father was."

Simon got to his feet. "*That* is not true. Our father would have fully recognized how deeply he was going to hurt others, only he wouldn't have cared. Perhaps he would have even taken pleasure in knowing he could do so without consequence. Rhys, you may be many things, but I know you'd never hurt me on purpose. Even at your worst, you weren't that cruel."

Rhys sagged as he leaned on Simon's desk. His friend sounded so certain, but Rhys didn't know anymore. Not about anything, even himself.

"This limits our options," Rhys began. "If you think the truth shouldn't come out—"

"I never said the truth shouldn't come out," Simon interrupted.

Rhys drew back in surprise. "But it will taint your family name as much as it will mine."

Simon shrugged, though Rhys could see he felt none of the nonchalance such an action implied.

"My father has done things that one day I'll share but are currently too *raw* for me to discuss. And I'm not opposed to telling the world the truth about his character, especially if it would protect you from greater pain. But I *do* think we shouldn't be hasty in this, Rhys. We aren't completely certain it is Warren who is behind this. I think we should obtain all the information before we decide what to do."

"You're correct, of course," Rhys said softly. "And I appreciate your willingness to sacrifice yourself for me if it comes to that. I'm not sure I deserve the consideration."

Simon came around the desk slowly. He looked at Rhys, and although his friend knew the truth, there was nothing different in his stare. Except that perhaps there was a greater connection between them now. One of family, not just friendship.

"Rhys, *long* before I discovered you were related to me by blood, you were my brother."

Rhys caught his breath, stunned once more by the kindness he had found in this man. "Thank you for that. And for standing beside me, even at my worst."

Simon smiled as he clapped a hand on Rhys's shoulder. "You know, I think Anne would do that, too."

Rhys moved away from the comforting touch of his brother. He hated that they had come full circle to his wife. He didn't want to hold out hope for a future with her. He didn't deserve it and he couldn't hope for it with so much uncertainty.

"I know she would," he said softly. "And *that* is why I must let her go."

Anne sat on the comfortable settee that faced the crackling fire, which pushed away the damp coolness the storm had brought outside. Lillian had a chair to her left, and the two women fidgeted in utter silence as the clock ticked loudly on the mantel. *Click, click, click* echoed in Anne's head until she wanted to scream.

Suddenly Lillian pushed to her feet. "Whiskey?" she asked.

Anne stared, but found herself bursting out, "Great God, yes."

The other woman laughed as she crossed the room, and suddenly the tension that had coursed between them since Rhys and Simon's departure melted away. When Anne took the drink her friend offered, she smiled, and it was a true expression no longer tightened by anxiety.

Lillian retook her place. Once the other woman was settled, Anne looked at her closely.

"May I ask you a question?"

Lillian took a sip of her drink before she nodded. "Of course. I hope we'll one day be as close as our husbands are. I've always believed true friends can speak of anything to each other."

Warmth filled Anne at the idea that she and Lillian would one day be as close as sisters, but could that ever be true? If Rhys succeeded in ending their marriage, she had no doubt Simon and Lillian would keep a stronger friendship with him than with her. It was simply inevitable. The very thought had her downing half her drink in one heated gulp, but she steeled herself and continued.

"You know this *thing* . . . this truth that torments Rhys, don't you?"

Lillian choked on her most recent sip of whiskey, coughing as she searched for a handkerchief in her pelisse pocket. Finally she regained her composure and dabbed her lips.

"I didn't expect you to be so direct," she said, though there was no censure or upset in her stare. Actually Lillian's frank gaze seemed to hold even more respect for Anne.

"Well, I can be direct when the situation warrants it," Anne said, setting her drink aside and leaning back to look evenly at Lillian. "And this is the most dire set of circumstances I've ever faced. If I don't ask the questions that plague me, I'll surely regret it later."

Lillian nodded slowly. "I'm far too familiar with the concept of regret, so I understand."

Anne wrinkled her brow. She could hardly picture Lillian as a person who harbored such feelings, but she put that aside as she asked, "Then will you answer me?"

There was a brief hesitation before Lillian nodded a second time. "Yes, Anne. I do know the truth, but I don't feel comfortable being the one to reveal it to you. As much as I believe you deserve to know, it isn't my place."

Anne rested her head against the soft chair cushion with a sigh. Of course Lillian wouldn't tell her what was really happening. Like Simon, she wished to protect Rhys's privacy . . . even from his own wife.

"I'm sorry," Lillian offered softly.

"You shouldn't be the one who is sorry," Anne responded as she finished her drink and held out her glass for another. "You're perfectly correct that it's my husband who should tell me the truth, though he seems determined not to do so."

Lillian was silent as she poured liquor into Anne's tumbler. It wasn't until she set the decanter aside that she asked, "Does it anger you that I know the truth and you don't?"

Anne pondered the question. Finally she shook her head slowly.

"*Anger* isn't the proper word for what I feel, I don't think. I *am* frustrated because it seems everyone is aware of what has caused all this pain and upset except for me. But my life is just as affected as anyone's . . . in fact, more than anyone else's will be, especially if Rhys goes through with his plans to abandon our marriage."

Lillian leaned toward her with a horrified gasp. "Abandon your marriage? You cannot be serious."

"I'm afraid I'm very serious," Anne said softly, though she kept her gaze from Lillian's as embarrassed heat flooded her cheeks. This was the second time she'd revealed her humiliating future to someone today, and each time it seemed to grow more difficult. How would she ever face the public if Rhys truly did leave her?

"He is an idiot," Lillian said with a shake of her head.

Anne shrugged. "Well, I thank you for that."

"And you've told him you don't wish for this?" Lillian stared at her.

"It seems my feelings on the subject mean very little to him," Anne said with a deeper blush. "Even his own heart seems to have no bearing on his decision. When we were in the countryside, I saw him changing as a person. Perhaps it was only wishful thinking, but I believe we bonded closer than ever before. I thought there might be a chance for us after all. But now that we've returned to London, he pulls away again. He's already separating from me, and I have no idea of how to bring him back."

Lillian moved closer, taking a place on the settee beside her. Her arm came around Anne and she hugged her gently.

"Oh, my dear, I'm so sorry. I had no idea the situation was so grim. I cannot imagine your pain."

Anne rested her head on Lillian's shoulder briefly, allowing herself to be comforted, though it wasn't Lillian's comfort or even Mally's that she desired. It was Rhys who she wished for.

But those wishes weren't to be, it seemed.

"I'm certain you cannot imagine what I am enduring," she said, straightening up from Lillian's embrace after a moment and turning slightly to face her. "Simon loves you. Even if I didn't know him so well, even if he didn't say it, one can see it from the glow within him. Every time he speaks your name, it's like a candle has been lit inside him. I envy you both for how easy your love seems to come to you."

Lillian dipped her chin with a happy blush, but when her gaze came up it was troubled and serious. "I'm very lucky in that, Anne, but the ease you see now hasn't always existed. I sometimes haven't deserved his love. I even tried to push it away, just as Rhys pushes at yours."

Anne tilted her head, not understanding. She'd

known Lillian was a little hesitant in the weeks leading up to their wedding, but she never would have guessed the other woman was actively trying to avoid a connection with the man she so clearly loved.

"But, my dear," Lillian continued, taking both of Anne's hands. "I'm so very lucky that Simon fought for my love, regardless of what I said, or even what I did. He fought for *me* because he loved me, just as you love Rhys."

Anne flinched, but didn't draw away. "Am I so obvious?"

Lillian smiled, warm and genuine. "I'm afraid you are, but only to a friend."

Words of contradiction died on her lips as she looked at Lillian. There was no use pretending, not if the other woman could see her heart so clearly. And honestly, Anne was tired of denying her feelings. Tired of pretending for the sake of propriety or the comfort of everyone else around her.

Finally Anne shrugged. "I've loved Rhys Carlisle for as long as I can remember. Those feelings are simply a part of the fabric of who I am, as much as my hair color or my eyes. I don't know what I would be without that."

Lillian cocked her head slightly. "And now it's my turn to ask an uncomfortable question."

Anne laughed despite herself. "It seems to be the day for them. What is it?"

"Today Rhys was kind to me and I sensed the beginnings of the shift in him that you mentioned," Lillian began. "But . . . but he has not always been so. His reputation is well-known and he is often feared, even hated. But you're so different, with none of his snobbery. Even before I met you, I'd heard the rumors of your compassion and your acts of kindness toward those around you. So I must know . . . *why* do you love him when on the surface you seem so very different?"

Anne dipped her chin and looked at her clenched fingers on her lap. "You aren't the first person to comment upon our match, to mention that I'm more accepting and ask if I could be happy with someone so hard. But you see, I've always seen something *more* in Rhys. I have always known it was there, hiding . . . perhaps being protected by that cold shell he presents to the world. I believe . . . no, I *know* he has a capacity for true nobility beyond his rank, beyond the blood and family history he holds in such high regard."

Lillian nodded, but Anne could see she remained incredulous and was driven to continue, not only to defend Rhys, but to offer some explanation of herself so Lillian wouldn't think her foolish.

"We were betrothed when I was still in the cradle,

though we didn't meet until I was six." Anne smiled at the memory, thinking back to that sun-kissed day that had stayed with her forever.

Lillian drew back with wide eyes. "You *were* matched very young."

Anne nodded. "Our fathers were friends and had always planned such a thing. It did frighten me a little to know my future was already planned. But the idea also intrigued me, even then. The first time I met him, Rhys came to my rescue, and from that day on I found myself observing him very closely whenever we met. As a child, he was open and friendly. He had a great capacity for kindness and often protected others who he felt were weaker. It was only over the span of years that I watched him change, both for the good and for the bad, and become the man who would be my husband."

Lillian tilted her head. "What a strange experience that must have been."

Anne laughed. "At times it was very odd indeed. But I think it also gave me a deeper understanding of Rhys. I saw things others might not have noticed because my attention was fixed on him in such a different manner. Yes, he is a hard man. He was trained to be that way by . . ." She shivered as she thought Rhys's late father. "Well, the last Duke of Waverly was not always a kind person, and *he* was the one who taught Rhys that he was better than anyone else around him. He told him that title and blood were the only important concepts when one looked at someone new."

Lillian frowned, and Anne couldn't blame her. Those very concepts had kept Lillian at the mercy of the *ton* and almost made her an old maid. It was no wonder Rhys and Lillian hadn't gotten along, though Anne had been moved to see Rhys try to make amends for his actions today.

"Still," Anne continued softly, "even as Rhys accepted that concept that he was better or more deserving, I still saw flashes of goodness in him. His friendship with Simon, which was so close and loyal, was one thing that gave me hope about his true heart. His warmth to his mother and sisters was another. And as for me . . ."

She trailed off as a long string of memories flashed through her mind. From the first time he'd kissed her hand, to the way they danced together with such ease, to all the moments they had shared while sequestered away since their marriage.

"He may not have always been loving, but he was never cruel," she whispered. "I know it's hard to see, but there *is* a man inside of Rhys who is worthy of love. Of saving. I believe that with all my heart, with all my soul."

As the words died on her tongue, Anne realized that at some point she had risen to her feet and now stood, fist clenched over her heart. Heat filled her cheeks at the passionate display she hadn't been able to control, and she sank back into her chair and kept her gaze slightly away from Lillian.

But instead of judging or denying what Anne had said to be true, Lillian reached out and gently covered Anne's hand with her own. When Anne glanced at her, it was to find a soft and friendly smile on the other woman's face, one without pity or even doubt.

"*You* are a very good woman, Anne Carlisle," she said softly.

"Either that or entirely foolish," Anne said with a nervous laugh.

Lillian shook her head. "I don't think so. But if you've loved him all your life, you must have pictured your life with him for an equal amount of time."

Anne nodded slowly. "I have indeed. I had such hopes—" She cut herself off, unwilling to ponder the details of what she had once desired and now feared was lost to her forever. "But that long-imagined future seems to be slipping away."

Lillian's fingers closed around Anne's upper arms and she squeezed gently. "Fight for it while you still can, Anne! I cannot believe I'm saying this, but fight for *him*. If you don't, you'll live with regrets, and as

I said, I have some experience with that. It isn't for you." She smiled as she released Anne. "I only hope Rhys will one day recognize how lucky he is to have a wife with your heart and passion. And that he'll endeavor to deserve your love and loyalty once you win this battle."

Anne tilted her head. She could well imagine how difficult it was for Lillian to say those words when Rhys had recently been so unkind to her. But that fact somehow gave her order more power. Lillian was telling her to love Rhys, not allow him to let go, even though Lillian didn't approve or even believe that Anne's thoughts about his good qualities could be true.

"Thank you," Anne whispered. "Thank you for offering me your friendship so willingly."

"You deserve it and so much more," Lillian said with an open and warm smile that touched Anne to her very core.

Before she could respond, the door to the parlor opened. As she and Lillian rose, Simon stepped inside with Rhys at his heels. From the taut expressions on the faces of the men, it was clear they had been having as intense a conversation as Lillian and Anne had shared.

"There you are," Lillian said with a smile and a light laugh as she crossed the room to her husband.

Her expression was purposefully blank, but Anne noticed that when she took Simon's hand she squeezed ever-so-gently in what was an obvious gesture of comfort.

Anne turned her gaze on Rhys. He appeared tired, rung out as if he had been twisted in knots during the time they were apart. She couldn't help herself, she crossed to him and stopped just before him. He stared down at her, looking at her face with a dazed intensity she'd never seen before.

Reaching out, she gently touched his hand, letting her fingers glide down the shape of it softly, but she said nothing. She could only pray he would feel her reassurance and that it would help him.

"Will you stay for supper?" Lillian asked.

Anne shook her head, the spell that had kept her eyes on Rhys suddenly broken by the interruption. She turned to face their hosts, but it was Rhys who answered.

"Thank you for the offer, but it's been a long day of travel. I think it would be best if we returned home."

"Perhaps another night," Anne offered.

Rhys's gaze shot to her and her heart dropped into her stomach. His expression clearly stated that there would be no other nights. Whatever he'd said to Simon, it hadn't changed his mind about leaving her.

They said their good-byes as Simon and Lillian led them to the foyer and watched them go to their carriage that was parked on the drive. The sun was setting, and as the door closed, only a dim light pierced the vehicle.

But even with little illumination, Anne could see clearly. She saw Rhys's pain. She saw his determination. And she saw that Lillian was right. It was time to make another stand in defense of her future, of her marriage, and of her love for Rhys.

It might be her last chance.

Chapter 15

Rhys paced the length of his office, restlessness plaguing him while the clock steadily ticked away the night. He'd been alone for the last two hours. Anne had said her good-nights just after a late supper and gone upstairs to her chamber.

He would never admit it out loud, but he missed her. Actually it went deeper than that. He *longed* for his wife. He ached for her touch, for her smile, for all the ways she'd comforted and aided him during their time alone in the countryside.

But he had sensed a shift in her today, both during and after their visit with Simon and Lillian. Anne seemed tense, distant, and distracted on the way home, barely speaking and never asking him what he and Simon talked about, although he was certain her questions lingered.

Once they arrived home, she had been nervous, only picking at her food and hardly engaging in conversation until she finally abandoned him for her bed.

The change was perfectly logical, of course. Rhys had made it more than clear that their marriage would soon end. Perhaps she was finally accepting that fact, surrendering to it. She might simply be attempting to make the ultimate end of them a little less awkward and painful.

He frowned as he stopped walking the room. Somehow he didn't like the idea that Anne would simply *accept* the end of their union. She'd fought so hard to stay at his side and sacrificed so much, the thought that she would then submit to his will actually caused a bit of a sting.

Which was markedly unfair and he knew it.

Rubbing a hand over his eyes, Rhys groaned. He had hoped today would somehow make his future path all the clearer, but Simon had muddied everything rather than clarified it. His brother's points about the fate Rhys would present to his mother and sisters if he revealed the truth of his parentage were good ones. And Simon's shock that he would leave Anne resonated in Rhys as well.

Whether he admitted it aloud or not, the fact was that the idea of losing Anne was beginning to make him feel physically sick. It was funny, he'd been betrothed to the woman for years, as close to her as he could ever wish to be, but he had taken her for granted.

It had taken *this*, it had taken the fact that he wasn't who he thought he was, that he couldn't have the life with her that he had so meticulously planned, it had taken her unexpected reaction to chase him when he left . . . *that* was how he had truly come to know the remarkable woman who was, at least for a short while longer, his wife.

And he would regret losing her for the rest of his days.

But if he never told anyone the truth, he could protect his family. And he could keep Anne. A bewitching thought, indeed. If only a blackmailer wasn't looming on the horizon, a harbinger of doom and scandal.

"Damn it," Rhys growled as he threw the door to his office wide and exited the suddenly stuffy chamber.

He was only tired, that was why he could almost convince himself he could keep his life. Once he slept, all the fog would clear and he would be able to stop allowing his emotions to lead him. He would remember what he was, who he was, and the duty he held to his father's title and its future. And then he would figure out how to handle all those unpleasant answers to equally difficult questions.

He moved up the stairs in the quiet. Most of the servants were already abed or finishing their daily duties. In these moments he could almost pretend he was alone.

Except he wasn't.

He reached the top of the staircase and looked down the long, dim hallway to his left. In a chamber just a short distance from his own, his wife slept. His beautiful, beguiling wife.

He moved toward her door and there he hesitated, looking at the smooth surface for what seemed like an eternity. If he knocked, she would allow him in. Even if she was distancing herself from him, he knew . . . he *hoped* on some level . . . that she still cared.

Certainly there remained a spark of awareness and desire between them that wouldn't be denied if he allowed it even the slightest opening.

But as exciting as that thought was, as much as he longed to fall into the shelter of her arms and spend the next few hours tasting her tempting body, it wasn't fair of him to consider such a thing. To touch her would be to give her false hope, and it would only serve to torment him more once the night was over.

With a sigh, he abandoned her door and went to his own chamber. He stepped into his dressing room. The bell for his valet was near, but he decided against it. He'd been undressing himself for some time now in the country. He could do it again.

He shed his jacket, cravat, and shirt where he stood, then sat down in the chair beside the fire to remove his boots. When he stood back up, clad only in trousers, that was when he saw her.

Through the open door that led to his bedchamber, his big bed was visible. And lying across it, her dark hair down around her pale shoulders and her slender body just barely clad in scraps of silk and lace, was Anne. She was on her side, propped up on her elbow, and all she did was watch him with those green-blue eyes that seemed to see his soul even when he tried to conceal it.

She didn't move or speak, she simply lay there waiting. For him.

She was temptation embodied. He moved toward her, almost against his will, and only stopped as he stepped over the threshold into the other room. He gaped at her silently, unable to help himself.

Even on their wedding night what seemed like a lifetime ago, Anne hadn't worn such sensual attire. Then he had found her in a plain cotton night shift, her hair back in a loose braid, the perfect picture of innocence. And it had driven him wild, almost out of control.

Tonight there was no innocence in his wife's stare,

nor in her nightgown. It barely skimmed her thighs, and the white lace that covered the rounded curves of her breasts couldn't conceal the thrusting pinkness of her hard nipples beneath. This gown was meant to seduce and tempt.

It did its job fully, for Rhys felt so hard that he might explode if she so much as touched him.

"Anne," he managed past dry lips. "What are you doing here? I thought you went to bed."

Slowly she pushed to her feet. The silky folds of her gown shifted, brushing over her bare skin the way he longed to do with his hands, his lips. She moved toward him in a few hip-swishing steps, and he caught a whiff of her subtle perfume on the air. God, she smelled like sunshine and lilacs and happiness. He wanted to bury his face in her hair and breathe her in until he never lost the scent.

Instead he clenched his fists at his sides and awaited her answer to his question.

"I did go to bed," she said softly. "Your bed."

He swallowed hard as she moved forward a second time. Now her body almost touched his, and he felt her breath on his skin when she looked up at him.

"*Your* bed is where I belong, Rhys. You know that to be true."

She reached a hand up and rested her fingers against the bare flesh over his heart. Rhys was certain she could feel it beating wildly, out of control because of her.

"No," he managed to croak out, but the denial didn't sound very convincing.

He squeezed his eyes shut in an effort to give himself some focus, but the image of Anne lingered in his mind, even when he couldn't see her. In a flash, he fantasized about all the pleasures they could share this night.

"No!" he repeated, this time with more force as he wrapped his fingers around her wrist and gently removed it from his chest. "I cannot do this. *We* cannot."

He thought he saw a brief flash of uncertainty as he released her, but then it was gone and the seductive hint of a smile tilted Anne's lips.

"Oh, I don't think that's true," she purred, moving closer again. This time the soft silk of her gown brushed against his naked skin. "I know for certain we are *able* to do this. We've done *this* and so much more before. To both of our great pleasures. Or do you now deny that?"

Rhys stared at her, wide-eyed. This was a new side of Anne. Another part of her he'd never been aware existed. But he could hardly resist her sensual tone, the way her fingers felt as she pressed the tips of them to his chest once again. Only this time she let them slowly glide down his stomach and to his waistband.

Rhys sucked in a breath at the lightning pleasure of that act. His cock, already hard, seemed to swell further, pressing with increasing discomfort against his pants front.

"Do you, Rhys?" she pressed, even as she slipped one button of his fly free. Her gaze never left his. The green-blue sucked him in, forcing him to look at her with an unblinking stare. "Do you deny we have been *most* proficient in pleasuring each other?"

He could hardly find breath, let alone speak, but somehow Rhys managed to force a few words past his lips. "No. I don't deny that, Anne, but—"

Before he could finish, she leaned forward and her mouth pressed to his, silencing his words, ending his denials, and setting his already edgy body on fire.

"God," he groaned into her mouth before he crushed his arms around her and drove his tongue between her open lips.

She cried out loudly, lifting up on her tiptoes to eagerly meet his aggressive tongue, sliding her silk-clad body against his until he was aware of each nerve ending he possessed because every one of them was screaming with intense pleasure.

He felt her hands moving, slower now because they were trapped by his embrace, but still able to unbutton his trousers after a few struggling moments. His pants waist parted and the fabric slid down a few inches. This time when she moved against him, he felt the delicious sensation of silk stroking the base of his cock.

He drew away with a gasp of pleasure as his head dipped back a fraction. Anne smiled up at him, a possessive, feral expression he had never before seen on her otherwise serene and kind face.

But he liked it. Probably far too much for his own good.

"You see, my love," she whispered as she shoved him backward toward the bed. "You need this. You *need* me, especially after what you endured today. Why do you fight what you can't deny?"

Rhys swallowed hard. *Need*. Anne was almost perfectly repeating his own thoughts in his office just a few moments ago. He did need her. And now, racked by pain, tormented by unpleasant, impossible choices, that need pulsed even stronger because he knew she could make him forget.

Couldn't he have just a short respite? Couldn't he accept this comfort she offered? He would end it before it went too far.

If he had an answer to his internal query, he didn't think it. Before he could, Anne pressed herself to him, leaning her full weight to his body, and kissed him a second time, this time tasting him, rubbing against him in a most pleasing and overpowering way.

His hands tangled in her soft hair, maneuvering her for the best access to her hot, soft lips. Leaning against the edge of the bed, he surrendered himself to the feel of her, the flavor of her, the erotic escape she offered with every fiber of her being.

Anne struggled for calm, for air as she held Rhys closer and kissed him with all the love, all the desperation, all the hope for their future she still held in her heart.

She'd never seduced him before. Oh, she'd made a lame attempt to do so in the countryside at their picnic, but tonight was different. Tonight she had one goal in mind and she had to hold fast to that goal.

Difficult considering how swept away she was by the pleasure of Rhys's touch.

She steeled herself and gently pushed. Rhys fell back across his bed without any resistance, but he clung to her and she fell with him. His pants slipped farther down as they moved and his cock came free to stroke against her bare leg when she landed atop him.

She reveled in the stroke of Rhys's skin, and in the way her body reacted instantly and intensely. With hardly more than a kiss, her empty body clenched, hot and wet and ready for him. Her nipples tingled, thrusting hard against the lacy fabric of the silky night shift she wore. Every touch, every breath seemed to resonate on some deeper level of her being, more amplified because she was only focused on joining herself to Rhys.

She drew back, shifting until she was beside him instead of on top of him. That would come . . . later. Right now she needed to make him long for her. To bring him to the very edge of his control until he was so blinded that he couldn't resist what she offered.

But he seemed to have other plans. Without any effort, he flipped her onto her back and drove hard into her mouth with his tongue. He stroked and thrust, driving her mad as his hard body writhed over hers with a promise of pleasure and desire. Then he drew back and scraped his teeth over her throat, gliding lower with his mouth even as he caught the lacy straps of her nightgown with his fingers to lower it away from her shoulders. The shift was delicate, and the strength with which he pulled tore it.

"I'm sorry," he groaned, though he never stopped dropping his mouth lower and lower.

"No you're not," she whispered, arching against him as he pushed the ripped fabric aside and latched on to her hard nipple with his wet lips. "And neither am I."

He sucked and her vision blurred. God, the things

he did to her, the way he made her feel. She was alive when she was with him. Womanly. Owned and cherished in the way she'd always dreamed.

She would *not* lose this. She refused.

He dragged his mouth lower, tasting her belly as he shoved the tattered remains of her nightgown away. She kicked it from her bare ankle and clenched her fingers into his hair as he finally reached the sensitive, throbbing place between her legs.

He tasted her delicately, with just the tip of his tongue tracing her waiting slit, but it was enough to begin the little tremors of release. It had been days since they joined together and Anne was on edge, more ready for him than she had ever been before.

If he sensed that, he didn't seem in any mood to tease. He pushed her legs open, holding her wide with rough hands, and dragged his tongue over her again and again.

She lifted her hips to meet him, sobbing out incoherent encouragement as he sucked and licked and tasted her in every way. And then, like a bolt from the sky, her release crested over her. Powerful waves of pleasure came one after another, never allowing her rest, never giving her peace. Nor did Rhys as he sucked and sucked her clit until she was weak against the pillows, unable to respond except to tremble when another blast of pleasure moved through her.

Rhys withdrew as the last shivers shook her, pressing a wet kiss to her thigh before he moved back up her body. She lifted into a passionate kiss and wrapped her arms around him, tasting her own essence on his lips.

"There is nothing better than seeing you come," he murmured as he pressed his lips to her temple.

"Nothing?" she teased as she rubbed herself against him gently. "I think there are some things."

Her heart throbbed. From excitement, yes, but also from nervousness. The time had come to enact her plan. Once she started, she wouldn't be able to go back. This was her final opportunity.

"I cannot think of one right now," he teased as he moved to his side next to her.

"I can," she murmured, then she rolled over, moving him to his back as she kissed him once more. She felt the tension leave him as their tongues tangled, the guardedness he so often possessed. Yes, she wanted his surrender.

He gave it when she did as he had done not a moment before. She glided her mouth down his body, nibbling on his flesh, tasting and sucking until he was arching and moaning beneath her. She reached his cock, thinking of the last time he'd been in her mouth. She had been able to steal his control, just a little, that day.

Tonight she needed it all.

She drew him between her lips, feeling the heat of him on her tongue, tasting the first salty drop of his essence that had leaked out while he pleasured her. Above her, Rhys let out a curse and clenched his fists at her shoulders while she took his entire length into her mouth and slowly withdrew.

"God, Anne," he murmured.

She looked up, watching the tension line his face. With a pop, she let his cock exit her lips.

"Let me give this to you, Rhys," she whispered. "Please."

He hesitated a moment, but then he nodded. When he flopped back on the pillows, she no longer felt resistance from him. He completely surrendered while she pleasured him.

With careful movements, she built his desire, bringing him closer and closer to the edge. But she never allowed complete satisfaction. Not yet. She kept him at the ready with her pace and the pressure of her tongue until she knew he was almost there. Ready to explode.

And then she executed her plan. With a swift movement, she slid up his body, spread her legs, and lowered her wet slit over him, taking his cock into her body for the first time since their honeymoon what seemed like years before.

He shuddered when her sheath squeezed over him and she couldn't help but do the same as his thick length stretched her. It had been so long, and the last time he took her the relationship between them had been so different. Then she'd been nervous, thinking about being right and "perfect" as he seemed to expect. And *he* had appeared distracted, not fully engulfed in the moment, but more fulfilling a duty.

Now she felt the true power of being joined to this man she loved. And the pleasure of that was more powerful than any she had ever known.

But the moment passed too quickly. When Rhys's eyes cleared and then widened as if he just realized what was happening between them, she knew she had to hurry, for he was beginning to remember all the reasons why he couldn't allow for this wonderful joining. She rolled her hips over him, thrusting his member in and out of her welcoming body with a swift, utterly intoxicating rhythm.

"Anne," he moaned, reaching for her hips, though she wasn't certain if that was meant to draw her closer or to push her away. It seemed he didn't know, either, for when his fingers closed around her flesh, he simply held there.

"Please," she gasped, continuing to jerk over him. "J-just for a moment, Rhys. Please."

He let out a strangled sound, but then he nodded. "A moment. God, you feel so good."

His hips began to lift beneath her and Anne gasped as the pleasure he'd brought her with his tongue mounted within her womb once more. Only this time it was different, more intense because they were joined as a man and his wife should be. He was hers. She was his.

The orgasm hit her hard and her hips increased their pace immediately as she cried out.

The veins in Rhys's neck began to throb and he shouted, "Anne, I must pull away."

The order drew her from the fog of her pleasure. But instead of removing her body as he requested, Anne locked her thighs at his sides. She collapsed over him, kissing him hard as she continued to thrust, thrust, thrust.

"Anne," he gasped into her mouth.

But it was too late. Every fiber of his being tensed and then, as he shouted a roar so loud it seemed to shake the bed, his essence pumped within her.

She collapsed over him, panting and sweaty as exhaustion and relief overtook her.

There. It was done. And it had been magnificent. Everything she'd ever dreamed she could share with her husband and more.

Rhys lay beneath her for far too short a time. Then he gently rolled her away and got to his feet. He said nothing, simply paced across the quiet room, his back to her and his shoulders shaking as he stared at the fire crackling in the hearth.

"That should not have happened," he finally moaned, pain evident in his tone of voice. "*That* was a terrible mistake."

Chapter 16

Anne flinched. The words Rhys said were painful, of course, but the tone of his voice hurt her even more. He sounded empty. Broken. Defeated. And all because of what she had done in the name of her love for him.

When he sank into a chair near the window and placed his head into his hands, her torment increased. He was naked, and not just in body. His emotions were naked as he sat there, for the first time, she saw them all. All the anguish, all the heartbreak, all the anger that had been caused by whatever secret he kept from her . . . they were alive on his crumpled face and in his shaking shoulders.

"You shouldn't have done that," he said once more, but this time it seemed it was meant for himself, not her. "I shouldn't have been so weak as to allow it. But it felt so good, *you* felt so good."

Anne slipped from the high bed, gathering a sheet

to wrap around her body as she did so. She moved toward him slowly, well-aware that she was now approaching something akin to a wounded animal. She would have to tread carefully.

"Rhys," she whispered as she reached out a hand for his bare shoulder.

He wrenched his arm away, his dark gaze flashing up as if he had only just remembered she was still in the room with him.

"No!" he cried as he returned to his feet and moved away.

She stared as he snatched up his trousers from the floor beside the bed and stepped into them, covering himself from her gaze in more ways than one.

But when he turned back, his wild eyes still glowed in the fire. In fact, Anne was shocked by how stormy they were.

"Please don't touch me, not now," he said, his breath coming in deep pants and his voice shaking. "You *shouldn't* have done that, Anne. You knew I couldn't have you this way."

She stared at him. Somehow she'd convinced herself that if only she could force Rhys to take the pleasure it was obvious they both desired, she would soften his stance toward her and their future. At the very least, she had reset the clock on whether she could be carrying his child. Certainly he couldn't withdraw from that.

But she'd underestimated the depth of his pain. His face did not reveal a softness toward her now or even a resignation that they might be forced to remain living as husband and wife.

No, she saw only betrayal and horror as he stared at her.

"Rhys," she whispered, her voice breaking just as his had. "I-I am *yours*. Tonight I hoped to remind you of that."

He shook his head. "No. You took advantage of what I told you in the countryside."

She opened her mouth, but he didn't allow her to speak.

"I told you then that I couldn't make love to you for fear of creating a child who would suffer from the events surely to come. A child who would only complicate those events further." He stared at her, his face blank again, his eyes no longer wild. But the dead emptiness of them disturbed Anne almost as much as his emotionality of before. "Isn't *that* why you made love to me?"

She fisted her hands at her sides and forced herself to draw a deep breath.

"Yes. Part of why I did this tonight was because

I knew if I became pregnant it would complicate your plans to abandon our marriage. But don't you understand? I can't allow you to separate from me without a fight! I love you, I love—"

"Stop!" he cried out in a rough tone that raked over her flesh and up her spine. With a long step, he grabbed her arms and shook her gently. "I *can't*! Why don't you understand when I say that?"

"Because you won't tell me why!" Anne shook free of his hands. "If this is to be our end, then you owe me that! And I won't give up on you or on us until I understand what drives you to do and say these terrible things."

He stared at her, as if he had never seen her before. He stared and stared until Anne shifted beneath his focused regard and fought the urge to turn away and run from the room. She could *not* back down.

"You want to know why," he murmured.

"Yes," she whispered. "If you truly want to send me from your life, I fear *that* is the only way to obtain what you desire."

A muscle in Rhys's cheek jerked. "Very well. If you want this secret so badly, if you want to carry this with you, I leave you to it. You can taste its bitterness and feel its sting just as I have since the moment it was laid at my feet and destroyed everything I ever thought or hoped for."

He returned to the chair he had first sat in and sank back into its cushions, almost as if he could no longer bear his own weight. Anne shook as she watched him in silence, on the cusp of finally understanding what had started this heartbreaking mess that threatened to destroy her life and her future.

Rhys looked up at her, his stare even and fully focused for the first time since he left her in his bed.

"Anne, I'm not the man you think I am. That fact has dictated my every action from the moment we returned from our wedding trip."

Anne's brow wrinkled. This wasn't an answer, only a deeper riddle. Her tone was sharp when she snapped, "I don't understand what you mean. Explain yourself."

He flinched. His naked shoulders had begun to shake and he swallowed hard before he said, "I tried so hard to protect you."

"I don't want your protection!" she cried, the anger she'd been repressing bubbling free once more. "I want the truth! Tell me now."

His gaze flashed up. "I have obtained irrefutable proof that my father was *not* the Duke of Waverly, Anne. It turns out I'm a bastard, and with that fact comes only utter ruin and scandal."

* * *

It was the first time Rhys had ever admitted what he knew out loud. Even when he spoke to Simon, he'd never laid out the facts in such clear and undeniable terms. Hearing them again made his stomach turn in disgust and his heart race.

Slowly he lifted his gaze to judge Anne's reaction to the awful truth she'd pursued with such dogged interest and focus. She stood rooted in the same spot, staring at him. But her expression was no longer one of frustration or anger or even love.

No, now all he could see when he looked at her was the absolute horror that glittered in her gorgeous, dark eyes. There was no room left for anything else now that she had heard the truth.

Rhys looked away. He'd expected as much when she found out what he was . . . or what he wasn't. What he hadn't anticipated were his own feelings in regard to her reaction. It hurt to see her look at him with such an expression of disgust. Actually *hurt* wasn't a strong enough word. Deep within his chest, down into his stomach, it was as if he had been lit on fire from within. The feeling was like a death.

But he supposed it was. The death of her love for him. An emotion that had been unasked for, unwanted when she first expressed it, but now . . .

Now that it was gone he realized how much he'd

come to depend upon her love for him. To want it, for it felt like the only true and good thing in his life.

Silence hung between them for a long time before Anne finally stepped forward. She moved with jerking steps, but eventually she reached him. To his surprise, she dropped to her knees on the floor before him and then her arms came around him. She held him, stroking his hair and wrapping her warmth about him.

"Oh Rhys, oh my dearest," she whispered, her tone so soft, so gentle that it felt like a caress. "How terrible for you to have carried this secret with you. I cannot imagine how its weight must have choked you. I'm so very, *very* sorry for the pain you're enduring."

Rhys stared straight ahead for a moment, confused by her reaction, but also undeniably warmed by it. He drew back from her a fraction and looked down into her upturned face. In the soft firelight, she was more beautiful than ever. And there was no censure in her gaze. The disgust he had thought he read there at first, he now realized was a deep and powerful pain on his behalf.

"Do you not understand me?" he asked, shaking his head in disbelief. "I'm not legitimate, Anne."

"I understand," she said softly, but her expression didn't change.

"I don't truly belong to the Waverly line or deserve all that comes with it," he insisted.

Still she did not falter. "Yes, I heard you."

He frowned, uncertain if she fully grasped what he'd revealed. "I'm not the man you married!"

Now her expression changed. She tilted her head, shock flooding her features, but then she lifted her hand and pressed it to his cheek, caressing his skin with her warm palm. He couldn't help but lean into the touch briefly.

"Of course you are. Because of the way you were raised, I know it's hard for you to understand, but I didn't marry your name or family history."

"But those things are why your father arranged this marriage for you," he protested.

She shook her head. "But I married *you*. You *are* my husband."

She smiled, and for a brief flash Rhys forgot his every trouble. For the first time since Simon had torn his world to shreds, he didn't feel the throbbing sting of disappointment, anger, and heartbreak. In fact, he felt a strange surge of hope when he looked into his wife's face.

She was a lifeline. And in her eyes, he could almost see a world where he could let all this go, where he could take her offer of love and acceptance. Where he could stay with her forever and never give a damn about bloodlines or blackmail again.

But the hope faded and reality returned within a few moments. With difficulty, he pulled away, rising from the chair and pacing to the window. He stared outside into the dark night, as mysterious as his own life had become.

"No, Anne," he said softly. "I'm not that man anymore. I can't be, and you must understand why now that you've heard the truth."

"Please look at me," she said from behind him after a long pause.

Slowly he faced her. Although she was clad only in his bedsheet and her dark hair was tangled around her face, she didn't look any less the powerful duchess. He had never seen her look so much like she fit that role. She was regal now in the way she stood and in the strength of her tone when she spoke.

"You can tell me anything you like, Rhys," she said in a voice that brooked no refusal. "But you cannot change certain facts. You and I were married. Our union was consummated, not only physically, but in the deep bond we developed in the countryside. And"—she looked around the room with a slight blush—"and in this very room tonight. You cannot deny those things."

"No, but—" he began.

She moved toward him. "There is no *but*. When

we wed, I vowed to stand beside you through all your triumphs and your pains, no matter how complicated or deep they were. I meant that promise."

Rhys shook his head with a growl of frustration. "And on the day we wed, I vowed to protect you, Anne. The only way I can do that now is to have you leave my side forever. If we're apart when this truth comes out, people will see you as a victim of my scandal, not a partner in it. Perhaps that will shield you in some small way from the pain and agony about to be rained down upon my head and the heads of all who are near me."

Anne stared at him, her eyes wide and mouth partly open. It was odd. In this moment she seemed more shocked than she had been when he told her of his unfortunate parentage. Finally she swallowed hard and seemed to gather her composure.

"And is that true?" she asked. "*Did* you make me a victim of your scandal? Did you somehow know the facts of your parentage before we wed and kept them from me as some kind of strange trickery?"

Rhys hesitated. He could lie to her, tell her that he'd been fully aware of who he was before they exchanged vows. But in the end, he wasn't sure it would matter to her. In fact, he wasn't entirely certain she would believe him. It seemed she could read his emotions even when no one else could.

So he slowly shook his head. "No. I found out the day I left London."

The color drained from Anne's cheeks. "Simon revealed your parentage to you when he came here that day."

Rhys squeezed his eyes shut. That afternoon seemed like years ago now, but the pain was as alive as if it had been five minutes before. He relived the encounter in a swift flash and shuddered as he forced himself to look at his wife.

"Yes," he whispered, and his voice broke.

Her bottom lip trembled slightly, but her tone was one of pure anger when she said, "Why did he tell you? If he knew something so horrible, something that would surely break your heart, why would he hand it over as a weight for you to bear?"

Rhys dipped his chin. She was only repeating the questions that had flowed through his own mind that terrible afternoon Simon had come to him. He'd been furious with his friend, until he knew the whole truth. He owed Anne the same.

"Don't judge our old friend too harshly," he said softly. "It's a complicated situation. For one . . ."

He trailed off, the next sentence almost too difficult to speak out loud. Slowly he composed himself as Anne waited, unspeaking and not pushing.

"Anne, my true father is the late Duke of Billingham. Simon and I are brothers, not just in the sense that we are close friends, but the same blood flows through our veins."

There was a long, shocked silence, not that Rhys blamed Anne for her stunned expression. Simon's father had hidden his true nature from everyone, pretending a kindness and honesty he didn't possess.

"But—but Billingham was revered as so pious, so faithful and true a man!" she finally stammered.

Rhys shook his head. "While we were in Billingham for Simon's country party, the two of us uncovered a great deal about his . . . *our* father that belies that exalted reputation. Apparently the duke hid a great deal about himself, including his penchant for producing some number of bastards. I'm not the only one."

She sucked in a breath at that admission, but after a moment of silence, she nodded. "You know, now that you've said you and Simon share blood, I can see the truth. There are a few similarities to your face, and sometimes Simon stands a certain way that puts me to mind of you."

Rhys blinked. "I hadn't noticed those things."

She smiled, but it was a sad expression. "Perhaps I was more focused than you were." She shook away the sadness. "The fact that Simon discovered you shared a father certainly gives me some indication of why he would want to tell you the truth, but he must have known what it would do to you."

With effort, Rhys refocused on his tale. "He tells me that his first reaction was to tell me what he knew, but then he realized exactly what you say. I think he was ready to keep the truth held inside of him for the rest of his life but something forced his hand."

Anne tensed. "What?"

He frowned. "It seems someone else knows about my parentage. And this person is no gentleman, but a villain who intends to blackmail my . . . my *brother* and me to protect this shameful secret. So you see, Simon had no choice but to reveal the truth to me so that we could determine the best course of action to deal with this blackguard."

Anne covered her mouth with her hand, but not before a gasp of pure shock and horror escaped her lips. "My God, Rhys!"

How much he wanted to comfort her, but he realized there was no solace he could offer. No way out of the situation that had been created. All he could do was continue to tell his tale and let her have the full weight of it so she would finally understand.

He sighed. "It seems the *person* will be in London within days to give us his demands. Once that has been done, a decision will have to be made."

Slowly Anne moved forward. Rhys watched,

mesmerized, as her hand moved out and then her fingers slowly wrapped around his bare arm. It was a gesture of comfort and love so pure and genuine that Rhys felt the sting of tears behind his eyes. He blinked, forcing them away.

"How much all this must have hurt you," she whispered.

The air left Rhys's lungs in a gasping sob, but then he regained his composure.

"Yes," he admitted, trying to temper his tone and his emotions. "To know that my entire life has been a lie and that someone is out there who will blackmail me or reveal this devilry . . . it sickens me, Anne. It disgusts me."

She swallowed hard, like she was fighting the urge to cry, but she didn't release him. "But perhaps this person can be reasoned with. Perhaps you can keep the truth from coming out, after all. There must be some way."

"Anne, you cannot hope for that to be true," he said gently. "Even if Simon and I were to be able to come to terms with this person or silence him in some other manner, I haven't yet decided that the truth shouldn't come out."

"You would reveal this yourself?" Anne gasped in surprise.

He shrugged. "I don't yet know. The fact is that I'm

living a lie and there are bloodlines to be upheld."

Anne released his arm suddenly and took a long step away. Her stare was filled with stark disappointment.

"*That* is your main concern? Bloodlines?"

He nodded. "Society will know the truth and judge me, but when I produce no heirs, they will also know that this shame against the Waverly name ended with me."

"And *that*, as much as 'protecting' me, is the reason you didn't want to make love to me," she whispered. "You believe denying this marriage the joy of children will somehow atone for the wrong that was done to your father when you were born another man's son."

He swallowed at her very precise summation. "Yes."

She let out a breath of what was obviously deep frustration.

"Have you learned nothing from all this?" she asked as she shifted the sheet around her higher. "Bloodlines aren't what matter. I think you have seen that *people* are what matter. Actions matter."

Rhys pursed his lips at that statement. Perhaps it was meant to soothe him, but all it did was conjure up a hundred memories of the ways he had treated those around him. None of them was pleasant.

"And my actions have proven I was a bastard in deed long before I knew that fact in name," he said as he clenched his fists at his sides. "Perhaps those I've hurt over the years deserve their moment to crow over my ultimate fall."

She tilted her head, but didn't deny his statement. She moved forward and touched his cheek once more, offering him that comfort and love he hadn't earned.

"You may not wish to admit it, but I've seen you change since we wed," she whispered. "For the better. And I believe you have the capability to change even more. I see so much decency in you, goodness you haven't yet allowed yourself to feel or offer because you've been so heavily influenced by rank. Now that you are free of it, think of what you could become! Think of what good you could do with the power you feel you don't deserve. You could earn it."

Rhys stared at her. There was no hesitation in her eyes or in her voice when she spoke of his potential. But how could she be so certain of his character when he didn't even know his identity anymore?

"You are blinded. Perhaps by the love I'm not worthy of."

She sucked in a breath at that statement. "Don't say that."

"Anne, your dreams sound wonderful on the surface, but they are just dreams. You must see now why we cannot be together. If I let you go many will empathize with you and gift you the friendship you have offered them again and again. You'll be damaged, but I don't think you would lose their acceptance. You could have a life—even . . . even the company of another man someday."

He swallowed hard against the bile that rose in his throat at that idea. Anne deserved the happiness a lover could provide. But every time he thought of another man touching her, holding her, it gave Rhys such a visceral reaction that he could scarce control himself. He wanted to break things, hit things, hurt anyone who dared to claim what was his.

Anne hadn't yet responded to his statement. She stared at him, lips parted. But finally she lifted her hand to cover his fingers, which still lingered on her cheek.

"I have a lover," she said softly. "I want no one but my husband and I never will."

He wasn't given the chance to argue. She lifted up on her tiptoes and kissed him. He tasted her anguish mixed in with her desire and of course her love, always that running undercurrent of her love for him that seemed to color his entire world. It made him want so much more than he could give and it made him pull her closer and kiss her with all the passion and heartache that tormented him. She relieved the ache, if only for a moment, and he selfishly allowed that.

Finally she pulled back, breath coming in short bursts as she stared up at him.

"No matter what you say or how you reason, you can't make me accept this," she whispered. He tensed and tried to pull away, but she held fast. "I do *not* accept it."

He cupped her cheeks, tilting her face up. He wished he could allow her what she desired, but it was folly. "Anne, in my life I've been wrong in so many ways. But this may be the first selfless thing I've ever wished to do. Please don't take it from me."

She moaned out a great sound of pain before she tilted her head forward. He did the same, and their foreheads touched. She rested there for some time before she spoke again.

"Must we resolve this tonight, Rhys?"

He hesitated. Every additional moment he spent with her would only add to the eventual torment when they parted, on both their sides. But, God, it was tempting.

"No," he whispered, loving the soft touch of her breath on his skin as they stood so close. "We have a few days more before my hand will be forced by the arrival of this man who is intent on blackmail and perhaps ruination."

She sighed. "Then let us wait to argue it out until then." He opened his mouth to protest, but she spoke first. "Please."

He pulled back to look down at her. Then he nodded as he took her hand and brought her to the bed. Wordlessly they lay down, arms around each other, bodies touching. And as he kissed her, he prayed that somehow this would get easier.

And knew it wouldn't.

Chapter 17

Morning sunshine flooded the bright and airy breakfast room, and for that Anne was happy. Life had been so dark and complicated as of late, at least she could take some solace in the weather. If there was sun, there was hope, and she clung to that hope with everything in her being.

While she was pouring tea from the service, Rhys entered the room. As their eyes met, time seemed to stop entirely and a world of unspoken communication and emotion flowed between them.

Last night everything had changed. The shift that had begun in the countryside had been completed when he finally confided his deepest secret and most devastating pain to her. She'd felt like his wife, perhaps for the first time.

She prayed it wouldn't be the last.

"Good morning," he said as he slid his gaze away and entered the chamber.

"Hello," she responded, as shy and awkward as she had felt after their wedding night. "Would you like tea?"

He nodded as she held up the cup she had poured. Carefully she added milk and honey and handed it over. Once he had taken the brew, she dared to lift up and press a quick kiss to his cheek.

"Good morning," she whispered.

For a moment Rhys didn't respond, but then he smiled. A real smile, one of the few she had ever seen grace his face. When he did so, the expression changed him. He seemed younger and less severe. All her hopes for his goodness and ability to love and be loved seemed attainable when he did.

Unaware of her deeper thoughts, he took a spot at the head of the table and looked down at the small pile of correspondence awaiting him.

She poured another cup of tea for herself and took a place at his right. It was odd how normal the situation felt, considering how out of control their current circumstances actually were. And yet here they sat, sharing tea and eventually breakfast like they were just another couple on just another morning. And if she could have this, even briefly, it was worth clinging to.

"Any interesting correspondence?" she asked as she sipped her tea.

He shook his head. "Not really. You might be surprised"—he lifted his gaze and shot her another quick grin—"or perhaps you might not, at how benign and boring the everyday workings of my position are. These are mostly updates on the various estates under my control, including questions about changes the managers would like to make to the way things are run or to the staff we have on hand."

"I never realized you were so involved in such things," she said as she wrinkled her brow.

He shrugged. "I'm responsible for the lives of a great many people." Suddenly a shadow passed over his face. "I wonder if they'll suffer for this scandal as well."

Anne swallowed past the tea that seemed to block her throat. For a moment Rhys had appeared to forget his troubles, but there they were, back again.

He shook away the emotion and continued, though now he spoke more slowly and his eyes remained distant. "At any rate, there are also a few matters to do with the House of Lords and some club functions." He tossed the majority of the pile aside. "Nothing that can't be dealt with later."

He tilted his head as his last statement trailed off. He looked at one letter that now peeked out from the bottom of the pile. "What is this?"

Anne craned her neck to see what he was looking at.

He pulled the missive free and turned it over to open it. "A message in my mother's hand. Damn, she must have been concerned about our disappearance."

Anne set her cup down. She'd never mentioned the worried letter from Rhys's mother that she had received the previous day, but before she could say anything he was on his feet.

"Great God, she says she is coming here this—"

He hadn't finished the sentence when Gilmour stepped into the room. "I'm sorry to interrupt your meal, my lord, my lady, but the dowager duchess has arrived. She seeks an audience with you both."

"—morning," Rhys finished his initial statement as he stared at Gilmour intently.

If the butler was concerned by this, he gave no indication, but simply waited patiently at the doorway for further instruction. Anne pushed to her feet. Since Rhys seemed incapable of giving orders at present, the duty fell to her.

"Will you give us a moment, Gilmour? Perhaps show Her Grace to the Rose Terrace. She's always liked the view there. And be sure to bring tea and some breakfast outside for us. The tables are already in place, are they not?"

"They are, Your Grace. I shall do so." The servant didn't hesitate at her order, but bowed slightly and exited the room.

"I'm sorry," Anne said once he had departed and they were alone again. "I did receive a message from your mother amongst the other correspondence yesterday when we returned from the country."

"And you didn't answer it?" Rhys asked, turning on her swiftly. "You didn't feel it important enough to share with me?"

Anne arched a brow, both understanding his peevishness and annoyed by it.

"You know," she said softly, past gritted teeth, "I was a little distracted by a wide variety of things yesterday."

The upset that lined Rhys's face slowly faded and he shook his head. "Of course you were. I apologize, Anne. I shouldn't have taken that tone with you."

Anne drew back. There were very few times she'd ever heard Rhys apologize and this one sounded very genuine, even easy. It seemed he was changing indeed.

"It's quite all right," she said, moving toward him. "You didn't expect her arrival and this is the first time you'll see her since you heard . . ." She trailed off, not wanting to speak out loud the thing that had hurt him so much.

He nodded in response. "Yes. But perhaps it's best, after all. This conversation was bound to happen, today is as good a day as any for me to confront her."

Anne hesitated, but then moved forward. Gently she slipped her arms around him and held him. For a moment he retained his stiff posture, but then he returned her embrace, holding her against his body and burying his face into her hair.

"You know I'm very fond of your mother and I'd like to say hello to her," Anne said as they parted. "But then should I excuse myself? Would you like to discuss this delicate matter with her in privacy?"

Rhys looked at her carefully. For a moment she thought he might ban her from the exchange entirely, but then he reached out and took her hand. His fingers tangled in hers and he lifted them to cover his heart.

"No. Please stay. It would . . . *help* me, I think, to have you there."

She sucked in a breath of surprise and happiness. Twice in as many days, Rhys had requested her assistance and admitted he needed her presence, not pushed aside her attempts at comfort as he had done so many times before. It meant more to her than anything to have him allow her to aid him, even in the smallest way.

"Of course I'll stay," she whispered as he led her from the room and down the hallway toward the Rose Room and its attached terrace.

The doors to the balcony were thrown open and the heady scent of blooming flowers greeted them even before they stepped outside. Rhys hesitated slightly at the threshold, glancing to Anne.

"It will be well," she whispered, though she realized that what she had just said might not be true.

But it seemed to be what he needed to hear, for he released her hand and stepped outside into the bright sunshine to greet his mother.

The dowager duchess stood staring out over the garden below, but she turned as the two came outside and smiled her greeting.

Anne had always thought her mother-in-law was a beautiful woman, with dark hair and eyes that matched her son's in their rich, brown color. But now that Anne knew the truth about Rhys's parentage, she found herself looking more closely at the dowager and seeing even more traits Rhys shared with her.

That was probably how she had kept up her ruse for so long. Rhys looked so much like his mother that the duke hadn't questioned why his son resembled *him* so little.

The dowager came across the terrace, both hands

extended. Anne held her breath as the mother and son met. Rhys was so tightly wound, she had no idea what he would do or say. After everything he'd endured in the past few weeks, Anne feared he might simply launch into a tirade against the woman who had raised him.

Instead he took his mother's hands and allowed her to press a kiss of greeting against each cheek.

"Good Lord, Rhys, I must admit I was worried about you," Her Ladyship said as she released her son and turned toward Anne to kiss her cheek once. "When Anne came to me and told me she didn't know your whereabouts, it frightened me."

Rhys's lips pursed. "It was a misunderstanding, Mother. But Anne . . ." He turned toward her with a slight smile. "Well, she found me."

Anne returned the smile before she motioned to a round metal table with matching chairs that was across the terrace. A tea service sat on its top.

"Shall we sit? I see the servants have already brought refreshment for us," she said, bound to keep up polite appearances if only because it gave her something to do as she awaited the confrontation surely to come.

Rhys's mother kept her eyes trained on her son for a long moment, then nodded. "That would be lovely, thank you."

As they moved to the table, Anne kept her worried gaze on her husband. He was controlling his emotions with the same efficiency as ever before, but as he pulled the chair out for his mother, she felt the tension coursing through him. She saw it in the way he held his body. After she seated herself, he took his place between the two women.

"I'm glad you're back. It isn't like you to disappear with no word," his mother pressed.

A muscle in Rhys's jaw twitched and Anne steeled herself for the floodgate of anger about to be opened. But he was quiet as he said, "I'm not sure what is 'like' me at all anymore."

Anne flinched at the rawness in his tone, and without thinking she reached out to cover his hand. For moment he simply stared, but then he smiled at her.

His mother also looked at their intertwined fingers and seemed surprised by their open display of affection. But she managed to tear her gaze away to address her son.

"I'm not certain I know what you mean by that statement."

Rhys looked at her, his face so sad and broken that Anne could have wept for him. Whatever ability he possessed to make himself the cold and distant duke, it was fading with every moment, leaving only the man inside. Only Rhys with his broken heart.

"Were you ever going to tell me?" he whispered, surprisingly soft.

The dowager's eyes widened and the blood slowly drained from her face. Anne was shocked by her expression. It was almost as if she had guessed what Rhys knew even before he said it. As if she had been waiting for this moment, perhaps for his entire life. And maybe she had.

Anne could hardly imagine the strain of waiting for that particular axe to fall. Despite the circumstances, she felt for her mother-in-law.

"I-I don't know what you mean," the dowager said as she absently fiddled with the edge of her cup. "What is it that troubles you, Rhys?"

He shut his eyes for a long moment. Anne felt the struggle within him to keep some kind of decorum.

Finally his eyes opened and he said, "I know about you and the Duke of Billingham, Mother. I know he was my real father."

When his beloved mother's face crumpled with utter devastation, it was quite possibly the worst thing Rhys had ever seen. It broke his already aching heart and torn spirit in a new way. But to his surprise, having Anne's hand in his actually helped. Although it was foolish, with her at his side he felt like he had a partner in this tragedy.

His mother got to her feet with a jerking motion that rattled the table and sloshed tea from her cup across the white metal top. Rhys shoved his own chair back to assist her, but she lifted her hand to stay his motion. Trembling, she slowly walked away to stand at the terrace wall and stare down at the garden below.

There was silence for so long that he lost track of how many seconds had passed, how many moments. Finally his mother turned toward him. Her ashen face was lined with determination and, to his surprise, almost relief.

"How did you find out?" she whispered.

Although Rhys had been certain of the truth almost from the first moment Simon revealed it, even though he had read every piece of evidence he possessed and found it to be solid, hearing his mother ask that question made his heart sink and his stomach turn. Some small part of him had held out a slender reed of hope that when he confronted her, she would deny the truth. That she would slap him or rail at him for the outrage of the accusation. And that she would give him a rational explanation for everything he had been told.

Now that final line of hope was broken and he

drifted away on the finality of the truth.

"Simon," he said, his voice cracking as he answered her question.

His mother drew in a sharp breath and lifted her hand to her heart. Tears filled her eyes.

"Dear Simon," she whispered. "So he knows the truth about his father, at last?"

Rhys could hardly find the words, so he instead nodded once. His mother shook her head slowly.

"That is most unfortunate. That boy loved his father so deeply, he had much faith in him. A child shouldn't be so disillusioned by a parent. I hope he's well."

Rhys pushed to his feet and moved toward her at last. He could scarcely believe what he was hearing. In this moment his mother was concerned over the well-being of her lover's other son?

"He's had quite a shock," he admitted, his tone as tense and emotional as he now felt. His voice elevated, almost of its own accord. "I can fully understand his feelings as I've had a great one of my own. Would you care to inquire after *my* welfare, madam?"

Behind him, he heard the screech as Anne pushed back her chair. She moved to his side and took his arm.

"Rhys," she said softly. "Please."

He frowned, hating himself as his mother's face

crumpled even further. He did deserve answers, but his mother deserved better as well.

"I apologize," he offered through gritted teeth. "That was out of line."

Anne moved toward his mother, her smile gentle and soothing. It seemed her nature to put others at ease, and he saw his mother relax when Anne's arm came around her.

"Your Grace, please understand how deeply this has affected Rhys, just as I'm certain it's affected you and your life over the years. You are the only one left who can provide him the answers I think we all know he deserves."

His mother looked at his wife briefly and then she nodded. Swiping at unshed tears, she straightened her shoulders and met his eyes with unflinching steadiness.

"*I* am the one who is sorry, Rhys," she said, and this time there was no trembling to her tone. Only strength and certainty. "Your wife is right that you are owed an explanation. Forgive my hesitance to offer it to you sooner. You see, this is a great shock to me as well. I'd somehow hoped this day would never come."

"And yet it has," Rhys murmured, wishing briefly that his mother's hopes had been realized.

The dowager nodded. "Indeed. I fear you will

judge me, but I must tell you the entire story for you to truly understand my actions."

Rhys glanced quickly at Anne. She nodded slowly, as if encouraging him to hear his mother's side. To give her the concern and care that the dowager had spent a lifetime gifting to him even as the last Duke of Waverly pulled Rhys further and further from her.

"Very well," he said as he motioned her back to the table. "I'd like to hear your tale."

They returned to their seats, and his mother took a long drink of her tea before she clenched her hands together on the table and let out a great sigh.

"What you must know above all else is that I loved my husband." She shook her head. "When we married, I had great hopes that we could one day be very happy and develop a love match. But I was a fool. To your father I was nothing more than a hostess for his parties and a mother to his children. He didn't care for me beyond what I could provide for his comfort. It only took a few months into our union before I realized he never would."

With every word from his mother's lips, Anne tensed beside him. From the corner of his eye, he looked at his wife and saw the pale sadness of her expression. In some way this was her story, too. Her path.

And he had been the one to place her upon it.

"What happened?" Anne asked, her tone surprisingly even and calm when he could tell his mother's words tore at the very core of her heart.

The dowager looked at her and smiled. It was a soft and sad expression. In that moment it was clear the two women had connected on a new level. That they each recognized the hopeless love the other felt for the man she had married. In their longing, they were sisters.

Only his mother had strayed away somehow, broken free of her bonds at least once, and sought happiness in someone else's arms. The very idea of Anne doing the same made Rhys sick, even though he'd given her his blessing to do exactly that one day.

"I was brokenhearted, of course," the dowager said, her words breaking through the haze of Rhys's thoughts. "I sank into my sadness and believed there was no hope for happiness ever again." She frowned. "*That* was when the Duke of Billingham took an interest in me."

Rhys couldn't hide his reaction to this part of his mother's tale, as the heat of blood rushed to his cheeks. Her reaction was just as powerful. Any joy, any happiness that normally touched her expression was gone. She appeared to be as embarrassed as he was by the indelicate subject.

"Although his reputation was one of goodness

and even piety, when it came to women, it seemed he could sense weakness and pain," she whispered, her gaze clouding with unpleasant memory. "He used it, manipulated it, until he had what he wanted. In my case, the attention was flattering at first, since your father had so little interest. And I admit I allowed Billingham to go too far."

Rhys pushed from his chair and paced away. He didn't wish to imagine his mother so compromised, or to think about the results of that indiscretion. But how could he not? There was no avoiding inserting himself into her most private mistake. After all, he had become its central consequence.

After a moment's pause, his mother continued her story, her voice wavering slightly. "I regretted the moment immediately, but it was too late. And I do *not* regret you, my dearest. You must know that."

There was an unexpected relief that accompanied that statement. How he would have hated to know that his mother despised him on some level each time she looked at him. That he was the physical manifestation of all her past wrongs. Her love had been so important throughout his life, he didn't wish to lose it.

He found his gaze slipping to Anne before he spoke again. She hadn't moved from her place at the table, but she was so fully focused on him that it felt as though she was at his side, regardless. Her continued comfort was, as always, greatly appreciated.

"Did my father—" He broke off with a shake of his head. "Did your husband know of what had transpired between you and Billingham?"

"No." His mother looked at him evenly. "And I didn't keep the truth from him in order to save myself, as you might imagine."

"No?" Rhys asked, his tone hard.

"I loved that man, even if he didn't care." The dowager's lower lip trembled ever so slightly. "When you were born, he was so happy to have a son. It was the first time I felt bonded to him in any important way. I refused to take that . . . to take you . . . away from him. So I didn't. It would have done nothing but hurt everyone involved if I had confessed what I'd done. And legally it would change nothing in our circumstances. I thought no one ever had to know."

Rhys moved back to the table and sank into his seat with a heavy sigh. "Unfortunately someone does."

Any remaining blood that colored his mother's already pale face drained away. In fact, despite the fact that she was seated, she seemed ready to swoon, and Rhys reached out to steady her on instinct.

His touch seemed to soothe her, for she whispered, "Someone knows?"

He nodded once. "The Duke of Billingham kept records. He made some kind of payment to you?"

His mother turned up her nose. "He tried, in the most vile terms, to buy my silence in order to protect his precious reputation. Of course I refused, but he continually sent me the same money over and over. Finally I donated it to the orphan fund of my ladies' group and that was the end of it."

"Well, he recorded the transaction, along with some other details and a few incriminating letters which passed between you during that time." Rhys sighed. "He trusted the wrong solicitor, for it seems that man was willing to share with another what he was meant to protect. Simon and I suspect a blackguard named Xavier Warren."

His mother's eyes widened. "Dear God."

Anne reached out and covered the dowager's hand in comfort. "The man is out of the country after being accused of treason, but Rhys and Simon say he's coming to meet with them in a few days. To arrange for some kind of terms for his silence, no doubt."

His mother flinched. "Then it is to be blackmail."

"Perhaps not." Rhys shrugged. "If we wish to avoid such a thing, then the best course might be for me to reveal this truth on my own terms. It would end any potential for blackmail now or in the future."

His mother gasped. "But the scandal, Rhys!"

"Yes, I'm well-aware of that," he said, unable to soften the bitterness of his tone. "But perhaps Society deserves its chance to revile me. To know the truth of my blood."

His mother lifted her hand to her eyes. "Blood, blood . . . you sound exactly like your father."

"He wasn't my father," Rhys snapped.

"He was in every way that mattered," his mother retorted with just as much heat. "And he was wrong in many ways. He taught you to believe bloodlines made more impact than feelings or behavior. He taught you that love and emotion were weakness. He somehow convinced you that families were only about history and purity, not *people*. I allowed it at the time because of my own guilt. But I cannot remain silent any longer. This secret has remained hidden for over thirty years. Revealing it now will only hurt you and everyone around you."

"I realize that, Mother," he said as he got to his feet again. "Do you not think that the consequences to you, to my sisters, to my wife weigh on me? But the man who raised me, the one I called Father, also taught me that right was better sometimes than good or easy. And there seems to be no escape from *right* if this Warren fellow knows the truth. This entire house of cards you've built is destined to come down now. I sometimes think I would rather tear it down myself than have someone else do it."

His mother's lips pursed, but she slowly got up from the table with all the regality that accompanied her rank. Anne scrambled to her feet and watched her as intently as Rhys did. His mother smoothed her skirts slowly.

"I know you, Rhys. And I can see this decision is not one you make lightly. If you do decide to reveal the past, I'm sure you will do it as a last resort in a desperate situation. But I hope it won't come to that. Not for my sake, as I know I deserve all the censure the revelation will bring. But for the others who will be drowned in its wake, including yourself."

Rhys cocked his head, filled with surprise at the fact that his mother didn't argue with him further. Although she had hidden the past for so long, she seemed willing to let him handle the future without question or comment.

And that made the idea that he might have to betray her all the worse. His stomach turned at the thought.

She looked at Anne with a smile. "You are much like me, I think, aren't you? Your story, it is similar to mine."

Anne sucked in a breath and cast a quick glance at Rhys before she jerked out a nod.

The dowager touched her daughter-in-law's cheek briefly. "I thought so. But I can see my son has deeper feelings than perhaps he admits, even to himself. Don't allow him to give up on you. And *please* don't give up on him."

Anne blinked, and in that moment all her pain was clear on her face. But then she squared her shoulders and the strength he had come to admire settled over her expression.

"I have no intention of giving up on him," Anne whispered, but she didn't look at Rhys.

"Very good." His mother shook her head and let her gaze fall on her son yet again. "Have I told you enough?"

Rhys nodded. "For now."

His mother let out a sigh. "Perhaps there is some way I can help. I still have some influence, you know. And I have a . . . well, a friend, someone who might be able to assist us if you allowed me to—"

Rhys barked out a laugh, though he felt no humor. "A friend, Mother? Do you really think some lady in your sewing circle could assist us in this?"

His mother pursed her lips, annoyance lining her face. "I'm not so foolish as to think that. This friend is not a lady but—"

He interrupted her again, this time with a wave of his hand. She was being utterly foolish and perhaps delusional in this line of thinking. It was better to cut her off now.

"No, Mother. No. While I appreciate the sentiment of your offer, there is no one outside of those who already know the truth who can help us at this point. Simon and I must meet with this person who is blackmailing us and only then can I determine the best course of action."

The dowager frowned and almost looked as if she intended to say more, but finally she shook her head. "I see what you are saying. It is only that I started this, if I could play some part in ending it, I would."

Rhys scrubbed a hand over his face in frustration. If only she was correct. The idea of escaping this situation was tempting indeed, but he could see no way.

"No," he said softly.

His mother's shoulders slumped. "So much like your father. I want to talk to you about this again, but not now. Now I'm exhausted and I need some time to reflect, as I'm sure you do. I'll see myself out."

She turned without allowing either Rhys or Anne to answer and slipped from the terrace quietly. When she was gone, Anne moved toward him. Rhys tracked her every move, anticipating her touch and unable to stop from expelling a sigh of relief and pleasure when she finally wrapped her arms around his waist and held him.

"You should hear her, Rhys," she said as she looked up into his face. "She has carried this secret a long time and her advice could be of use."

He shook his head slowly. "I realize that, but it's different now. She might have been able to pretend away the secret, but I can't."

She pulled away, and he saw the frustration on her face. "Then you have much to plan. I'll leave you to it."

She moved toward the door. Rhys longed to call her back, to give her what she demanded, if only to see her smile and revel in her warmth.

But instead he only watched as she left the terrace, left him alone once again.

Chapter 18

The alleyway was dark, with a dank smell of human desperation and sweat all around, as well as far more unpleasant odors. It was no place for a gentleman, that was certain, and Rhys felt Simon on alert for attack the same way he was.

"Are you certain this is the place?" Rhys whispered, continually scanning the darkness for any sign of a trap.

Simon bobbed out one nod of his head. "Indeed it is. And we are right on time."

In the distance there was a scrape of boot on cobblestone and then a voice hissed, "You got *that* from your father."

Rhys and Simon tensed at the same moment, and both of them pivoted to face the voice in the dark. Rhys watched as a haggard, thin man moved into the dim light of a lamp. Dragged himself was more like it, for one of his legs had apparently been injured and healed improperly, rendering it almost useless. It twisted oddly behind him and scraped along the sidewalk with a gut-wrenching sound.

"*I* always told him that being early was better. For the element of surprise, but perhaps you already guessed that when you received my missive a full week before you expected it." The other man smiled, revealing a row of rotting teeth. "But your father was always a punctual man. Perhaps that was one of his few admirable traits."

"Are you Xavier Warren?" Rhys asked, his voice low in the quiet. He had no idea who else was lurking about. There was no need to project their woes to every vile person within earshot. He and Simon had enough problems as it was.

"Oh, so you figured it out? Excellent deductive skills," the man said with a sarcastic snort. "Though I can see that statement shocks the new Duke of Billingham here. Do I meet your expectations, boy?"

Rhys looked at Simon from the corner of his eye, and what Warren said was true. His brother was staring, clearly taken aback by the man he saw before him.

"Now that I see you, I do remember you vaguely from my childhood. You came a few times to talk to my father," Simon whispered as he looked the man up and down with an expression of horror. "You have *changed*."

Warren began to laugh, but the thick, wet sound soon changed into a coughing fit that forced him to bend at the waist and hack in a thin, sickly fashion. Rhys stared in horror. He could almost pity the poor bastard.

Until he spoke again.

"I have your father to thank for my current failing condition," Warren said as he spit something foul across the alley and straightened up. "You see, at some point Billingham decided having me banished to the Continent as a traitor wasn't enough for him."

Simon caught his breath and shot Rhys a side glance. In that brief moment, Rhys saw his friend's pain reborn over the disappointment his father had truly been. He hated Warren for that as much as for the havoc he intended to bring down on Rhys's life.

Simon's voice was hollow when he asked, "Are you saying that my father—"

"Sent men to kill me. And almost did the job, too." Warren motioned to his twisted leg with a rage-filled scowl. "I suppose I knew too many secrets, after all." He looked at Rhys. "Eh, *Your Grace*?"

Rhys fisted his hands at his sides to prevent himself from launching across the expanse at the other man and finishing what his father had not. With a few deep breaths, he managed to calm himself.

"It seems there are a great many secrets to be had. The question is how much you want for them, Mr. Warren."

Warren stared at Rhys in silence for a long moment. In the other man's eyes Rhys saw madness and mental decay, but he also saw rage, pain, and a thirst for revenge that would probably never be quenched, no matter what he did to Rhys and Simon. It made Rhys shiver to see such intense and ugly emotions on another person's face.

"For decades I did everything Billingham asked of me like a trained dog." Warren spat, fists clenching and unclenching at his sides. "I was his right-hand man, I fought when he told me to fight, I brought him his women when he desired them, I strong-armed his opponents, and when someone couldn't be convinced through money or threats to do as he required, well . . . I even killed for him."

Simon turned his face as if he had been struck and Rhys swallowed past the bile that rose in his throat. Billingham had been quite the actor indeed to hide such terrible truths about his character from everyone around him. And now all those hidden facts were coming to rain down on his sons, both the legitimate and the illegitimate.

"He turned on you," Rhys said softly, encouraging Warren to continue, for the man had seemed distracted as he stared at Simon. Warren looked to be reveling in the other man's pain and disbelief, as though it fed him in some twisted way.

"Yes," Warren said, shaking his head and refocusing. "After an argument over a job he ordered me to do, Billingham told me it was time for me to go. At first having me banished for doing the very things he had asked of me was enough for him. But after I wrote to him, asking him to increase the pitifully small consideration he sent me for my years of loyal service, the duke became determined to see me dead."

The other man's face twisted, his haunted eyes telling his tale as much as his shaking voice. "I lived for years in hiding, growing sick from the holes where I was forced to cower, in constant pain from the bullet still lodged in my hip. And all the while Billingham became almost sainted in the eyes of the *ton*."

Rhys sucked in a breath, torn between utter disgust and total pity for the shell of a man who hunched before him. "I think both Simon and I appreciate the torment you've been through. But we need to understand what it is exactly that you want from us. Perhaps we can come to terms."

The other man's eyes lit up with greed and a fevered

desire that made him look even madder than he had at first glance. Rhys fought the urge to step away.

"Yes, my terms. First, I want ten thousand pounds a year for my silence."

Simon blinked as he repeated, "Ten thousand pounds?"

Rhys stared as well. That was a large fortune. Certainly together he and Simon could spare it without much financial hardship, but it was an outrageous annual sum.

"I think I've earned it," Warren barked as he motioned to his broken body.

"I wonder what the families of your murdered victims would say about that," Simon snapped.

Warren made a sudden move for his pocket and Rhys leapt forward, positioning himself between the men. It was an odd thing. This blackmail involved *his* future, but for some reason he was able to remain far calmer than Simon, who was so angry he shook like a leaf in a storm.

"Gentlemen," Rhys said softly. "There is no need to resort to this." He locked eyes with his brother. "Please."

Simon pulled away with reluctance and disgust. "Very well."

Rhys returned his gaze to their blackmailer. "Is that all? Ten thousand pounds will end this?"

"No, not quite. There is something else I'll require."

Rhys's heart sank. "And what is that?"

"I want to return to England," the other man said, his tone changing. There was a faraway longing in his voice now, in his clouded eyes. "I want my name cleared of the charges of treason. I want to see my sister again. And I want to be invited to Society functions. I want to be returned to the position your father took from me when he threw me to the wolves."

"He gave you that position as well, you know," Simon said as he glared at the other man.

"I earned it, boy, and don't you forget it," Warren growled.

Rhys reached up and rubbed his temples. "And *that* is all? If we arrange for these things, it will settle our debt and you'll keep your tongue about your knowledge of our father's dealings."

Warren looked at him with another putrid smile. "I don't know, Your Grace. I might think of other items I desire, but for now let us call it a start. It will hold my silence for at least a year at this price. We can renegotiate then."

Nausea rose in Rhys, for this was just what he had expected and feared. Somehow he tamped the reaction down as best he could.

"As you might guess, my brother and I will require

some time to discuss your terms," he choked. "May we meet again after we've talked?"

"Oh yes," Warren said. "I'm not an unreasonable man, but neither am I a fool. I'll meet with you, but at a place of *my* choosing."

"And where is that?" Simon asked, his brow arching.

"The Earl of Rythsdale is holding a ball in two days, is he not?" the other man asked.

Rhys nodded, trying not to think too hard about how this man could have obtained that information.

"Good," Warren said. "Then I'll meet you there."

Simon snorted out a laugh. "You must be jesting. You'll never be allowed entry, Rythsdale is the soul of propriety. He wouldn't allow a traitor in his midst."

Warren's brow arched slowly. "You are likely right, but I have ways of *taking* what I'm not allowed to have. I will be there, I assure you, and I'll notify you when I'm ready to speak to you."

"And why there?" Rhys cocked his head.

"Because, my lord," Warren said with a sneer, "if you refuse my terms, you will have to deal with me in the most public way possible."

"You—" Simon began, his face twisting in a mask of rage.

Before his brother could reach the other man,

Warren pulled out a pistol and pointed it directly at Simon's chest. At such close range, even the worst shot in the countryside would kill him, and Warren's hand didn't shake even a fraction.

Rhys caught his brother's arm and held him steady, praying Warren wouldn't get it in his addled mind to pull the trigger and obtain his revenge in another, even more devastating fashion.

"We understand, Mr. Warren," Rhys said softly. "And we'll see you at the Rythsdale ball with our answer."

"Good," Warren said as he backed into the shadows. "I look forward to it."

There was only one loud scrape of his injured leg and then silence as Warren faded into the blackness like the experienced criminal he was and left the two brothers to themselves.

Rhys stared at Simon. Without a word between them, they walked back to the carriage they had come in together and got inside. It was only when the door was closed and they had ridden away a reasonable distance that Simon spoke.

"It's worse than I anticipated, though perhaps that was a foolish oversight on my part." He shook his head. "I knew he had done vile and even criminal things, but I never knew my father . . . *our* father participated in murder."

The pain in Simon's voice was plain, but Rhys had no idea how to address it. There was nothing he could say or do that would ever change the disillusionment his friend now faced. Or the horror Rhys himself faced. This Pandora's box had been opened, the secrets would never again fit back inside.

All they could do now was to deal with the consequences.

"This will never end, you know," Rhys murmured, resting his head back against the leather seat and letting out the breath he had been holding in a sighing *whoosh*. "In fact, judging from Warren's demeanor and his hatred for our father and for us, it will only grow with each passing year. Hell, it might even be passed on to our children if Warren can manage it."

Simon was silent for several blocks, merely staring out the window in troubled thought. Finally he nodded. "And some of the things he asks for are impossible. The money we could give him, we might even be able to somehow clear his name if we use enough of our combined connections. But can you imagine trying to obtain him entry back into Society?"

Rhys shuddered at the thought. "His years in hiding have broken his mind, as well as his body. No one will have him, I agree."

"Warren is driven by greed, but also vengeance,"

Simon said quietly. "Seeing him so destroyed, I can almost understand why."

Rhys darted his gaze to his brother's face. "Don't you dare pity him, Simon. Or forget that he was a killer, a blackmailer, and a thief. Our father may have taken advantage of those things, but Xavier Warren was willing to perform those acts out of pure greed and I think a little pleasure at causing pain and heartbreak. He doesn't deserve your consideration or understanding on *any* level."

Simon shrugged one shoulder. "It hardly matters now. The man holds our shared fate in his hand."

Rhys squeezed his eyes shut as nausea washed over him a second time. He had always been in such firm control of his life that this entire concept was entirely foreign to him. And hateful.

He had truly tried to find another option, but now he could see there was but one way out. The path he had feared he would have to tread from the first moment he heard the awful truth about his birth.

"No, Simon," he murmured as he straightened up and squared his shoulders. "Warren *wants* to hold our fate, but he only has that power if we give it to him. We *can* take it back. There is a way and you know it, though you've fought against it in the past."

The carriage slowed and Rhys glanced past Simon to see that the vehicle had pulled into his own drive at his London home. Simon stared at him.

"You're talking about setting this secret loose in your own way, on your own terms," his brother whispered.

Rhys nodded. "I am. It would end this, you know that as well as I do."

His brother remained silent for a long moment, resting his head back against the carriage seat and staring up at the ceiling with unseeing eyes. Finally he nodded, though the action was jerky.

"You may be right. This may be the only option we have left."

Rhys reached out to squeeze his brother's shoulder, relieved that Simon wasn't arguing with him now that the moment of truth had finally come.

"I'm going to take back my fate, Simon," he said softly. "One way or another, I won't let a blackguard like Xavier Warren own the keys to my future. For better or worse, I'll ruin myself before I let him do so."

Chapter 19

Anne paced across the chamber floor one more time, her night shift flapping about her ankles as she snapped out each pivoting turn. Her gaze darted to the small clock on the mantel for what seemed like the tenth time or more. The hands had advanced only a few short moments since she last looked, but that gave her no solace. It was after two in the morning and Rhys had not yet returned from his meeting with whatever villain wished to blackmail him over his true parentage.

She lifted a hand to her trembling lips. She couldn't help but think of all the ways their meeting could have gone wrong. What if there had been a fight? Or all this was just a trap meant to bring Rhys and Simon to a man with questionable intentions?

What if Rhys was hurt and couldn't reach her?

The possibilities bombarded her from every side, making the tick of the clock ever louder, like a drumbeat in her mind. She could have screamed down the house in frustration and fear, but at that very moment the door behind her opened. She pivoted and watched as Rhys stepped into the chamber, his face lined with emotion, but his body whole and unharmed.

Without thinking, Anne launched herself toward him, racing across the room. She clung to him, shaking with relief as his arms came around her and stole her breath with the force of the way he crushed her to his chest.

"I thought—I thought—" She hiccupped, burying her face in his shoulder.

"Shhh," he soothed as he maneuvered to look down at her.

In that brief, utterly unguarded moment she saw the broken heart he wouldn't normally reveal to anyone, even her. She saw how badly the meeting must have gone. And she recognized, just from that one glance, how desperate their situation had become.

Then his mouth was on hers and all the thoughts melted away. She ached to comfort him in the only way he had ever allowed. She longed to feel his touch as her own comfort and forget, even just for a moment, all that stood between them.

He pushed her toward the bed and she fell across it with him half covering her. His weight was delicious against her body, his mouth so hot and wet as he dragged it away from hers to trail down her throat. She arched beneath him, helplessly reaching for the pleasure his touch promised and the delicious escape these precious moments would provide for them both.

"God, Anne," he groaned as he maneuvered one breast free from her shift. The cool air of the chamber tightened her nipple and made her suck in a breath. "I want you so much I can feel it in every vein, in every pore."

"I'm yours," she whispered, gasping as his mouth closed over her nipple and he sucked hard enough that pleasure merged with pain in a most delightful fashion. "I will *always* be yours."

He lifted his head at the second statement and there was a deep and abiding sadness in his eyes as he stared at her. He moved forward to kiss her lips once more, but the passion he had first exhibited was now muted. There was something else about the kiss now. A gentleness, a deep caring . . . and a statement of farewell that she tried desperately to ignore.

She could hardly breathe, let alone speak, but it didn't seem as though Rhys required either of those reactions. Instead he moved his mouth down her body a second time, hesitating at her one naked breast and suckling there for a moment before he let his mouth press lower across her cotton-covered belly.

His warm hands caressed her legs through her night rail, massaging the sensitive flesh and making her arch against him with ever-increasing desire. Slowly he glided the fabric upward, sliding it along her tingling skin until she was unable to contain a moan of pure pleasure.

The fact that he could make her come undone so easily gave him all the power, but she didn't care. In this moment, she surrendered willingly, with no further thought to the future or the past.

When he had bared her from the waist down, he drew back. In the firelight, he stared at the slight parting of her legs, at the rise and fall of her breasts as she panted out breath. His eyes glazed with a desire that created such triumph in Anne.

For so long she had believed he didn't want her, she'd tormented herself with those fears and wondered constantly about her failings. But now she knew how wrong she'd been. The longing for her within him was clear in his every move and breath now. He had only hidden it before in some misguided attempt to protect her. To protect himself.

Rhys cupped the insides of both thighs gently and she sucked in a harsh breath. His fingers were so warm, so rough on the delicate skin there. He pushed and her legs parted, revealing her sex to him. No longer did she feel embarrassment or vulnerability when he stared at her. She *wanted* him to see her, to touch her, to do everything he wanted to her. She needed that as she needed breath and food and water.

He positioned himself between her legs, and without preamble his mouth covered her. Anne cried out, hands fisting in the fabric of the coverlet. His tongue drilled into her aching sheath, his thumbs spreading her open as he licked and licked until her entire body shook with anticipation and rapidly mounting pleasure. Within moments she was trembling out of control, and then the orgasm hit her like one of the angry waves on the beach back at the country cottage.

Her hips arched wildly as the pleasure of release spiraled ever higher, with ever more intensity. Rhys gave her no quarter, tormenting her with the same passion even as her cries grew louder and her body thrashed beneath him. He never stopped, punishing and pleasuring her with his tongue, with his fingers until tears streamed down her face and she collapsed, weak against the pillows, her only remaining movements a few tremors as he gently lapped at her a few more times.

Utterly spent, Anne looked down her body at him. She wanted more, though she had nothing left to give. She waited for him to strip off his clothing and at least offer her the chance to pleasure him as she had done so many times before.

But he didn't.

Though she could see his raging erection pressing insistently along the front of his trousers, Rhys made no move to obtain his relief. Instead he slid up the bed to lie on his side next to her, brushing her hair away from her face as her breathing slowly returned to normal.

"You are beautiful," he finally whispered, his voice cracking. "I never told you that enough."

Anne squeezed her eyes shut as she attempted to control her wild emotions.

"Then why not make love to me?" she asked, though she knew the answer in her heart. She heard it in his voice, felt it in his touch.

But she needed to hear it out loud. From him. *Now*.

"I wanted to. God knows I want nothing more. But I can't. Because . . ." he said, touching her cheek gently. She opened her eyes with reluctance and met his even gaze. "Because the meeting tonight didn't go well, Anne."

She nodded, though it felt jerky and strange. "I guessed as much from your expression when you entered the room. Please, won't you tell me about it? I've driven myself mad with worry and wondering since you left."

Now Rhys's face was grim, all the desire and joy gone from it.

"We were correct in our guess that the blackmailer is my father's old minion Xavier Warren," he began slowly. "It seems the two of them were involved in activities far deeper than mere political intrigue. What I saw and heard tonight, Anne . . ."

He trailed off, pain lining his face. She lifted her hand and stroked his cheek. How she wished she could help him. To take away the agony he now experienced.

He shook his head, as if banishing the ugly memories, and his gaze cleared. "What I learned in the time Simon and I spent with the man is that Warren will never stop. He's driven by forces that aren't in anyone's control, even his own. If we surrender to his ridiculous demands, he'll only reign over us for the rest of my life, and possibly for the lives of the next generation."

Anne flinched. Rhys spoke of the children he said he would never give her in order to protect his precious title, and it tore her heart to shreds once more.

But Rhys continued, "I won't allow it. I won't live with an axe hanging over me, over you, over everyone I love for all time, not to protect a legacy I don't even deserve. No, it's time to end this the only way I can. I'm going to reveal the truth myself, Anne."

She stared at him. His words sank into her skin, into her soul, into her heart. They weren't unexpected. He had been saying this could be his course of action for some time, but still she could hardly believe him.

She waited for sadness, regret, for all the pain she'd been barely controlling over the past few terrible weeks to make its way to her surface and bubble free at last. If there was ever a time to let emotion loose, this was it. But those feelings never came.

No, it wasn't pain that bombarded her as she stared at her husband. And it wasn't regret, though she was certain she would experience a great deal of that feeling later.

What hit her now, in this charged moment, with the force of a slap . . . was *anger*. Anger at the situation, anger at the blackmailer who crushed all her precious hopes, but the deepest and darkest anger was directed at Rhys. And there would be no stifling it, no controlling it. Tonight she would finally say everything she had held inside as she fought to keep him. Tonight she would indulge her own feelings instead of thinking of him and his.

"After all the time we spent together, I was foolish enough to believe you had changed," she whispered as she pushed off the bed. She smoothed her nightgown to cover herself. "But you are the same selfish ass you have ever been!"

Rhys stared at his wife as she paced across his chamber. She was shaking with rage, and her pointed barb about his selfishness stung him like no other.

"I have tried so damned hard," she continued, almost as if she couldn't stop now that she had begun her outburst. She stared at him with green-blue eyes filled with heated anger. "I gave you *everything* you wanted, *all* you asked of me and more. I offered you my sympathy and my hand and my heart because you needed them. Most of the time I offered them at my own detriment."

"And I appreciate that—" he began, getting to his feet.

"No, you don't," she snapped, stepping toward him and then coming to a halt as she fisted her hands at her sides.

He stared at her, her eyes on fire, her skin flushed with emotion. At one time he would have called this reaction a weakness. He would have judged her for her out-of-control release of emotion. But now he ached as he looked at her, for he knew his wife was anything but weak. She possessed a strength he envied. She would fight, even if the battle was one she could never win. *They* could never win.

"You must see," he whispered. "This is my most selfless act."

She was silent for a long moment, staring at him with her eyes wide and hands shaking at her sides. Her lips parted and from them came a long laugh, but it wasn't like the beautiful one he had come to love. No, this sound held no humor and no warmth. Instead it was filled with both contempt and disbelief.

"No, my darling," she finally said with a shake of her dark head. "What you are doing is *anything* but selfless. I call it cowardice, plain and simple."

Rhys moved forward as his own anger bubbled to the surface. His nostrils flared and he barely reined in the urge to raise his voice when he responded.

"You cannot mean that, Anne, not knowing what you do. To reveal myself will destroy me. It will open me up to every barb and sling and arrow that have been held at bay by my family name and history. You call that cowardice?"

She nodded without even an ounce of hesitation. "I do indeed. If you were brave, you would *fight*, Rhys, not surrender. But you won't. You won't sacrifice your damned obsession with rank and your infatuation with what you call honor even for one moment."

Rhys stared at her, silenced by the passion with which she spoke and the pointed words she hurled at him like daggers. Even when he hadn't recognized it, she had always looked at him with love and respect. Now all he saw was fury, disappointment, perhaps even a fraction of disgust.

And each emotion shamed him.

Anne shook her head, clearly not even close to being finished. "You won't do it for your mother or for your sisters, certainly you won't do it for me. *Never* for me."

She turned away as she bit back a loud, pained sob that cut through the room with the power of a gunshot. For a long time she remained with her back toward him, the chamber around them silent.

Rhys stared at her shaking shoulders, wishing with all his heart he could comfort her, but too shocked and pained to do so. And perhaps she would not accept that. Not from him. Not anymore.

"Oh Rhys," she finally sighed, her voice shaking as she turned to face him.

Her eyes were dry, her face solemn, the fierceness of her anger now tempered by the one emotion he had prayed he would never see in her. Pity.

"You could do so much good with the life and the power you were given along with the name Waverly," she said with a dismissive shrug. "But instead you choose to do *nothing*."

Rhys took a step back, moving away from the

accusations that rocked him to his very core. They challenged everything he had been telling himself for his entire life, and certainly what he had believed over the past few weeks. They made him question his heart, his bravery, his very existence. And he wanted to make them stop. To make *her* stop.

"I'm sorry," he finally said, his voice barely carrying in the chamber.

Her gaze slipped up and down his frame and she nodded.

"Yes. You are. I love you, Rhys. Nothing has ever changed my heart, perhaps nothing ever will, even this. But if you are so willing to throw away the life we could have together . . . if you are so willing to throw *me* away after all the times I've proven myself to you . . . then perhaps you don't deserve me after all. And that has *nothing* to do with the blood that pumps through your veins or the name you call yourself by."

She turned her face. In the firelight Rhys saw a tear slide down her cheek, but she didn't acknowledge it. Nor did she speak again as she slowly walked past him to the chamber door. He stared as she opened it and stepped into the dark, quiet hallway.

Only then did she turn back and whisper, "Goodbye."

She was gone before he could say anything. The

door shut behind her and she left him in the chamber they had shared, the bed they had shared. She left him alone, just as he had been asking her to do since he discovered the truth about his parentage.

But his reaction was anything but triumph or relief. Without realizing he had done it, Rhys found himself on his knees, staring at the door, staring at the spot she had last stood.

In that moment, in that place, every emotion he had ever avoided, mocked, and feared slapped him in the face. He felt each in turn, though one pushed its way above the rest. One tormented him like no other.

In that moment, he knew with utter clarity just how very much he loved Anne.

His wife, his unwanted duchess, somehow *she* had become his entire world. His reason for rising in the morning, his meaning for living. He loved her without hesitation or doubt, without reservation or qualification. He loved her and she had just left him, not because she didn't return his feelings, not because she wanted something or someone else.

No, she had left him because he wasn't willing to fight for her.

Nausea rose up in him as he struggled back to his feet.

"I must fix this," he said, needing to hear the words out loud. "There must be a way."

He had spent so long believing there was only one option to end this blackmail, this nightmare Simon had revealed to him, that he had stopped searching for another answer, a way to fight as Anne had said he would not. Now his mind raced as he frantically prayed for another alternative.

Because now that he recognized how dear to him she was, there was no way he could let his wife go. There was no way he could protect her by abandonment.

He found himself running for the door, tearing it open, and hurrying into the hallway. He wanted to go to her, but he resisted. He couldn't. She needed him to fight now, that was the only way to make her see he loved her. The only way to be certain that the future he offered, when he finally laid his heart bare, was the future that she deserved.

So instead of going to her chamber, he ran down the stairs and called for his horse. Because the beginnings of another plan had come to Rhys's mind. A risky plan, but perhaps the only way to have what he wanted. What he needed. For once in his life, he knew what that was.

And that was Anne.

Chapter 20

Anne smoothed her shaking hands over the silky folds of her spring green gown before she offered a weak smile to one of the ladies who passed by and said hello. The Earl of Rythsdale's annual summer ball was in full swing, but she could hardly concentrate on the gaiety around her.

Not when she was fully aware of the horror about to come.

"Here you are," Rhys said as he slipped up beside her and handed over a drink. She took the cup with a slight nod of acknowledgment.

"Thank you."

He shook his head. "No, I thank you for coming tonight. I realize how difficult this is."

Anne arched a brow as she sipped her drink. *Difficult* was something of an understatement. Since their last passionate and angry encounter two nights before, Anne had been tormented. She had returned to her father's home the morning after their argument, mostly because she couldn't bear to stay in the same place as Rhys when she knew what he intended to do to himself, to her, and to their marriage. Surprisingly he had allowed her to go.

But then when had he ever asked her to stay?

"I wouldn't want to miss your grand exit tonight," she said, unable to keep the bitterness and sarcasm from her voice. "I am certain it will be the talk of Society."

Rhys looked at her evenly and Anne squirmed slightly under his scrutiny. Since he had picked her up at her father's home earlier that evening, he'd been behaving strangely, watching her with an expression she didn't fully understand. It was as if he was trying to glimpse her soul and coming quite close to doing so.

"I hope that what happens tonight *will* be the talk of Society," he said quietly.

Anne pursed her lips and turned away. How he could so callously destroy everything around him was beyond her, but there was no use arguing anymore. Her husband was a stubborn man and he obviously cared little for her thoughts on this or any other subject.

Rhys glanced down at his pocket watch briefly. "The message I received upon our arrival said that Simon and I are to meet with Warren in a quarter of an hour in one of the salons attached to the ballroom."

Anne nodded as her gaze flitted around the room. She found Lillian and Simon at the edge of the dance floor across from them. They both appeared as nervous as she felt, though they stood close together, a united front against the evil bent on destroying their happiness.

Anne shot a glance at Rhys. She had nothing of the kind. By the end of tonight she would be utterly alone.

"Will you dance with me?"

She blinked as she stared more closely at her husband. "I beg your pardon?"

He smiled, a knowing, odd expression. "I realize you're very angry with me, Anne. You have every right to be. But I hoped you might put that aside for a few moments and dance the waltz with me. It has just started, and I think it was always a favorite of yours."

Anne stared at the dance floor. She'd been so wrapped up in her own thoughts that she hadn't even noticed the music change or the couples begin to move together. Rhys was correct. The waltz had always been her favorite dance, perhaps because it forced him to hold her close.

Tonight that made her heart sting.

"I don't know—" she whispered, trying desperately to keep her voice from cracking with emotion.

"Please," he whispered as he took her hand and began to back toward the floor. "Please, dance with me."

She followed him without answering, mostly because she couldn't help herself. He had always been able to lead her with ease, and truth be told, she longed for this touch, especially if it was to be the last dance, the last embrace he allowed them to share.

Rhys's hand was warm on her back as he twirled her into the crowd of dancers. His gaze held hers, even and strong, as he gracefully maneuvered them in and out of the steps, and soon she forgot everything around her. She forgot the other dancers, she forgot Lillian and Simon, she even forgot the blackmailer who waited in the wings. There was only Rhys, there was only her, there was only the heartbeat they shared as they held each other.

But the music ended far too soon, and Anne blinked as the rest of the room came back into focus once more.

"I—" she began, staring at Rhys.

He took both her hands and lifted them to his lips to kiss each one gently. "I know. Now go and be with Lillian. Simon and I must meet Warren. You may need her support for what happens next."

Anne blinked as sudden tears stung her eyes. She nodded, unable to stop the things about to come. Unable to even try anymore.

"Be careful," she whispered as she pulled away from him.

He nodded and then he disappeared into the milling crowd, off to face a villain, off to end her life as she knew it. And all Anne could do was watch him go.

"Are you ready for this?" Simon asked as they hesitated before the salon door just off the ballroom.

Rhys nodded. "There is no longer a choice, is there?"

Simon arched a brow. "There is *always* a choice, my friend."

Slowly Rhys turned to face his friend and brother. "You think my plan to be folly?"

His brother shrugged one shoulder. "Perhaps, but in truth, it may be the only way to save us all. I suppose we'll find out, one way or another, soon enough."

With that, Simon reached out and opened the door. The salon was empty and cold, unlit by a fire since it was not meant to be used by the guests who filled the Earl of Rythsdale's glittering home. Rhys hesitated as his eyes slowly adjusted to the darkened room. He didn't like this, it felt like a trap.

"Warren?" Simon called out, as hesitant and on edge as Rhys. "Where are you?"

There was a rasp of flint, and suddenly a lamp glowed across the room. In the rising light, Xavier Warren limped forward and stared with utter triumph and even a touch of mad glee at the two men who had come to meet him.

"You are late," he said, tapping the clock on the desk beside him. "Perhaps you should be punished for that."

"What more can you do but what you have threatened already?" Rhys said with a snort of derision.

"I can think of a few things," Warren said with a thin smile. "Your wife is a beautiful woman, Waverly."

Rhys stalked forward a step. "Do not speak of my wife."

"Why not?" Warren's smile broadened. "Perhaps *she* could have some involvement in this. That was always your father's favorite game, I think it might be fitting to make it mine as well."

Rage flowed through Rhys as he stared at the vile person who stood, so smug, across from him. This man had murdered, he had stolen, he had threatened, he had done everything in his power to hurt others, and it was all in the name of greed. All in the name of Rhys's real father.

"You know," Rhys said as he cocked his head and let his gaze flow over Warren once more, "I think I might enjoy what is about to happen even more than I thought I would."

"Enjoy it?" Warren asked, drawing back a fraction. "What are you talking about?"

Rhys lunged toward Warren, hitting his body with all his weight. Because of his old injury, the other man was already off-kilter and he fell backward, sprawling across the floor with a yelp of pain.

Rhys dug his hand into Warren's coat, searching for the spot where the villain had kept his gun during their last encounter. He hit upon it just as Simon threw open the salon door and allowed three other men into the room, their own weapons drawn.

"What the hell is this?" Warren squealed as Rhys tore the gun loose and thrust it across the wooden floor with a clatter.

Rhys got to his feet, grabbing Warren by the lapels as he did so and dragging him up. He pushed him toward the other men with a nod.

"You see, gentlemen," Rhys said as he watched Warren stagger into the arms of the military officers he and Simon had asked to come here tonight. "It seems our intelligence was correct. May I present Mr. Xavier Warren, traitor to the Crown. I think you've been looking for him for some time now."

As two of the men held Warren by his arms, the other withdrew a sketch. He held it up and pursed his lips with a quick nod.

"This looks like him indeed. Mr. Warren you are under arrest for the crimes of treason, murder, and a list so long that it will take hours to present it to you."

Warren's face crumpled as he yanked and jerked in the arms of his captors.

"No! *You!*" He glowered at Simon and Rhys. "You idiots. Do you think this changes anything? I'll utterly destroy you and all you stand for! I have the power!"

Rhys arched a brow. "I have no idea what you're talking about Mr. . . . . Warren, is it? But you are a traitor to the Crown and I'm happy I could play a part in bringing you to justice. Gentlemen, perhaps you could take him away before he spoils the Earl of Rythsdale's party."

"Indeed, Your Grace," the main officer said as he bowed slightly. "And our thanks to both of you for helping us with this matter."

Warren howled as they dragged him out of the room. Simon and Rhys exchanged a look before they followed the group out into the main ballroom. Already the faces of the crowd were turned toward the ruckus, but all sounds in the ballroom ceased as the officers stepped into the room with their screaming, squirming quarry at their sides.

The Earl of Rythsdale hurried forward. He was a younger man, near Simon and Rhys's age. Rhys's stomach turned as he vaguely recalled mocking Rythsdale when they were boys. But then he pushed those thoughts away as he refocused on the matter at hand. If he survived this moment, he could make up for all the others.

"What is the meaning of this?" Rythsdale snapped as he looked from Simon and Rhys to the officers and back again. "Who is this *person*?"

"A traitor to the Crown, my lord," one of the officers said with a quick bow for the earl.

Rythsdale looked at Warren with an expression of pure disgust. "In my *home*?"

"Indeed, sir. Planning something terrible, no doubt. But the Duke of Billingham and the Duke of Waverly helped us bring him to justice." The officer acknowledged Rhys and Simon with a quick bow.

"Bring me to justice?" Warren howled. "No, they only covered their own asses."

He struggled and managed to free one hand briefly. With it, he motioned to the crowd. "Do you think you know these men? These paragons of virtue? These elevated mice?"

The officers grabbed for Warren and caught him

into their grip again, but it didn't stop him. And Rhys could only watch and wait for what was about to come.

"The Duke of Billingham, this man's father," Warren screamed as he tilted his head toward Simon. "He wasn't the saint you believe him to be. He fucked half the women of your rank and most of them far below it."

"That's enough, you!" the officer who held Warren snapped as the crowd let out a collective gasp at both his language and the images he had just put in their minds.

"You can't stop me now," Warren cried out as he smiled at Rhys and Simon. "You could have, but not now. And this one—" He nodded toward Rhys. "His mother spread her legs for Billingham. The great Duke of Waverly is nothing but a bastard brat of his best friend's father. He's no better than most of the pickpockets on Bond Street. Remember *that* when you look at him."

A murmur rolled through the crowd as the people around them began to whisper to each other, to stare at Rhys with question, perhaps even glee that he was being humiliated before them in such a fashion.

But Rhys didn't look at them. He simply stared at Xavier Warren and focused on what he had to do. Because here was the moment. Everything hung on this.

Slowly he moved forward, fists clenched at his sides. He stopped mere inches from his accuser and looked the man up and down with all the disdain the man who had raised him had instilled in him. He returned his thoughts, his demeanor, his tone to the man he had been before all this happened. And it was easier than he would have liked to admit.

"What in the world are you going on about?" he asked with a sniff worthy of the prince himself. "Of course I'm the Duke of Waverly's son. And how *dare* you insult my mother in such a fashion? I should have you flayed from head to toe for such disgusting accusations."

Warren stared at him, eyes wide. "I have proof!"

"Do you?" Rhys asked more calmly than he felt inside. "Please produce it, I'm sure we are all agog at the idea."

The other man blinked. "I-I wouldn't be such a fool as to bring it with me," he stammered.

Rhys shook his head as he rolled his eyes at the crowd in general. "Oh, of *course*. You have proof of this ridiculousness, but not on your person. I'm sure everyone believes you, though. You certainly look like the sort of fellow who can be trusted. What is it you are accused of again? Treason? Murder?"

The crowd murmured in unison and he gave them another look of incredulity before he returned his attention to the officers who held Warren. "Honestly, what kind of job are you doing that you would allow such a vile dog into our midst? Take him away, his stench is overpowering."

The officers did not seem to know what to say in the face of his dismissive disgust, but began to drag Warren toward the door. Rhys faced the crowd, hoping desperation didn't line his face. Many nodded, and he heard snatches of their whispered conversations.

"Waverly has always been as much of an arrogant braggart as his father ever was. Who could doubt his paternity?" one lady snickered.

Her companion nodded. "And the Duke of Billingham was far too good and decent for this foolishness to be believed."

Rhys sagged in relief, for the two women seemed to represent at least two-thirds of the crowd. But to his dismay he also saw the shocked and questioning looks of others. It had been a risk to allow Warren to spill his poison and hope a cold denial would be enough to combat the response. Some of these people would forever distrust that he was who he said he was.

"Excuse me!" a man's voice called out from the crowd.

Rhys turned toward it and was surprised when his mother came forward with a man at her side. The gentleman was of an age with her, with graying hair but a handsome, friendly face. As for his mother, her face was splotched with humiliated color as she looked first at Rhys and then the stranger who was her companion.

"I am a physician," the man explained. "May I examine this person?"

Rhys blinked. What the hell was going on here? But the crowd leaned forward, almost as if they were watching a play on the stage. Here was a new character on scene, forget the fact that someone in trade like a doctor shouldn't even be at this glittering social event. They didn't care about that, they only wanted to see how it all played out.

The Earl of Rythsdale stared at this apparently uninvited guest, but then looked at the crowd. It seemed he saw the same scene that Rhys did, for he nodded. "Please do."

The men holding Warren exchanged puzzled looks, but didn't dare protest when this person, this doctor Rhys's mother apparently knew, approached Warren. The stranger looked him up and down, ignoring the other man's struggles as he pulled down his lids to look at his eyes and examined his sallow skin. Finally he shook his head slowly.

"Poor man, he seems to be utterly mad. He may not even know who he is or where he is. You would do best to take him to an asylum rather than a prison, gentlemen."

Rhys's eyes widened as he looked at the crowd. The remaining doubts of all those around them suddenly faded as people began to nod and the talk began again.

"Of course it's madness," a gentleman said, looking over the people in his group.

Another nodded. "He is a traitor, after all, he couldn't be right. And if he is mad as well, then . . ."

"How unfortunate that Rythsdale's party was ruined by such a person," a countess whose name Rhys couldn't remember said with a theatrical sigh.

The lead officer shook his head in confusion and then looked at Warren with new wariness.

"Well, perhaps you are correct," he said.

"Correct?" Warren spat as he began to struggle wildly. "What the hell are you talking about? I'm perfectly sane! Everything I said is true."

He was dragged from the room with every word, and finally the sounds were only echoes, and then the echoes faded.

A panicky Rythsdale waved to the orchestra wildly. After a few moments of shuffling, they began to play. Slowly the crowd fell back into its regular rhythm. Rythsdale turned to Rhys and Simon with a shrug.

"Bad luck that madman turning up here. I apologize for his outburst."

Rhys's eyes widened. Here he and Simon had arranged all this, but it had been believable enough that Rythsdale was apologizing to *them*!

"Well, I suppose you might have better security in the future," Rhys snapped, hoping this was the last time he would ever have to use the superior tone he had once reveled in and now reviled.

Rythsdale nodded and excused himself. Rhys turned toward Simon, but he was already across the room with Lillian. He looked around, but Anne wasn't with them. Hadn't she seen? Where was she?

But before he could look for her, he turned to find his mother standing close by. She smiled at him, but didn't speak before a few of her oldest friends approached.

"How *dare* that person speak of you in such a fashion?" one of the ladies huffed.

"Really!" his mother agreed as she met his gaze. "Goodness, he must have just randomly chosen me from the crowd. Why, it could have been any one of us he said those horrible things about."

That seemed to set the gathered women into a flutter and they all began talking at once in hushed and rather excited terms about the drama that had just unfolded. But from their smiles toward him as he backed away, Rhys could see not one of them had even an inkling that Warren had told the truth. Between his own denial and the mysterious diagnosis of madness from a man who shouldn't have even been in their midst, the situation was defused. It was over.

"Hello."

Rhys turned to find Anne standing at his side. She smiled up at him, but he saw raw emotions in her eyes.

"I want to take you away from here," he whispered.

She nodded. "And I want to go with you. But not yet. We must stay awhile longer in order to maintain appearances. But we have much to discuss."

"We do," Rhys said as he looked down at her. A swell of powerful love overtook him. "There is much for us to talk about indeed."

Chapter 21

When Rhys said he wanted to go home with Anne and talk, he hadn't pictured that he would soon be standing in his parlor with Simon, Lillian, his mother, and the mysterious doctor who had been his savior. But here they were, and until he dealt with all of them, there would be no private reunion with Anne. There would be no explanations and declarations that burned within him as he stared at his wife, so far away across the room.

She blushed as she turned her face from his and covered her reaction by saying, "Now that we are all gathered here, perhaps someone could explain to me what happened tonight?"

Rhys stepped forward and slowly stared at the doctor who had come forth and offered him a final salvation. "As much as I appreciate this man's state-ments at the ball, I'm not certain I feel comfortable speaking on this topic with someone who is a stranger to our family."

The older gentleman smiled, but it was his mother who spoke. "He may not be known to you, but he is no stranger to me. Rhys, this is Dr. Graham Langrish. He is a—" She stopped and sent a side glance toward the other man. "He is a dear *friend* of mine. When I mentioned I knew someone who might be able to help, this was who I meant."

Rhys stared at the two, now standing together. Slowly his mother slipped her hand into the crook of Dr. Langrish's arm. The stranger covered her fingers briefly in an unmistakable gesture of affectionate comfort.

It was Anne who moved closer.

"Oh," she said softly as she looked at the couple. "Oh."

"Yes, my dear," his mother responded with a girlish blush. "*Oh*. And the doctor knows the particulars of our situation already. I didn't think it fair to deny him that truth when he might be affected by it himself in the future."

Rhys hadn't stopped staring at the apparent couple who stood before him. He had never once pictured that his mother would involve herself with a man again, and certainly not one of no rank. But here she stood, a light in her eyes that he had never seen before.

And this man had saved him, perhaps *because* he loved Rhys's mother. So Rhys pushed his lingering snobbery regarding rank and bloodline away and slowly extended a hand to Dr. Langrish.

"Sir," he said stiffly.

Langrish's handshake was firm and brief. "Your Grace. Anything I know stays with me to the grave. I hope you'll soon see that I only have your mother's best interest at heart. I'd never do anything that could cause her pain."

Rhys nodded, discomfort making him shift ever so slightly. But didn't his mother deserve love? She'd spent a lifetime longing for it but never having it returned by her husband. That desperation had driven her to do things she most certainly regretted. But now, with this new man, she appeared . . . content. And that was enough for Rhys.

"I hope I'll soon know you better," Rhys said quietly. "And I thank you for the part you played tonight. Without your statement that Warren was mad, I fear many at the gathering would have given more credence to what he said about me and my family. Your performance during what transpired defused much of the gossip."

The doctor shrugged. "I don't think what I said was so very far from the truth. There *was* a certain madness in Warren's eyes, caused by whatever twisted evil made him what he was. But I think it was also created by ill health and fear. An asylum may be the best place for him. If you'll help me find out where he was taken, I'll visit him later and see if I can be of some assistance. And also make every effort to determine where he hid the proof he claimed to possess so that you or your brother can obtain and destroy it."

Rhys almost sagged in relief. That was the last piece of this puzzle, and if it could be found, he thought he could put the matter to rest.

He nodded. "I would appreciate that greatly, Doctor. When Simon and I met with him earlier, he mentioned he had a sister who he greatly wished to see again. Perhaps if she could be found, it would ease his anger and his struggle."

Anne sucked in a breath, and Rhys turned to find her staring in disbelief at him.

"You—you would offer solace to a man who tried to destroy you tonight?" she whispered.

He nodded slowly. It seemed odd, but what she said was true.

"He didn't succeed," he explained. "And Simon's father—" He stopped and glanced at his friend. "*Our* father did terrible things to him in the years since he left England. Perhaps everyone deserves some comfort, some kind of second chance." He returned his gaze to Anne. "I have to hope we can *all* change and perhaps find acceptance again."

Without reply, she dipped her head.

Lillian slipped her hand into Simon's. "Do you think it's over, then?"

Simon looked first to his wife with a reassuring smile and then to Rhys. "I don't know. We know my father had more bastard children who are out in the world, and perhaps even other solicitors who made devil's bargains with their incriminating information. But all we can do is hope to handle whatever comes our way, and not live in fear."

Rhys nodded. "Someone very wise once told me that fighting was sometimes the best option. And if anyone threatens this family again, we *will* fight. I know now that it is very much worth the battle."

Simon reached out and the two men clasped hands briefly before he sighed. "Now it is late and I think we should talk more about this tomorrow. Dr. Langrish, I thank you again for what you did for my family. And Lady Waverly, you were most excellent tonight in how you handled the situation, despite how difficult it must have been for you."

"I was happy to help after all these years of silence and guilt." The dowager duchess smiled. "You've been through a great deal, Simon, but I'm glad you have such a bride to help you."

Simon smiled as he took Lillian's hand. They said their final farewells and departed, followed by the doctor. When they were gone, Rhys looked at his mother.

"Are you happy?" he asked.

She hesitated only a moment before her face lit up. "I am, Rhys." She looked at Anne. "I hope you shall be, as well. Good night to you both."

Then she slipped from the room and quietly closed the door behind her. Rhys turned to face his wife, painfully aware that two very happy couples had left this chamber, entirely certain of their love and their futures. But he wasn't. And now he had to face that, this final challenge of his wife, who stood stone-still in the middle of the room, watching him. And what terrified him most was that her normally open face was now utterly unreadable.

Anne stared at Rhys. They had been alone so often in the past few weeks, but tonight it felt awkward. *She* felt awkward and utterly uncertain of what to do next. Her only comfort was that the situation seemed to be equally difficult for her husband, for he shifted from one foot to the next like a green schoolboy who wasn't sure how to say hello to a girl who caught his eye.

She eased toward him one step, unwilling to

move closer for fear she would launch herself into his arms. And until she understood what had happened, what his thoughts were, she refused to do that. Not again.

"I thought you had decided to end this situation quite differently," she whispered.

He nodded. "I had."

"When Warren came out of the room bound and led by officers of the Crown, I could scarcely breathe," she continued. "And you denied him so forcefully. Even before Dr. Langrish said Warren was mad, there were many around me whispering it couldn't be true. That only a true descendant of the late Duke of Waverly could conduct himself as you do."

Rhys drew in a breath and shook his head. "I suppose if there is but one benefit to the terrible way I behaved in the past, it is this. But I hated doing it. I hated speaking that way, acting that way. Somehow it's no longer second nature to me. Thanks to you."

"Thanks to me?" Anne laughed, humorless as she shook her head. "I have had no effect on you whatsoever, my lord."

"Is that what you think?" Rhys asked, and now he crossed the room to her, the green boy gone, the man she loved so desperately returned. "Why do you think I changed my mind about revealing my parentage to that room tonight? Why do you think I took the risk to deny Warren's charges in that public place?"

Anne swallowed, drawn in by how close he now was. By how much passion snapped in his dark eyes. "I don't know, Rhys."

He caught her hands and drew them to his chest, forcing her to step forward as he did so. She felt his heart beating against her palms, a strong, wild rhythm that spoke of his continued anxiety.

"Because of *you*, Anne," he whispered.

"Me?" she breathed, hardly able to hear her own voice over the sudden rush of blood through her veins.

He nodded. "I was ready to throw away my life, but then you walked away from me two nights ago. In that moment, I realized fully what it would mean if I declared myself a bastard and surrendered to the scandal that would surely follow."

Anne blinked, hardly able to comprehend this confession. "I don't understand."

"I could have lived with being denied in public. I think I could have survived the hatred, the crowing, and endured the whispers," he explained, maneuvering her closer with each word until his arms were around her back, cradling her to his chest. "But when I fully felt the power of losing *you*, I realized I would do *anything* to prevent that."

Anne's lips parted in complete shock. She had spent a lifetime being denied by this man. Even when they were at their closest, he'd never surrendered himself completely. But now he was saying . . . he was telling her . . .

"You told me a few nights ago that I didn't deserve you," he said.

She cringed as she recalled all the things she'd said that night. Her anger had overflowed, words she had held in for years had bubbled forth.

"Don't look so guilty," he soothed, smoothing his hands along her spine. "You were absolutely correct. I *don't* deserve you. I've been arrogant and wrong my entire life. Only when you forced yourself into my veins did I see how very wrong I was. And only when you told me you would leave me before I could destroy us did I realize how much I loved you."

Anne couldn't help it. A sobbing gasp escaped her lips. She could scarcely breathe as she stared up at Rhys. He didn't seem to be in jest, or compromised in some way that he would say something he didn't mean.

"You love me?" she repeated, fighting to control her tone. "After all this time, after everything we've endured, you're now telling me you love me?"

He nodded, utterly solemn and completely without hesitation. "I do, in so many ways. I love your spirit,

I love the strength I've seen you exhibit over the past few weeks. I love your kindness and your ability to teach me something new about myself with just a look. I love *you*, Anne, with everything I am and everything I hope to become. Everything you once believed I could be."

Now her tears flowed freely. She couldn't have stopped them for anything in the world, nor did she wish to. Finally, after all the waiting and wanting and hoping, she was receiving the one thing she had ever desired.

"If you'll allow me," he continued softly, "I'd like to try to earn the love you once felt for me. Perhaps, in time, you'll come to feel even a shadow of it again."

The joy that rushed through Anne was something unlike anything she'd ever felt before. The heady feeling overtook her, and she knew that in that moment she could fly if Rhys asked her to do so.

Instead she carefully slipped from Rhys's warm embrace. Slowly she wiped her eyes before she looked at him with a small smile.

"Oh, Rhys, you don't know how like me you sound right now, hoping for the love of your mate. And thinking that somehow time can change things."

Rhys swallowed hard. "You think it cannot, then?"

"When it comes to some things, yes," she said, but then she shook her head. "But not when it comes to me."

The blood drained from Rhys's face and his knees buckled before he caught himself and straightened up. Anne was shocked to see the sparkle of tears in his eyes, the utter disappointment that lined his face.

"Then I've lost you," he whispered, his voice thick. "You don't think there is any way I could ever change your heart?"

She moved toward him. "No, Rhys. Because I have *never* stopped loving you. In fact, in the weeks since we were wed, no matter how trying they were, no matter how angry I was, I've grown to love you more with every passing day."

A sharp exhalation of breath escaped Rhys's lips as he stared at her.

"Y-you love me still?" he choked, moving toward her in a few long steps. But he didn't touch her.

And she realized why. Like her, he was in awe of the feelings she declared. In awe of the idea that they could love each other, without barriers, without exception, for the rest of their lives.

"Of course," she whispered as she touched his cheek. "I will *always* love you."

He caught her arms and pulled her close, and then his mouth was on her with a fiery possessiveness that was like nothing she had ever experienced before. She clung to his neck and lifted to her tiptoes to meet his crushing kiss. And she didn't resist as he pushed her back to the closest settee and laid her down across it, then covered her with his heavy, heavenly weight.

He pulled back. "I've never claimed you as my wife."

She blinked up at him. "You have. We consummated our union."

"No." He cupped her cheeks gently. "I have never *claimed* you, not like I wanted to."

"Then do it," she murmured as she lifted her mouth for another kiss. "I'm yours, so *show* me now that you are mine. I have waited for that forever."

He growled out an answer and quickly went to work on the little pearl buttons that flowed along the front of her gown. Quickly he freed the row and pulled her to a seated position to glide the fabric away, along with the thin chemise beneath.

She arched her back as he stared down at her, eyes dilated with a desire unlike any other she had seen from him. She realized it was because this time there would be no holding back, no regrets or withdrawal. Tonight he would truly become hers and hers alone.

The very idea made her shiver with delight and anticipation.

"Are you cold?" he murmured as he slipped to his knees on the floor below the settee and turned her so that she was seated. With a tug, he slouched her down, half naked and spread out before him.

"Will you offer to keep me warm if I say yes?" she asked, smiling.

He grinned up at her. "Indeed, my lady. As your husband, it is my duty to attend to *all* your needs."

"I look forward to that," she whispered.

He laughed as he lifted up on his knees and cupped her breasts, bringing them together before he dropped his mouth to one tight, hard nipple. Anne relaxed her head against the settee cushions and surrendered to the wet tugging of his lips that brought electric pleasure to her nipples and seemed to arc through her entire body, settling in a pulse between her already damp thighs.

She tangled her fingers into Rhys's hair, holding him steady against her body, stroking his scalp with lazy brushes as he lapped and tasted each breast in turn.

Soon she was writhing against the settee, swept away by the rising pleasure just this simple touch inspired.

"More," Rhys growled from below her, and gently urged her to lift her hips so he could pull away the remainder of her gown and under things.

"This is a familiar position," Anne said as she lowered her bottom back on the cushion. "Me naked and vulnerable to you, but you utterly clothed and in control."

Rhys stared at her a moment before he pushed to his feet. Never breaking eye contact with her, he slowly untied his cravat. He shoved his jacket away, then went to work on his embroidered vest and the shirt beneath.

Anne clenched her fingers into useless fists on the settee cushion as she watched more and more of her husband's skin revealed. God, he was beautiful naked. And hers. All hers from now on.

He hesitated at the trouser buttons. "Do you really think I'm in control?" he asked as he tugged the buttons free. "That I have *ever* been in control when touching you? Even when I pretended it at the beginning, in truth, I wanted to take you and claim you and touch you in ways that were far from gentlemanly. Far from polite."

The pants dropped away and Anne sucked in a breath. His cock was fully hard, thrusting proudly against his stomach. She moved to the edge of the settee and reached for him, taking him in hand and stroking him from base to tip in one smooth motion, just as she so often had during their time together.

Rhys groaned and Anne smiled at him.

"I wish you had done all those wicked things to me, Rhys," she whispered.

He cursed and returned to his knees before her, pushing her back on the settee. "Don't worry, love, I intend to do them all and more tonight."

His mouth came down on hers, stealing her breath, and at the same time he positioned his cock at her dripping entrance and glided forward.

Rhys almost lost himself right then and there, as his wife's hot body welcomed him in, closing around him even tighter than her fist had, enveloping him in wet heat that felt like heaven. It had been so long since he breached her, and the last time it had been under duress and followed almost immediately by regret.

But tonight there would be no regrets. Only love. Only her. Only this.

He cupped her backside, dragging her forward to fully seat himself in her. She whimpered as her mouth came down on his shoulder. She was already on the edge, close to coming, and he wanted to feel her do that not against his mouth, not around his fingers, but while he drove into her.

He thrust, rolling his hips as he held her tightly to him, driving against her and within her as her legs wrapped around him and her head dipped back. She let out a wild, wanton cry and came almost immediately. The release was hard, her sheath tightened around him, rippling as the pleasure overtook her. He shut his eyes and groaned as her body milked him, urged him to take his own pleasure.

But no, not yet. He wanted to make her come at least once more before he joined her. And as her eyes fluttered open and her breathing rate lowered, he knew now he could mete out that pleasure over a long time. He could make her ache and beg and surrender in ways he had only dreamed of before.

He braced his arms on either side of her head and lifted up to look at her. Her gaze was glazed and unfocused as she smiled up at him. He returned the smile, then slowly rotated his hips. She caught her breath with a small gasp of "Oh!" and then looked at him in wonder.

He chuckled. "Did you think this was over? No, my love, it has only just begun."

He repeated the swirl of his hips before she could answer and instead of words she uttered a low, gurgling groan. He continued the gentle thrust and swirl, bringing her back to the edge of release, but never allowing her to fall over.

"You torment me," she finally gasped, grasping for his lower arms and digging her fingertips into the flesh as she reached for purchase.

He laughed, but in truth, this exercise was as much

torture for him. He had always been so careful to hold back, but now doing so was too difficult. He wanted to unleash his passion onto his wife. He wanted to show her how intense his feelings were for her.

And he wanted to pour his seed deep within her flesh.

"You are correct and it is time to end the torment," he whispered, his breathing harsh and broken.

She smiled and lifted her hips but he shook his head.

"No, love. I want you to roll over for me."

Anne withdrew a fraction. "Roll over?"

He nodded as he reluctantly withdrew his damp cock from her body. They both moaned in unison as he parted from her, but he managed to choke out, "Trust me. It will be most pleasurable for us both."

She didn't argue. Slowly she rolled over on the settee and Rhys stared. God, how he loved her naked body. The curve of her shoulders rolled so elegantly into the valley of her back and the smooth roundness of her bottom. He lowered his lips to the spot just above her backside and kissed her there.

Anne bucked as she let out a cry of pleasure. Rhys stared. Apparently he had found a most sensitive spot. Very good information for later, but for now . . .

He wrapped an arm around her stomach, moving

her until her backside was lifted and he could see the damp entrance of her sex. He positioned himself carefully and then drove forward.

Anne's back arched and her cry filled the air. She glanced over her shoulder at him, completely unaware of how sensual she looked at that moment.

"My God, it's entirely different!" she gasped as he drove forward again. "Rhys!"

"Come with me, angel," he ordered as his thrusts grew more erratic. He could scarcely control himself anymore. Not when her body gripped him so tightly. Not when she pushed back to meet him and cried out with wicked and wild abandon.

"Yes!" she finally screamed, her inner walls tugging harder, pulling him deeper.

He no longer held back. With a roar that filled the room, Rhys pumped his seed into her, his thrusts becoming wild and hard as he lost himself in the pleasure of her body.

He didn't know how much time had gone by when he finally came back to himself. He was still bent over Anne's body. Her breath came in shaking heaves and her arms shook.

He withdrew reluctantly and took her into his arms as they settled back on the narrow settee, lying face to face, as close as two people could be.

Anne was silent for a long time, but her wide,

loving smile said everything he needed to hear. He kissed her, gently, and when he pulled away, he said, "I love you."

Her smile grew even larger as she whispered back, "And I love you, Rhys. I will always love you."

"And *I* will always fight for you, from now on. You are the only thing worth winning."

She settled her head against his chest, their breathing merging as one. For the first time, perhaps, in his entire life, Rhys was content. No matter what happened, no matter what came, the love he felt for her and the life he would live with her . . . they were worth fighting for.

Epilogue

Six Months Later

When the occasional whisper about the parentage of the Duke of Waverly arose, it was generally squashed immediately by the reminder that if anyone in the world acted as if he had the most exalted title a man could hold without actually being royalty, it was Waverly. Those who still questioned were silenced by the fact that his accuser had been proven quite mad before he died in the asylum, his beloved sister at his side.

Of course this conversation almost always led to a discussion of how very much improved Waverly was, how marriage had softened and changed him, making him a far better man.

If Rhys had overheard any of these exchanges, he wouldn't have disagreed with that last statement. He certainly *felt* like a better man now that his mind was not forever consumed by rank and privilege and power struggles. There was only one person to thank for that gift, and she sat across the parlor from him, chatting with Simon's wife. Anne glanced at him, almost as if she felt his stare, and smiled.

"You are utterly besotted." Simon laughed as he clapped a hand on Rhys's shoulder and forced his brother's attention back to him.

"I am indeed," Rhys said with a chuckle of his own. "Quite blissfully so."

"I'm very happy for that fact." Simon's expression grew serious. "For a while I didn't think you would ever feel this way. That you would let happiness pass you by in exchange for less important things."

A shiver rolled through Rhys's body at the thought. "I don't like to consider what would have happened if I had done so."

His brother's eyes softened and then he lifted his glass and addressed the room. "On this Christmas Eve, then, I would like to say a toast to our family. Secret as it may be, it remains *ours*."

Rhys grinned as he lifted his glass. Yes, he did have a new family. He had grown closer to the sister he shared with Simon, and Simon sometimes hinted there was more to know about their family that he would one day reveal.

Each person in the room drank, and then Anne cocked her head.

"It has been six months since we discovered the truth about your father, gentlemen. We all know there are other children that he sired. I often wonder if you intend to seek those other people out?"

Lillian nodded. "Yes, I find I'm curious about them myself."

Simon and Rhys exchanged a look, and Rhys saw that his brother seemed troubled.

"Do you know something you have withheld?" he asked, setting his drink down behind him.

Simon nodded. "As you know, I have been kept very busy not only by my lovely wife"—Lillian blushed deeply but laughed—"but also by the work I must do on my father's old town home here in London. Just like in our country home in Billingham, he has left his records in a state. It takes hours to sift through them. But recently . . . just this very week, in fact, I found some new information about one of the remaining children he sired out of wedlock."

Rhys swallowed hard. He had wondered about his other siblings, but had kept those thoughts at bay, focusing instead on his own future with Anne. But now he steadied himself on the nearest chair as the world briefly spun before him.

Anne seemed to recognize his difficulty, for she

got to her feet and moved to his side. When she touched his hand, everything was set to rights again. He smiled at her, drawing from her strength and her love in the way he had come to depend upon over the past few blissful months. He had never thought it possible, but it seemed his love for her grew with each day they spent together.

"I wish you had told me," Lillian said softly as she joined her own husband. "I realize this situation continues to cause you great pain."

Simon smiled as he touched his wife's cheek briefly. "We've been busy with the holiday celebrations. And I wasn't certain how to approach the situation. You see, the man is another son of a titled gentleman."

Rhys shut his eyes. "Someone titled."

"No, this time he is a younger son. But one we are acquainted with," Simon said. "In fact, it's someone you have not always gotten along with."

Anne's fingers tightened in Rhys's hand as he said, "Who?"

"Caleb Talbot," Simon said softly.

Rhys didn't react for a long moment as he thought of his last encounter with Talbot. He had reached out to the man, sensing his pain, but Talbot had rebuffed his overtures. Since then, he had disappeared from Society once more. Rhys thought of the anguish he had seen on the other man's face. Although he denied

Rhys, Talbot had suggested he understood Rhys's difficulties.

"It may be possible he knows the truth already," Rhys said softly. "It would explain his sudden and complete departure from Society and his separation from his brother, the Earl of Baybary, when they were once thick as thieves."

Simon nodded. "Yes, I thought the same. But I learned my lesson, Rhys. I don't think it is wise to approach Talbot and force this truth upon him."

"No?" Rhys said, thinking of all the ways his life had changed since he learned the truth. The journey had been difficult, but so much worth the pain. Without the truth, he might not have ever allowed himself to love Anne. Or to change as a person.

"If he does have an inkling about his birth," Anne said softly, "he might come to *you* in time."

Rhys looked at her, then to Simon again. "And if he does, we'll welcome him."

Simon nodded. "Indeed we will. As we would any of the children our father sired over the years." There was a long silence, but then Simon shook away the maudlin thoughts. "But this is Christmas! We shouldn't moon over facts we cannot change. Come, let us go to the salon where we'll have some mulled wine and make promises for the new year that we will instantly break!"

Lillian laughed as she took her husband's arm, and the couple left the room. Rhys turned to Anne and offered his own arm, but she didn't take it. Instead she looked at him, exploring his face with those seeing eyes of hers.

"I would like to give you your present," she said softly.

Rhys lowered his arm. "My present? Do you not wish to wait until our families join us tomorrow?"

She shook her head. "I don't wish to wait another moment."

His eyes widened. Her gown didn't have pockets and she didn't hold a package, so he could imagine there was only one kind of gift she could offer him. He grinned.

"You know, people will look for us. The possibility of being caught in a rather awkward situation is very high. You are a naughty little minx."

Anne laughed as she swatted his arm playfully. "Not that, you oaf. Not yet." She stopped laughing. "Although my present is related."

He stared at her, brow knitted together. Her hand shook as she reached out and took his, then moved it to cover her belly.

"I'm having a baby, Rhys," she whispered, tears springing to her eyes. "Right now your child grows inside of me. I've known for two weeks, but wanted to surprise you for the holiday. Yet seeing you tonight, loving you so much, I couldn't wait another moment to share this with you."

Rhys continued to stare, his mouth partly open as he felt the warmth of her body beneath his hand.

"A-a child?" he finally repeated.

She nodded. "I hope you are happy."

With a shout of pleasure, Rhys swung her into his arms and spun around the parlor. "Happy! I am the happiest man in the country! A baby, Anne, great God that is good news!"

He set her down and looked into her face, which had softened with relief.

"Were you afraid I wouldn't be happy?"

She shrugged. "I couldn't help but remember when you said we should never have children to protect the Waverly line."

He touched her face. "Darling, that was another life. Another man who said those terrible things. The Waverly line is perfectly protected by me, and if it is a son who is born, I'm sure he will be a good and decent duke. I couldn't be happier. With this news and with you."

Then he bent his head and kissed her once more.

Unforgettable, enthralling love stories,
sparkling with passion and adventure
from Romance's bestselling authors

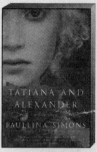

At Avon Books, we know your passion for romance—once you finish one of our novels, you find yourself wanting more.

May we tempt you with . . .

- **Excerpts** from our upcoming releases.

- Entertaining **extras**, including authors' personal photo albums and book lists.

- Behind-the-scenes **scoop** on your favorite characters and series.

- **Sweepstakes** for the chance to win free books, romantic getaways, and other fun prizes.

- Writing **tips** from our authors and editors.

- **Blog** with our authors and find out why they love to write romance.

- **Exclusive content** that's not contained within the pages of our novels.

Join us at
www.avonbooks.com

AVON

An Imprint of HarperCollins*Publishers*
www.avonromance.com

Available wherever books are sold or please call 1-800-331-3761 to order.

FTH 0708